E.D. HACKETT

Farm Cove Bliss

A Small Town Sweet Romance

It's the
little
things

E.D. Hackett-Fiction Author

First published by E.D. Hackett 2023

Copyright © 2023 by E.D. Hackett

This novel is entirely a work of fiction. The names, characters and incidents portrayed in it are the work of the author's imagination. Any resemblance to actual persons, living or dead, events or localities is entirely coincidental.

Designations used by companies to distinguish their products are often claimed as trademarks. All brand names and product names used in this book and on its cover are trade names, service marks, trademarks and registered trademarks of their respective owners. The publishers and the book are not associated with any product or vendor mentioned in this book. None of the companies referenced within the book have endorsed the book.

First edition

ISBN: 978-1-7374679-4-6

*Cover art by Cover Design by Jillian Liota, Blue Moon Creative Studio
Editing by Granite Editorial*

*This book was professionally typeset on Reedsy.
Find out more at reedsy.com*

This story is dedicated to the Sizzle King. Without your imagination, my story wouldn't be nearly this exciting.

Acknowledgement

This novel would still be brewing in my mind if I hadn't stumbled across Kindle Vella. With the help of my husband, we created an entertaining plotline that was fun, funny, and probably not nearly as spicy as he wanted.

My family continues to be my top four cheerleaders. Without their constant interest, conversation, and support, this novel would sit in a drawer until the end of time.

My critique partner, Gail, has become a good friend, and I rely on her for all book-related decisions. She continues to be my sounding board and has helped me fill in the holes and expand upon the drama. With her suggestions, I created two flawed individuals who needed each other's strengths to fulfill their wants and needs. I know you will love them just as much as I do.

Thank you to my editor Nicky, from Granite Editorial, and my cover designer Jillian Liota, from Blue Moon Creative. This novel has turned out better than I could have imagined.

It takes a village to write and publish a novel. I am proud of Farm Cove Bliss, my first romance novel, and I hope you enjoy it too.

Keep Reading,

Edy.

CHAPTER 1: CRYSTAL

"**M**s. Whitman?" an unfamiliar, deep voice said through the phone.

"Yes, this is Crystal," Crystal said, glancing at her watch.

"This is Declan O'Halloran from O'Halloran Long-Term Care. I'm sorry to call, but your mother passed last night." His rough voice grated in her ear—if he were in Crystal's house she would have offered him a glass of water.

"I'm sorry?" she asked, not quite sure she had heard correctly.

"Your mother. Evelyn," he clarified, like Crystal and Evelyn had never met before. "She died in her sleep last night. It was peaceful but unexpected. The nurse went into her room around six this morning to administer medication, but she was already gone. I'm sorry for your loss."

Crystal held the phone tight against her ear, focusing on the cars zipping down the busy street outside her classroom window. She looked at her watch. Just ten minutes remained of her lunch break before her students would filter back into the small, overcrowded classroom. She knew she needed to say something to end this call, but wasn't sure what. "It's okay," she comforted him. "What do you need

1

from me?" She felt crass for being so direct but needed to get herself sorted before 12:07p.m.

"You're her one and only next of kin. We need you to come here and finalize the paperwork. Her body will go to the morgue and you will have to arrange any further plans directly with them. We have her documents in a safe to give to you for your review." He spoke with authority and ease, as if reciting his speech from memory.

Crystal finger combed back her bouncy brown bangs before securing them with a headband and jotted down **haircut** on a sticky note. She wondered how many times a week he made these phone calls. "It's a three-hour drive. When do you need me by?" she asked.

"As soon as possible," the man on the other end replied. Crystal couldn't remember his name. She knew she shouldn't have picked up her phone since she was working, but the Saratoga number drew her in. The only person she knew who lived in Saratoga was Evelyn.

Crystal glanced at the calendar, scanning the end of school year activities and last-minute meetings she needed to attend. There were three more days of school before summer vacation. *Can I leave a mob of six-year-olds with a substitute for the last few days of school?* She knew she should, but didn't want to pull Mason from his final days of fifth grade.

"I have a son who is finishing up school in three days." She didn't share that she had three days left of work. It felt easier to blame the delay on Mason. "I can get there by Tuesday of next week. In the meantime, I'll make all the phone calls to coordinate the services." Crystal stood from her desk eyeing the door and her half-eaten lunch. "I have to go. I'm available after 3:30 if you need me." She quickly hung up the phone and placed worksheets on all the desks.

Dead. A mix of emotions flooded over Crystal and she wondered if she was somehow defective for not breaking down at the news. It had been three years since Evelyn entered the nursing home. Crystal had helped her settle into her new facility, and once Evelyn appeared content, Crystal had never returned. She had told herself that she lived too far away and was dealing with enough drama in her personal life. She had assumed Evelyn wouldn't even know she was alone.

Crystal knew that normal people would have cried into the phone, left work in a hurry, and drowned their sorrows into a pint of mint chocolate chip ice cream, or alcohol, or whatever vice they craved. But, instead, an emptiness spread through her limbs.

First her marriage had died, and now her mother. Fifteen years of teaching had forced her to carry the burden of being a second mother to all her students. Mental exhaustion had become her constant state of mind and her marriage had suffered because of it.

All I have left is Mason.

The children bounced into the room, tossing their lunchboxes into the coat cubbies and filed to their desks.

"Hello," Crystal called out, her face welcoming and her voice comforting. "This afternoon we're going to do a science experiment." She emphasized the word science and her brown eyes widened like checkers. This was a surprise for the students.

"Yay," they cheered.

Crystal worked through the afternoon, focusing on her teaching, and pushing all thoughts about her personal life down to her toes. She forced Evelyn's scowl into the recesses of her mind, refusing to let her mother's disappointment loom over her.

Crystal decided to prioritize the last few days of school and savor her chaotic yet consistent life. She knew she had to go back to the town where she was raised and face the demons that kept her away for most of her adult life, but she wasn't ready.

* * *

That night, Mason sat on the oversized, tan couch while Crystal passed him a glass of pink lemonade. The cushions sagged in the middle from too much use and the pillows were permanently flattened from Lulu's favorite sleeping spot.

Two years ago, she had found the dog roaming around the park during Mason's baseball game. When no one claimed her from the dog pound, Crystal took her home. Lulu and Mason had immediately become best friends.

Crystal plopped Lulu next to Mason to break the news. "Mase, I need to tell you something."

Her ten-year-old son fidgeted on the cushions, fiddled with the buttons on his shirt, and bounced his legs, causing the dog to rise and fall like ocean waves.

"Mason," Crystal repeated.

He sat on his hands to keep them from moving. This had been a strategy he learned years ago when teachers would tell him to 'sit on his pockets' and he misinterpreted the direction to sit on his hands. Either way, it worked.

"What's for dinner? I'm hungry," he asked.

"Mason, hot dogs and homemade macaroni and cheese. But that's not what I have to talk to you about."

"Does it have bread crumbs on top?" he interrupted.

Crystal narrowed her eyes. "Yes. Mason, Grammy died." Mason knew about death, but he didn't know much about Grammy. He had only seen her a handful of times throughout his life.

Mason looked at her silently, waiting for more. After a long pause, he said, "Okay."

"Do you have any questions, or do you want to talk about it?" Crystal asked.

Mason shook his head.

Crystal sighed, but continued explaining anyway. "She died in her sleep. It was old age. We need to go to Saratoga so I can arrange the funeral. After school on Wednesday, we'll go on a long car ride. We'll stay at her old house, which should be empty. I don't know, I have to call. I haven't been there in a while." At this point, Crystal was talking to herself, but needed to formulate a plan. She only had a few days before the nursing home expected her.

Mason put his hands in his pockets and bounced on the edge of the cushion. "How long will we be gone for?"

"Not long, just a few days. Do you want me to see if you can stay with Daddy?" It wasn't his week but, if Jeremy felt generous, he might swap. If Crystal explained it was due to a death in the family could he really say no?

Mason looked torn, and Crystal could see he was debating between what he wanted to do and what he thought he should do.

"You know what, Mase, I'll call Daddy. I shouldn't have asked you to come." *Stupid, Crystal. He's just a child.* She heard Jeremy in her head reminding her that she put Mason in impossible situations. That he was a child and shouldn't need to make adult decisions.

Mason smiled. "Sure, Mom. How long until dinner?"

Crystal rubbed her face up and down, focusing on her temples. "Ten minutes." She got up from the living room chair and busied herself in the kitchen.

Memories of the last time she saw her mother flooded her like a tidal wave. She struggled to breathe and grasped the counter to steady herself. Three years ago, the police had called Crystal explaining that Evelyn had been outside wandering the rural town of Farm Cove, where Crystal was raised. Hikers found Evelyn in the state park near the farmstand she frequented. The seventy-five-year-old woman had collapsed in a ball due to weakness, coldness, and dehydration, the police officer reported. They had carried her to their vehicle and driven her to the hospital. She didn't have any identifying information on her, and couldn't tell the orderly where she lived or if she had any family.

Thank goodness their neighbor, Mr. Dole, had happened to be in the Emergency Room for a severed finger and recognized her. He had promised Crystal he would keep an eye on Evelyn and would check in on her at least once a week.

Crystal had driven home that day in a panic. Mason had just turned eight, she was fighting with Jeremy, and had just gotten written up at work for taking off too much time. When she arrived at the hospital, Evelyn mistook Crystal for her own mother and lashed out at her, blaming her for everything that went badly in her life. The doctor said that her dementia was advancing and she would have fewer moments of lucidity. Crystal's sanity was already teetering on the edge of collapse, so she researched nursing homes and moved Evelyn into O'Halloran's.

Crystal stood in the kitchen and wept for Evelyn. She prayed the nurses were right and hoped her mother had passed peacefully. Perhaps she believed she was dreaming and she flew into the clouds to greet Crystal's dad, who had been patiently waiting for her.

Crystal's shoulders shook and her nose ran, but she didn't care. Pent up guilt, anger, and trepidation slipped out of her eyes like a raging river. She breathed slowly, straightening back her shoulders, wiping her face, and biting her lip before the tears flowed again. She knew this day was coming, but wished it hadn't come so soon. There was still so much to say.

CHAPTER 2: DEREK

◈

The rickety old truck came to a stop at Phil's Diner. Derek pulled the lever up and put the truck in park before hand-cranking the driver's side window closed. He pulled his ball cap over his eyebrows and glanced in the rearview mirror, sighing deeply.

Molly's Toyota Camry sat beside him. It was newer than Derek's truck but still required the heat on in the summer to prevent the engine from overheating. Molly had asked Derek to fix it before the summer heat rolled in, but he forgot. The driver's seat was empty. Derek checked his watch, wondering if he was late for their breakfast, as he strolled into the diner.

"Hey, Phil!" He gave his younger brother a slight wave. "Hi, Margie." He followed the waitress. Her curly ash blonde hair bobbed as she walked.

"Morning, Derek."

She led him to the back corner of the diner where Molly sat, focused on the menu.

"Hey, Mols. Don't you know the menu by heart?" Derek smiled, but his tone of voice remained stern.

"Morning, Dad." Molly stared at the menu. "Yeah, I can't decide. I like it all."

Margie sat a hot cup of coffee in front of Derek. "Here's your coffee, just how you like it. Do you want your regular?"

He nodded.

"I'll have the short stack of pancakes and a side of bacon," Molly said.

Margie scribbled onto her receipt pad and winked at Derek. "Coming right up."

"How are you?" Molly asked.

Derek removed his hat and rubbed his dark brown hair. "Good. Are you excited to be done with school?"

Molly rolled her iridescent blue eyes. Every time Derek looked at her, he saw Vanessa's loving gaze. "Dad, I've been home for almost a month now."

Derek nodded, pouring six sugar packets into his coffee cup. "Sorry, I didn't get much sleep last night. I was trying to balance the finances for grandpa's business."

"Don't you mean your business?" Molly's long, wavy hair swayed as she talked.

"Technically, yes, but I can't think of it like that. Grandpa built it. He should have given it to Uncle Phil. Obviously, Phil knows how to run a business. I'm practically running Fischer Home Services aground."

Molly gazed at him from above her coffee mug rim. "Not true, Dad. You're a great businessman and a great carpenter. Other things distracted you, that's all. Sorry about last night. I didn't wake you when I got home, did I?"

"Nah, I don't think so," Derek said.

"I went to Lucy's farm for a party, and I don't think I got home until after two." After a pause, she continued. "I wanted to talk to you about school, Dad." Molly smiled, and Derek watched excitement cascade through her face. "You know my old roommate? Ali? She got an apartment, but apparently, one of her new roommates bailed. I want to move in with her."

Derek drummed his fingers on the table and leaned against the red vinyl booth. "What does that mean?" His stomach rumbled, and he looked around for Margie.

"Well," Molly cleared her throat and continued. "It means that I wouldn't be living on campus next year. I would be in an apartment with Ali and another girl, Sunny, from her major."

"By next year, do you mean three months from now?"

Molly nodded vigorously. "Next school year," she clarified.

"Mols, do you think that's a good idea? What if you don't get along with this other girl?"

Molly played with her napkin, slowly ripping it into shreds. "I do. I don't know her great, but I know her well enough. And besides, I'll have my own room. Plus, I'll save money in the long run because rent and food costs less than room and board."

Derek smirked and nodded. There it was. "How are you going to pay for it? Westchester County isn't cheap. It's at least double of what you'd pay in Saratoga County."

"I'll get a job," Molly countered.

"You're in school full time. You can't work enough to cover your rent."

"Come on, Dad! Can't we come to some kind of agreement? I can pay half and if I have to take out a loan to cover the other half, I will. I really want to do this."

"Short stack with a side of bacon." Margie turned the corner and placed the plate in front of Molly.

Molly turned, her face tense. "Thanks."

"And for you, big guy, the Lumberjack." She placed three plates with eggs, pancakes, French toast, and bacon in front of Derek.

Derek nodded, and Margie slinked away.

"How much is half, Molly?"

"I don't know, like six hundred. I can easily save three hundred a month for rent. All I need is another three hundred for food and utilities, and the rest of the rent. I can make it work, Dad," Molly pleaded. "I'll work three jobs this summer if I have to or dip into Mom's savings."

Derek dropped his fork and it bounced off his plate before clattering to the floor. "You will not tap into your mother's savings. She specifically wanted that money to go to your wedding or first home, whichever came first."

Molly's face contorted at his outburst. "Dad! What if I never get married? Will that money sit there until I die? That money was for me, and I'm over eighteen! We agreed on this. Legally I can take out that money for whatever I want. This apartment is like my first house. Please."

Derek's heart rate quickened and then slowed. He felt his pulse beating against his temple and down his neck. Molly's words ran through his head, and he quickly did the math calculations. He thought about Vanessa and what she would say if she were still alive. He remembered their first apartment and how hard it was to make ends meet without help from family. He and Vanessa acquired a significant amount of debt during their early years of marriage, and he didn't want that stress for Molly. The settlement from Vanessa's car crash let him erase all the hard financial times from their past, but it cost them her life. He wondered if they would still be in debt if Vanessa had survived.

"Fine."

Molly jumped up from the table, ran to the other side, and threw her arms around Derek's shoulders. "Thank you, Daddy!"

"Fine," he repeated. "We'll make it work, but you must uphold your end of the bargain. You pay half and you keep up your grades.

Otherwise, the help is gone." Derek smiled to himself, imagining Vanessa high-fiving him for setting clear expectations. It was a condition Vanessa would have instilled. Derek looked at the ceiling. *Even though you're gone, you're still raising our baby.*

CHAPTER 3: CRYSTAL

S chool had ended the day before, and the sense of accomplishment for getting through another year mingled with her grief. The drive to Saratoga from Rochester was long and tedious. Crystal drove close to eighty down the New York State Thruway while listening to self-care podcasts and whatever radio stations came in clearly.

The anxiety crept in at the thought of seeing her mother. *My dead mother.* Crystal shivered, afraid to imagine how much more Evelyn had deteriorated over the past three years. Guilt seeped into her heart for being unavailable. Remorse lay over her like a heavy, wet blanket. *What do the nurses think of me?* She knew she should have been more integral to her mother's long-term care, but the divorce and her son's learning disability zapped her into an empty void. There wasn't any room left to worry about Evelyn.

The only person who understood the intricacies of her relationship with her mother was Jeremy, and he was off-limits. Crystal could barely stomach her ex-husband, and needing to lean on him made her nauseous. He may have watched Crystal and Evelyn's relationship decline over the past twenty years, but Crystal couldn't trust him with her emotions. He lost her the night he came home with fuchsia lipstick on his neck.

Day turned to night, and the old farmhouse from Crystal's childhood came into view. Her mouth dropped to the floor of the car. She had arranged for Mr. Dole to check in on the house from time to time, but she rarely heard from him. She assumed he was keeping up with the maintenance.

A paralyzing thought crept through Crystal's mind and swept down her body as she took in the current state of the house. *What if Mr. Dole is dead?* Crystal couldn't hypothesize any other reason for the disarray of her old home.

She stared, unsure if she even had the right house. The overgrown front bush pushed up to the second floor, and the vines wrapped up the shingles to the second-floor windows. The once white house now appeared gray from dirt and mildew. The shutters hung cockeyed, and the shingles looked worn and weathered as if they had barely survived a category five hurricane.

The long, curving gravel driveway was now green from grass and weeds taking root in the crevices. Crystal cupped her hands around her eyes to eliminate the sun's glare and struggled to find the driveway's edge. The place where the mailbox used to be was empty, and the grass was high enough to house thousands of hungry ticks.

This was not the house she remembered from her childhood, or even from three years ago. She pulled out her old house key and wondered if she would even need it.

Fear penetrated Crystal's body, and her heart raced as she contemplated her choices. She could stay here, or she could leave. Mason's face flashed through Crystal's mind, and she promised to call Jeremy and thank him for keeping Mason for a few days. Seeing her childhood home in such disorder flooded her with embarrassment and shame—at least she hadn't brought her son here.

Crystal's car crept to the front of the house, where she found a broken window leading into the living room. Broken windows equaled animals, and Crystal trembled at the thought of mice and rats running around. She stood in shock, unsure why Mr. Dole hadn't contacted her about the house's dilapidated condition.

Crystal couldn't stay here. It wouldn't be safe with a broken window and the possibility of animals living inside. She drove to the nearest motel and questioned if it would be any cleaner or safer than the house, but it was all she could afford. *Two nights and then this nightmare will be over.*

* * *

That next morning, she drove to the nursing home to meet with the director. Her chest thumped as the long driveway to the white one-story building came into view. The majestic maple trees provided shade to a handful of residents sitting outside in wheelchairs. Crystal waved to a nurse standing next to the main walkway as she climbed out of the car.

"Hello," she called. The woman held open the door for Crystal, and she entered. The aroma of roses and hydrangeas masked the scent of the aging residents, but Crystal still sensed death, and she shuddered.

"I'm here to speak with the director," Crystal told the receptionist.

She waited in the lobby until a young man approached, probably in his early thirties. "Ms. Whitman?" he asked. The fluorescent lights made his already orange hair and freckles stand out harshly against his pale skin as he held out his hand to greet her.

"Yes," Crystal said, immediately standing. She smoothed her chestnut hair and tried to pull it in a ponytail, forgetting she had cut it too short. She pulled the sides back before dropping her hands, and her hair fell to its natural bob, cupping her jawline.

"I'm Declan O'Halloran," he said, sticking out his hand. "We spoke a few days ago. We can meet in my office."

Crystal followed him and sat across from him at a small table in the corner of the room which had scattered papers spread all over it.

"First off, I am terribly sorry about your mother's passing. She was a wonderful woman," he said.

Crystal nodded, a lump forming in her throat. Flashes of Mason danced through her mind, and guilt followed for not allowing him to know his grandmother. She was happy he wasn't here with her. "Thank you," she mustered.

"I have all her legal documents. You're her only next of kin and power of attorney, so I will be passing this to you."

Crystal's head perked up. "About the farmhouse," she said. "I was always under the impression the house was being cared for by our neighbor, Mr. Dole. Do you know anything about that? I drove by yesterday, and it looks abandoned."

Mr. O'Halloran shook his head. "Sorry. Toward the end, she pulled into herself and didn't talk about much of anything. I can check with the receptionist, but she never had visitors. That name doesn't ring a bell."

Crystal swallowed back tears, the hot saliva burning her throat. "Thanks. And where is her body now?" Images of her dead mother lying in a coffin traveled before her, and nausea built up. She blamed herself for not being around during her mother's final years. *I'm a terrible daughter.*

"At the funeral home. You need to meet with them to make the final arrangements."

Crystal nodded. "Thank you."

She returned to the car, carrying a box of her mother's belongings. She walked with her head down, avoiding eye contact with the office staff who hung around the lobby. That box represented the Evelyn that Crystal never knew. The finality washed over her, and she cried giant tears of regret as she drove away from her mother's final home.

Crystal returned to the hotel and settled on the flat, lumpy mattress. She picked up her phone and called Jeremy.

"Hi, Jer. How's Mason?"

"Fine. He's been jumping on the trampoline all day. We're going to a cook-out tonight. He's fine." His stern voice drained Crystal even more. She rubbed her eyes, unable to muster enough energy to analyze his vocal intentions.

"Tell him I'll be home tomorrow. I'll pick him up around twelve."

"Great. Is everything okay?" His voice softened, and Crystal recognized the man she fell in love with a lifetime ago.

"Yeah, fine. Just overwhelming, you know? Tell Mason I'll call him to say good night tonight."

Crystal hung up the phone, took off her shoes, and wondered if she would pick up bed bugs if she walked in her socks on the thin, worn carpet. She decided it was worth the risk. Even though it wasn't yet noontime, she climbed under the covers and turned on the television.

She called the funeral home and listened to the ring. *One-two-three-four...Come on, pick up.*

"McDaniel's Funeral Home," a cheery high-pitched voice answered.

"Hi, yes, I'm calling to work out the details about Evelyn Whitman's passing," Crystal said, still focused on the television. "I was looking through Evelyn's will, and she would like to be buried with my father. He's in St. Paul's cemetery."

"Yes, of course. We are sorry for your loss. We are waiting on confirmation of the service details. Are you free tomorrow morning?"

Crystal glanced at her watch. "Yes. I can come down first thing."

"Great, " the woman replied. "We can decide on the type of services you'd like."

"Um, actually, there won't be any services right now." Crystal thought about her home, three hours away. Mason's summer schedule was jam-packed with camp and therapy. Her life was out in Rochester, not here, in Saratoga County. The overwhelming gloom pressed upon her.

"No services?"

"No, sorry, I can't. I'll plan a celebration party for next month. Can we arrange to have a priest bless the body before she's buried?" Crystal's voice cracked.

The woman stumbled over her words. "Um, of course, ma'am. We can talk more about this tomorrow. Is 8:30 a.m. okay?"

"Sure. That'd be great."

CHAPTER 4: DEREK

"Hi, Margie, I'll have my usual." Derek stretched his arms over his head. He looked out the window and watched the cars travel along the quiet road. He needed to get a few more jobs before Molly got evicted from the apartment she hadn't even moved into yet.

Margie meandered over with a pot of coffee. "Just brewed, Derek. Nice and hot." The thick, white ceramic cup steamed with liquid energy. "Is anyone joining you today?"

"Nah, just me. I got a busy day today." He didn't want to talk to Margie but enjoyed the distraction. "Is Phil here?"

"Not yet. He'll be in later."

Flashbacks from the night before shot through his brain like the brilliant colors from a spinning disco ball. He'd had the nightmare again. It had occurred so many times he could describe every uncomfortable, painful sensation that continued to haunt him during his sleeping and waking hours. In his dream, he watched young Molly walk into the bathroom at Fischer Home Services. Somehow, a fire broke out. Derek rushed to the bathroom but couldn't disengage the lock. He heard her through the door but couldn't verbalize directions on how to unlock the deadbolt. She screamed, panicking. He pulled and threw his body into the door, but nothing happened. The heat behind him crackled louder, and his body tingled. Everything went black. Suddenly, a firefighter grabbed him, and Derek screamed at him to help Molly first, but nothing made sense. The firefighter couldn't hear him. Molly died, and the business disappeared into black smoke. Everything in his life had perished.

Like every nightmare, he had jolted awake in bed drenched in sweat. His heart had pounded out of his chest, and he couldn't catch his breath. He had stumbled from his bed and sat on his porch, watching the sunrise and thinking about Vanessa. He sometimes wished he had been in the car that night instead of her.

The bell above the diner door dinged, bringing Derek back from his thoughts. He watched a harried-looking woman walk in. Derek knew everyone in this tiny town, but he had never seen her. *She looks lost.*

She scanned the restaurant, unsure if she should sit or wait to be seated. Her cropped dark hair, rectangular-shaped glasses, and black, fitted suitcoat didn't match up with the locals at 7 a.m. on a Thursday. She looked like a fish out of water.

He wanted to tell her to take a seat because her awkward hovering and fleeting eye gaze made his body tense against the uncomfortable seats.

"Excuse me!" She waved her arms at Margie like she was catching a taxi. "Do I sit anywhere?" The patrons at the counter turned and looked at her.

"Yeah, take a seat," Margie said. "Wherever you'd like."

The woman walked toward Derek and sat at the counter. The round, red vinyl stool swiveled as she adjusted her weight. She stepped on the footrest to add some inches and dropped her purse on the floor.

The woman sat with her head in her hands and pulled at her eyebrows. The menu sat in front of her, untouched.

"What can I get you?" Margie asked.

"Coffee, please. And a bagel with cream cheese. And fruit salad, if you have it."

Margie shook her head, her poofy blonde hair swaying above her shoulders. "Sorry, we don't have that, but I can get you a banana."

The woman pushed back her hair. "Sure."

Derek noticed the black pumps, briefcase, and gold jewelry. *She's not from here.*

The woman looked around, her feet tapping against the footrest. She took two small sips of coffee and then dumped six sugar packets into the steaming cup. Derek smiled. *A woman after my own heart.*

"Here you go, Mr. Fischer." Margie placed multiple plates before him, and Derek dug into the eggs first.

"Thanks, Margie."

Before Derek could ask, she poured another cup of coffee, and he immediately added six packets of sugar. He looked up and caught the woman's gaze. He smiled and she dropped her eyes to her phone. He watched her eat her meal while texting or searching the web.

She was pretty, he decided. *Pretty in an unusual way.* She reminded him of a librarian. Quiet, mousy, comforting, and safe.

Derek shook his head and pulled out a photo from his wallet. Vanessa's elongated features and almond-shaped sky-blue eyes stared back at him. She looked so happy.

This woman slumped over the counter was the opposite of Vanessa. Short, round, and cute, when Vanessa had been tall, thin, and beautiful. Every time he looked at Molly, he saw Vanessa staring back at him. When Molly scrunched her nose when she was excited and threw her head back in laughter, he saw Vanessa's enthusiasm and excitement to try new things. When Molly crossed her arms to defend herself or negotiate, he saw Vanessa's passion to help others. He knew Vanessa was with him through Molly, which made him feel at peace.

The woman pushed her plate forward and grabbed her briefcase. She dug through, removing an umbrella, sunglasses, and receipts before finding her wallet. She tossed a ten-dollar bill on the table and exited the diner. "Thank you," she called to Margie.

She looked at Derek as she passed and gave a small smile. He felt heat run up his neck to his cheeks, embarrassed she caught him looking at her. He averted his eyes and stared into his coffee.

I'll never do it, Vanessa. You're the only one for me.

CHAPTER 5: CRYSTAL

༄

C rystal arrived at the funeral home and sat in the large empty parking lot. The regal building sat to her left, opposite the generic town library. Two men wearing matching black suits stood at the door. The immaculate building stood out amongst the neighboring homes, sprinkling them with a little of its grandeur.

She took a deep breath and approached the door. Her hands felt cold, and her parched mouth begged for water. She had read Evelyn's documents the night before, paying close attention to her will. Any assets remaining after the nursing home payment went to Crystal, including the house. Crystal didn't want the responsibility. She just wanted to go home.

In the old Victorian lobby, Crystal met Jennifer, a woman about her age who wore too much makeup for the hot summer sun. She wore a black dress suit with a pencil skirt and blazer, hugging her tight bosom. Crystal saw beads of sweat forming around Jennifer's brow.

"Nice to meet you." Crystal loosely shook her hand. She wiped her palm against her jacket to remove any transferred sweat.

"Right this way." Jennifer slowly walked down the hall into a small room.

"Thank you. This is a beautiful room." Crystal admired the tall ceiling and high windows. The perimeter created a perfect square with a fireplace against one wall. Against the other wall, Crystal saw a large oak desk with claw feet and engraved designs along the side. In the middle of the room stood a lopsided card table, breaking up the magnificence of the surroundings.

"During the Victorian era, this was the morning room, which was the women's domain. It's where the women would handle all the responsibilities. Today we call it the office." Jennifer smiled at Crystal and motioned to the card table.

Crystal sat and Jennifer handed her a glass of water. "Ms. Whitman, we are sorry about your mother's passing. Thank you for coming out today."

Crystal swallowed the pit lodged in her throat.

"I understand you don't want to hold a service," Jennifer said.

"Correct. I would rather have a celebration party once I can get everything organized. I don't live nearby, and I don't have any family. I do have a child, though, and I need to be home with him. Right now, I don't have time to organize a funeral."

Jennifer nodded and appeared to contemplate the situation. She shuffled the papers on the table, probably figuring out how best to maximize their profit. "Let's go through the process, then."

After much debate, Crystal picked out a simple yet elegant casket.

"Would you like to be present for the blessing?"

"Yes, if I can," Crystal said.

Jennifer scheduled the blessing to occur the next day, and Evelyn would be buried immediately after.

Crystal left the funeral home, saddened by her lack of feelings. Her mother had died, and all she could think about was going home. *Is this normal?*

She called Jeremy and diplomatically explained the situation. "Two more days," she promised. "I'll pick up Mason and keep him for next weekend." Everything in their marriage was tit for tat, and she needed to remind him that she knew she was due for an extended custody visit.

Crystal drove past the old farmhouse, and pulled into Mr. Dole's driveway. The pristine white saltbox home stood away from the main road. Crystal knocked on the door, internally practicing her speech. *Hi, Mr. Dole. I was wondering who was taking care of my mother's house?*

The heavy door creaked open and a young man looked at her. "We're not interested." He began to close the door and Crystal thrust her arm out to stop him.

"No, wait. My name is Crystal. My mom is Evelyn. We lived next door. Is Mr. Dole here?"

The young man stood between the door jamb and the edge of the door. "He passed away about eighteen months ago. My name's Daniel, his grandson."

Crystal stepped back, her face long and her eyebrows raised. "Oh, I'm so sorry for your loss."

He scrunched his eyebrows. "Can I help you with something?"

"Oh, no, nothing. I was back in town and wanted to thank him for helping my mother a few years back. She recently died. It was nice meeting you." Crystal turned quickly and climbed into her car. She stepped on the accelerator and sped out of the driveway.

She pulled down the driveway of her home and considered her dilemma. The farmhouse once stood tall and proud, but now was in shambles. Evelyn prided herself in her garden, ensuring the meticulously planted flowers bloomed during each season between early spring and late fall. Crystal often found Evelyn outside in the early morning, digging in the dirt, planting bulbs, and pruning the bushes. Now, Crystal couldn't identify where the bushes or flowers used to stand. She couldn't even see the first-floor windows.

Instead of going inside, Crystal walked around the perimeter and climbed into the thorny bushes. She cupped her hands against the dusty window and peered through. Her parent's filthy kitchen table sparkled in the sunlight.

From what she could see, only one window was broken on the house's far side, which could have occurred during a heavy rainstorm. Crystal recalled her father complaining about those trees being too close to the house, but Evelyn had persuaded him that the shade was worth the risk of a limb breaking in the wind. *It looks like Dad was right.*

The house was hers since there was no mortgage. *I could have convinced her to sell this house if I hadn't been so angry or if I had known Mr. Dole had died. Now I'm stuck with it, and it's probably only worth a dime.* Crystal wished she had taken more interest in Evelyn's affairs when her dementia worsened, but it was too overwhelming. When Evelyn got sick, Crystal was already busy navigating a divorce and single parenthood.

Now, she faced a bigger problem. She had a house that could potentially make her a lot of money and set up Mason for years, but nothing in life came for free. She had to fix it up. Otherwise, the profit potential was next to nothing.

Crystal pulled out her phone and searched for help.

CHAPTER 6: DEREK

❧

"Fischer Home Services," Derek said into the red plastic telephone receiver. The cord tangled within itself, and he stretched it out before it released back into the narrow twist.

"Hi." He heard uncertainty in the woman's voice as she hesitated before continuing. "Hi," she repeated. "I don't know if you can help me, but I recently inherited a house in town that's falling down. I need a quote to fix it. There's a lot wrong. It's been empty for a few years now."

Derek glanced at his nearly empty calendar and flipped to the next month. *Yep, nothing.* "Sure. What type of things do you need?"

"The bushes are all overgrown, and the driveway needs to be paved. The house has broken windows and needs new paint. I haven't quite made it inside yet. I'm sure there's more. The thing is, I don't have a ton of money. I know there's a lot, and it won't be cheap, but I have no idea how much it could cost."

Derek tapped his pen against the table. "Are you looking for inside or outside?"

"Everything. Both," the woman quickly replied. "But I also need to know the cost breakdown because I don't think I'll be able to afford it all. At least not right now."

Derek glanced at his empty calendar again. "Are you free now?"

"Yes!" Enthusiasm penetrated his ear. "That would be great."

She gave him the address, and he promised to be there within the hour.

Derek knew the house. When he and Vanessa had first moved to Farm Cove, NY, they often drove around looking for their dream home. Her college was nearby, and her first teaching job was five minutes away, so settling in the small village made sense. Derek hadn't wanted to move to an old hick town without a stoplight or a grocery store, but Vanessa convinced him that it would be a great place to raise a family. He and Vanessa drove up and down every rural street, admiring the quaint houses, searching for their perfect home.

As he pulled up to the dilapidated house in Farm Cove, he remembered the flowers, the pristine paint job, and the welcome sign on the door. He and Vanessa loved that house. He noticed when the house started to fall apart and wondered if the person living there had died. Occasionally, he would drive by, looking for an auction or sale sign, but nothing appeared. Now, he would meet the person behind the home. His heart thudded against his chest.

The truck door clanged shut, and the metal vibrated against the frame. A woman wearing a black pencil skirt and blazer stood before him. He recognized her giant briefcase and the sudden uncomfortable feeling he carried at the diner presented itself again.

"Hello. My name is Derek." He wasn't sure if she would recognize him from the diner but recalled making eye contact before she left.

"Hi. Crystal. This was my parent's home, and I need to fix it so I can sell it."

Derek nodded, scanning the damage to the exterior of the home.

"I haven't been inside. I'm kind of afraid to walk in there. Spiders, raccoons, mold...I can't do it."

Derek scanned the house and yard, rubbing his hands through his thick, dark hair. "Let me survey the outside. Then, I'll go inside and check it out if you want to follow behind."

Crystal sat on the stoop, her legs making a ninety-degree angle with the broken concrete, and Derek roamed around the exterior, making notes in his notebook.

Yard, driveway, paint, new windows, he wrote.

"I'm ready to go in if you are." He approached her from the opposite corner.

She unlocked the door, and Derek led, asking for directions on where he would find specific rooms. The house's interior was rougher than the outside. Cracked and crumbled sheetrock in some rooms, faded and peeling wallpaper in others, and mildew-infested bathrooms greeted him.

"The good news," Derek said, "is that I didn't see any animals. Just spiders, but we can get rid of those."

He noticed that the woman shivered at the mention of spiders.

"Based upon what I see, you need new everything. Furnace, walls, flooring, bathrooms, possibly foundation. It's a full overhaul, and it might be cheaper to tear it down and start over again."

"No," Crystal said. "I don't have time for that, and I need to fix it and sell it so I don't have to worry about it anymore. What would be the bare minimum to get it functional and sold in the quickest amount of time?"

Derek pursed his lips and scrunched his nose. He was a one-person show and probably couldn't do it all. He would have to subcontract out, which meant he'd have to work with other contractors. He hated being around people, but maybe they would use him for future jobs if he included them in this monstrosity. His calendar was empty for the next few months. And he needed money to support Molly for all of next year.

He looked around, considering his options. "Interior and exterior paint, new windows, landscaping, and sheetrock. The furnace hasn't been used in a few years so if you want to sell you need to get a new one. That's a big expense. The roof looks good, and the water valve was shut off, so your pipes are good. You're lucky it isn't worse." Derek smiled brightly at Crystal's good fortune. "I think we can spruce up the kitchen and bathroom. Maybe new appliances for the kitchen, painted cabinets, and updated bathrooms. You can market it as having character and probably as a fixer-upper."

Crystal looked at him and back at the house. "Can you send me a quote? I have a few other contractors coming over, and I live three hours away. I can give you a call in a week after I get my finances straightened out."

Derek nodded and gave her his card, which Vanessa designed years ago when she helped him run the company during the summer months. Vanessa always told him to carry his cards because *you never know when someone needs work done.* The card, although newly printed, listed their old phone number, so Derek crossed it out and penciled in his cell.

Crystal took one of his cards and wrote her number and email on the back. "Email is better. I try not to answer my phone."

Derek stuffed it in his wallet next to Vanessa's weathered photo from their wedding and Molly's school picture from kindergarten.

The woman didn't seem to remember him from the diner. She never said where she lived, but he imagined a city with large buildings and actual businesses. She didn't live in a rinky-dink town like Farm Cove, with its empty main street, dwindling population, and overabundance of farms.

"So, what's the story with this house?" he asked her.

"I'm not really sure. My parents bought it in the sixties. Supposedly it was a working farm, but the town bought all the land and sold it as individual lots. All we had was the house and that old barn in the back."

Derek nodded, imagining who had lived in the house a hundred years ago. Probably a family of ten crammed into the three bedrooms, the older kids minding the younger kids or working the farm. Life was tough back then.

Derek had considered leaving Farm Cove after Vanessa died, but he stayed for Molly. He needed a job to absorb Vanessa's teaching salary, and his father agreed to teach him the ropes of the business. Eventually, Derek became a partner, and then when his father passed, he became the sole owner.

But now that Molly's in New York City, why am I sticking around? Derek looked at the house and at Crystal. *Maybe this is the break I need.*

CHAPTER 7: CRYSTAL

‿❦‿

He's cute. Not celebrity-cute. But good-guy-cute. I bet he'd make a good father. Crystal shook her head in disbelief. She lived hours away, her mother had just died, and she had a son. She did not have time in her chaotic life to pursue a man, even if it was only in her imagination.

"Are you from around here?" She stuffed the business card into her purse. "You look familiar."

He grinned at her. "Not from this town, but from upstate New York."

Crystal pushed her bangs to the side of her forehead and peered into his ocean-blue eyes. They pulled her towards him like a light at the end of a dark tunnel. She had a hard time looking away. She cleared her throat and stuck out her hand. "Thank you again for meeting with me."

He gripped her hand gently and squeezed. "We'll be in touch."

Crystal smiled and followed him down the crumbled driveway toward her car. She sat in the driver's seat and turned the engine. She put the car in reverse, pressed the pedal, and lurched backward before falling forward again. The heavy revving of her engine echoed off the clouds. She tried again, and nothing. Her front wheels spun, but her back wheels stuck like bubble gum.

Crystal threw the car in park and jumped out, racing around to the back of her vehicle. Two flat tires stared back at her, and she threw back her head and screamed in aggravation toward the canopy of trees. She turned to face the road and bumped nose-to-nose with Derek.

"Sorry, I didn't see you," she mumbled. "I have a flat. Or two." She pointed toward the wheels. "I have no idea how that happened."

Derek looked around at the dilapidated house. "I do. Check out all those beer bottles smashed in the bushes. Kids must come here to party on the weekends."

Crystal bit back tears and turned away from Derek to wipe her eyes. "What am I going to do?"

"Are you hungry?" Derek asked. "I know a great place where we can grab some lunch."

Crystal turned toward him and narrowed her eyes. "Lunch? I'm stuck here, and you're thinking about food?"

He leaned forward and peered over her shoulder. "Relax. I have some connections. They'll be able to get your car fixed. I'll take care of you."

Crystal blushed. *He'll take care of your car, Crystal. He'll help you right now; not take care of you forever.* She turned to face her old home to hide the redness traveling up her face. When she returned to Derek, she smiled brightly. "Sure, that would be great."

She climbed into his old truck. The ripped seats and metal floor reminded her of her father. The antique dial radio played music through the round speakers in the door. "I love this song," she commented.

"I hope so, because this is the only station I get."

Derek turned toward town, and Crystal wondered if she had made a big mistake. In a car with a stranger. She tightened her grip around her pocketbook and leaned toward the door. "Where are we going?"

She pulled out her cell phone to remind him that she could get help if something terrible happened.

"My brother's place." He kept his eyes on the road, and Crystal scanned the car for a potential weapon if needed.

"I thought we were going to eat." Her voice quivered, and she halted her thoughts. He turned toward her. *Oh crap. Now he knows I'm scared.*

"We are. He owns Phil's Diner, and Phil's my brother."

Crystal's heart slowed, and the pit in her throat melted. "I was there this morning."

"I know. I saw you."

Crystal's head whipped toward Derek, and she saw him smile behind his beard. Hints of gray sparkled as rays of sunshine infiltrated the truck. "That's why you looked so familiar," she said.

"Probably. It's not every day you see a beautiful woman in this small town."

Is he flirting with me? Crystal moved her hand closer to the door pull and looked away.

Derek pulled into the empty parking lot, and his jalopy kerplunked to silence.

Crystal followed him into the diner and scooted into the vinyl seat facing him.

"Well, well, look who's back." The waitress from breakfast sauntered over. She placed her hand behind Derek's head and leaned toward him. Crystal couldn't help but notice her perky breasts poking through her scoop neck t-shirt.

Derek looked up and smiled. "Hi, Margie. This is Crystal. I was helping her on a job, and her tires are flat." Crystal couldn't help but wonder why he felt compelled to explain their situation to her. "Crystal, this is Margie. She's been working for my brother since the diner opened."

Crystal smiled sweetly. *She's pretty. Perky boobs, plush lips, straight teeth, thin, petite body. I can see why he likes her. I wonder what their story is.* "Nice to meet you."

They ordered lunch, and while waiting for their food, Derek called a few friends.

He placed his phone on the splotchy table. Looking at the screen, Crystal saw a woman with crinkled eyes, silky hair, and a broad smile. She was caught mid-laugh, with her head thrown toward the sky for emphasis. She held a fruity drink, and the blue ocean water and blue sky created a fairy tale backdrop. "The problem is," Derek said.

Crystal jolted her eyes up and away from the illuminated phone.

"It's a small town, and everyone's busy. My buddy, Joe, said he could tow your car to his garage and have it for you in the morning. Do you have roadside assistance? That might be quicker." The phone dimmed, and Crystal wondered who the beautiful woman was to Derek.

Crystal shook her head. She forgot to renew her membership months ago when dealing with Mason's issues at school. Every time the caller ID showed the school phone number, Crystal cringed and ignored it. Usually, they left a voicemail explaining that Mason was in trouble for being disrespectful to his classmates or teachers. Crystal couldn't call back until she processed the offense. Last school year's academic and discipline problems took up most of her attention, and renewing roadside assistance was the least of her problems.

"Well, it looks like you're here until tomorrow." Derek smiled at her and shrugged his shoulders. Margie slid their order on the table, and Crystal unfolded her paper napkin, placing it on her lap. Derek took a sip of soda, and she couldn't help but imagine the taste of his sugar-coated lips. A burning sensation rumbled near her belly button. She wiped her mouth with her napkin and rummaged through her purse to keep her mind occupied.

"It's fine. My mother's blessing is tomorrow at eleven at the funeral home. Do you think I'll have my car back by then?"

Derek took a bite of his sandwich and nodded. "Yeah, I'll tell him you have an appointment in the morning."

Crystal felt her body relax against the hard seat. "Thank you so much. But what am I going to do about all the other contractors? I had two other appointments today and one in the morning. Should I cancel?"

Derek grinned. Crystal noticed a gap in his two front teeth that was wide enough to fit a toothpick. *How didn't I see that earlier?* "Well, you have no car, so I guess you're stuck with me." He stuck a fry in his mouth and bit down while smiling.

Crystal shook her head, a grin spreading across her face. She leaned on her hand and stared into his playful eyes. "I guess that's it then. I guess you're my guy for the next few months. But only if the price is right." She paused and took a sip of soda from her straw. She looked at him from the top of her eyes. "I guess you'll be busy tonight working the numbers. Hopefully, we can meet up tomorrow to go over everything."

Derek chuckled. "That sounds like an ultimatum, but you'll need a ride tomorrow, right? To get your car?"

Crystal nodded.

"Don't worry. I'll drive you. We can talk about details then."

"I guess I'm yours." Her cheeks reddened, and she grinned. *What am I doing? I thought this guy would kill me a few minutes ago, and now I'm all his?*

CHAPTER 8: DEREK

Who's the girl?" Margie asked the next day at breakfast. She tipped her head back and rolled her shoulders.

"Hello to you, too. Are you feeling okay?"

"Yeah, just tired. Haven't had a day off in almost a week. My back is killing me." She looked around the empty restaurant and slid in next to Derek.

Derek felt her hand brush against his thigh and shifted further toward the window.

He poured sugar into his coffee and stirred. The clanking of metal on ceramic filled the booth.

"So, who's the girl? She's cute."

Derek sighed and turned to face Margie, but her face was inches from his. He turned his head back to the center. "Her mother died. She wants to sell the house on Clearview but doesn't have much money. She wants it to be habitable but not perfect. I was at the house yesterday with her, and her car got two flats. I called some buddies, but the car wasn't available until this morning."

"You know, Derek, I've always wanted what's best for you. Maybe it's time you branch out. Meet people and have some fun."

Derek's left leg bounced rhythmically under the table. "No thanks. I'm not interested."

"Your life, but what would Vanessa say? She'd want you to live whatever years you have left. You're no spring chicken, you know. And how many years has she been gone?"

Derek drummed his fingers on the laminate table. "Twelve years, Margie."

Margie whistled and leaned closer to Derek. "Twelve years is a long time to be alone."

Derek bit his lip and took a sip of lukewarm coffee. "I wasn't alone. I've dated before. The problem is that there aren't many single women around here. Everyone in town knows what happened and Vanessa's name always came up. Usually on the first date. It was 'I'm so sorry. How are you? How's your daughter?' I don't want to be reminded of my dead wife while on a date. I just don't. Besides, I have Molly. And work. They both keep me busy."

Margie dropped her voice and touched his hand. "You need to open your heart, Derek. It's time."

A booming voice from the kitchen interrupted them. "Margie! Order's up. Come on. It's gettin' cold."

Margie ignored the command and leaned closer to Derek. "Molly's gone now. She's living her life, so it's time for you to start living yours." She hoisted herself up from the narrow booth, stretched her back, and walked toward the kitchen. "I'm coming, I'm coming," she said.

Derek stared out the window, thinking about Vanessa and the inconceivable pull to Crystal. He shook his head. *This is stupid. She's leaving today and lives three hours away. Why am I even wasting my time stressing about this?*

Derek recalled Crystal's gaze when he had added six sugar packets to his coffee. He sensed her recognition in that tiny detail about his life, just as he had noticed it when he first saw her. He chuckled at the image of her screaming into the sky, thinking no one saw her. He'd been watching her, analyzing her movements, and he hadn't even realized.

He checked his phone and saw a missed text from Crystal. **Car's ready. Could you pick me up at ten?** Derek responded with a thumbs-up emoji.

They had spent the evening prioritizing projects for the house. Crystal wanted to get the house renovated and sold before Thanksgiving. That gave him four months to overhaul the inside and outside, cutting it close. He didn't know if he would be able to pull it off.

Phil approached the table and placed Derek's meal in front of him. "Here you go."

Derek stood up and hugged Phil. Phil could be taken away from him at any moment, just as Vanessa had, and Derek didn't want to risk the guilt of taking his brother for granted. "Hey, man, busy morning?"

Phil adjusted his apron. "Nah, not too bad. We got a guy back there training on the grill. Mind if I sit with you?" He slid in before Derek could answer.

Derek poured ketchup on his home fries and put jelly on his toast. "You want some?" He motioned toward his plate.

Phil shook his head. "So, how'd it go with the house yesterday?"

"Good. Better than I thought. She's looking at a thirty-to-forty-thousand-dollar reno, which is awesome for me. It'll keep me busy and line my pockets, but I gotta find a crew. She wants the house on the market by Thanksgiving." The home fries tasted extra oniony today.

"Are you going to use Dad's contacts?"

Derek bobbed his head. "I think I have to. I may have burned those bridges already, but I'm willing to take that chance for this job. Go back with my tail between my legs."

"Let me know if you need any help. I can swing a hammer."

Derek scoffed. "You? You practically sleep here. Thanks for the offer, but I think I'll be okay."

Phil grinned. "Sure, whatever you want to do. The Fourth of July cook-out is coming up soon. Are you up for another Home Run Derby tournament?"

Derek laughed. "Yeah, man. The reigning champion must defend his title. I'll be there."

"I don't know if you're up for it, but Amy's new stylist at her salon is coming. She's single. Amy thinks you'd be great together."

Derek threw his hands on the table and pushed his plate away. "C'mon, man! I love your wife, but I don't want to see anyone. I'm not there yet."

Phil threw his hands up in the air and leaned his body back. "No pressure, man. She'll be there, but I'll tell Amy no pressure."

The last thing I need is another woman being thrust upon me because people are trying to help. I don't want it. As he spoke to himself, a petite woman in a black suit with a briefcase poked her head into his mind, and he couldn't help but shiver in anticipation. Warmth filled his core, and his heart rate sped up like a jackhammer. "Phil, I gotta go. Thanks, but no thanks. I'm not interested."

CHAPTER 9: CRYSTAL

"Mom! Where are my basketball shorts?" Mason stood at the top of the stairs, holding a duffel bag and his pillow. "In the wash. Let me grab them." Crystal had been home for two weeks and now it was time to return to Farm Cove to help with the house. Jeremy agreed to take care of Mason for three weeks, so she had to make every day count.

She opened the basement door with the empty laundry basket on her hip. "Lulu, no." Crystal nudged the door closed before Lulu could escape into the basement. Three piles of dirty clothes and towels greeted her in front of the washer and dryer. She pulled out the warm clothes and trekked up the stairs. "Mason, here."

Mason unzipped his bag and stuffed the shorts into any available air pocket. "Are we going yet?"

"Yes. Do you have enough clothes for all seasons? Chilly nights, hot days, swimming, and enough underwear to last a week? Dad doesn't do laundry often." Crystal scanned the room and grabbed the dog bowl, a bag of food, and her rolling suitcase.

"Yeah, Mom. I have it all."

Crystal stopped and turned toward Mason. "Okay, great, because you're going away for three weeks. A week of camp, a week at Nana's, and a week with Dad. I'm really going to miss you." She leaned in for a hug, but Mason's body stiffened and he pulled away.

"Yeah, Mom. I got it. I'm ready to go."

They made three trips, loading the car with bags and food. Crystal stuffed her rolled-up sleeping bag and air mattress into the trunk and slammed it down. "Let's go. But first, the dog." She ran into the house, hooked up Lulu's leash, grabbed her crate, and passed her to Mason.

"Mom, are you sure you're going to be able to take care of Lulu? She might get hurt."

Crystal pulled out of the driveway, looking over her shoulder and smiled at Mason, who had Lulu sound asleep in his lap. "She'll be fine. I have her crate, so she'll be safe if anyone needs to work in the house. Derek said the bedroom, kitchen, and bathroom are habitable. I don't know what that means, but I'm going to cross my fingers that it's habitable to my standards." She looked in the rearview mirror and smiled. "Don't worry, Mase, Lulu'll be fine."

Mason petted Lulu's soft fur and snuggled into her face. "I'm gonna miss you, Lulu."

"It's only a few weeks, sweetie, and we'll be home a full month before school starts."

As they drove the ninety minutes to Jeremy's apartment they talked about Mason's upcoming basketball camp, trip to Lake Ontario, and week off with Jeremy. When they pulled into the parking lot, Crystal texted Jeremy, and within a few minutes he stood outside her car.

"Hey, buddy." He rubbed Mason's head. "You're getting so tall! You're going to be taller than Mom soon!"

Mason hugged Jeremy and took Lulu out of the car to stretch her legs.

"Thanks, Jeremy. I appreciate you taking him an extra week." Crystal smiled at her ex-husband.

Jeremy leaned against the hood. "Don't thank me, thank my mom. I couldn't get off work for two weeks."

"I will." Crystal looked down and slowly raised her eyes. "Well, I'm halfway to Farm Cove and want to get there before dark, so I should probably go."

"Why are you going again?" Jeremy ran his hands through his hair and leaned close. Crystal inhaled his familiar aftershave.

"If I want the house on the market, I need to pitch in. Plus, I only have so much money in savings, so I need to do what I can. I can paint and do yard work, which should save a few thousand dollars."

Jeremy scanned the area behind Crystal. "Mason, not too far," he hollered. He turned his eyes back to Crystal. "I mean, why do you need to go back? Why not just sell it as is? Why bother?"

Crystal sighed. "Because I owe it to my mom, and the least I can do is honor the life she built, even though I chose to walk away."

Jeremy kissed her on the cheek, and Crystal recoiled at his closeness. "You have a good heart," he whispered.

Crystal stepped back and narrowed her eyes. *What was that?* She walked toward Mason across the lush, green grass. "Mason, sweetie, I have to go." She leaned into him and wrapped her arms around him. "I love you. Call me if you need anything. Just say the word, and I'll come get you."

Mason hugged Crystal's waist, familiar with the parent hand-off. "Bye, Mom, love you. Bye, Lulu. I love you too."

Crystal watched Mason and Jeremy walk away from her, and her heart sank. Mason may have adjusted to the parent hand-off, but she hadn't. She missed him already, and he was still in her view. She drove the hour-and-a-half to Farm Cove in silence. She thought about Jeremy and could still smell his cologne. The kiss on her cheek surprised her, and she wondered why he felt comfortable doing that.

The last time they saw each other, he asked her if he could introduce

Mason to his new girlfriend. Crystal couldn't ask if it was the woman with the fuchsia lipstick because she didn't want to know. She agreed but never asked about her again. The wall between them thickened, but somehow Jeremy decided to knock it down with a sledgehammer. *What did that kiss mean?*

The house slowly came into view, and it looked the same. It had been two weeks, and the driveway was still broken and overgrown, and the vines still pressed against the second-floor windows. Someone covered the broken window with a board, and Crystal gained some comfort that a wild animal wouldn't eat her in the middle of the night.

Crystal saw Derek's jalopy closest to the house, and two newer construction vehicles sat behind it. She slammed her door shut, grabbed Lulu, and entered. "Hello?" she called.

The circular saw buzzed in the distance, and banging ricocheted off the empty walls. "Hello?" she called again. She carried Lulu into the kitchen.

Derek slid the brand-new stove against the wall, wedged between two cabinets. He pulled off his protective eyewear and smiled at her. He wore a tight, white tank top that squeezed his torso and accentuated his pectoral muscles. Her gaze fell across his biceps, shiny from sweat. A toolbelt hung loosely around his tight jeans, and Crystal's mouth salivated.

"Hi," she breathed. "Uh, this looks great." She motioned toward the stove.

He pulled a pencil from his ear and jotted down notes in a small notebook on the counter. "Hi." His wet hair framed his face, and Crystal's heart thudded against her breasts.

"Uh," she looked around the kitchen to avoid his blue eyes. "This is Lulu. She'll be staying here with me for a few weeks."

Derek smiled at Lulu and petted her head. Lulu snuggled up against him, and Crystal smiled. She always trusted Lulu's instincts when judging someone's character.

"She likes you."

Derek looked up, and their eyes locked.

"That means I like you too." Crystal's breathy voice caught in her throat.

Derek chuckled. "Good thing, because we're going to be spending a lot of time together the next few weeks."

Crystal took a step back and leaned against the fridge. Her legs weakened under the weight of her body. "I can't wait."

CHAPTER 10: DEREK

S he looked cute in her denim overalls, Converse sneakers, and a white tank top that hugged her curves in all the right places. She didn't know how to do anything, but at least she tried. Derek spent most of the day supervising Crystal's inability to swing a hammer or paint in a 'Y', but he didn't mind.

He had hired three contractors to help him flip the house, and he could see the progress they had made, but Crystal wanted to help with the renovations. She had been in the house three days and, so far, they had torn down the wall between the dining and living rooms and painted the upstairs hallway. Just that one coat of paint had transformed the space into a breath of fresh air.

"Crystal, when you paint, you want to go left-down-right-down-up." He grabbed her wrist from behind and modeled the movement. A zap of electricity flowed from her wrist to his hand and up to his throbbing heart. "That way, there're no streaks." He applied pressure to the wall and extended her arm as high as she could reach. The scent of her shampoo filled his nostrils, and his heart thudded harder.

She dropped her arm and turned toward him, pressing against him to avoid the wet paint on the wall. Heat lingered between their bodies.

"Thanks, I'll remember that," she whispered. He stared into her eyes and recognized apprehension and confusion.

She broke his gaze and ducked under his arm to escape the box he created around her. She scurried to the far end of the hall and continued painting.

Derek watched her roll paint on the wall with long strokes. "Tell me about your kid. What's he like?" Derek picked up another roller and tackled the opposite wall.

Crystal's shoulders seemed to relax, and she smiled at him. "He's ten years old and is a sweet boy, but has a hard time in school. It's not the school work; it's all the other stuff. Personal space, staying seated, blurting out when the teacher's talking. It's hard because he's kind and smart, but sometimes he can't control himself."

Derek nodded. "School's tough. I was the kid that couldn't read, so they always made fun of me. I hated when the teacher made me read aloud in front of the class. It was humiliating." Derek recalled the shame that had grown deep inside when he stumbled over the word 'mischievous' and the cool kids in the back snickered. The day he graduated high school was one of the happiest days of his life. He could finally move on and away from the bullies. "Have you talked to him since you've been here?"

"He's at camp this week. Last night, I talked to his dad, Jeremy, and he said all was well. I'll pick him up in two and a half weeks."

Derek continued painting as the quiet sat between them. The echo of chatter downstairs muffled by eighties rock music filled the silence.

Derek's voice caught in his throat, but he pushed through. "Are you married?" He had looked for a wedding ring, but hadn't seen one.

She snapped her head toward him. "What? No. God, no. Divorced. I caught him cheating and that was that."

Derek's heart rate sped up and slowed down. He didn't want to pry because they barely knew each other, but he was curious. Instead, he offered her a bottle of water, which Crystal opened and guzzled in its entirety.

"What about you? What's your story?" Crystal glanced at him as he dipped the roller in more paint.

"My story? Let's see. I moved here when I got married. My wife was a teacher. We had a daughter, and a few years later, my wife died in a car crash. Hit by a drunk driver at four-thirty in the afternoon." He focused on the wall before him, but felt Crystal's stare. He didn't want to see her pity. Feeling it was bad enough.

"I'm so sorry," she said. She elongated her words and over-emphasized the word 'so.'

Derek shrugged, his shoulders tensing again. "Eh, it was a long time ago."

Crystal stood back and scanned the hallway. They were two-thirds of the way done. "Tell me about your daughter. What's she like?" Crystal scratched her forehead, and gray paint smeared along her hairline.

Derek was relieved to talk about Molly. He walked over to Crystal's end of the hallway and tossed her a towel. "Here. Your face." He reached over her to paint the area she couldn't reach. As Crystal wiped her forehead and retied her bandana, her midriff peeked out of the corner of her overalls. Derek averted his eyes, aware of their proximity. "Molly's almost twenty and goes to school in Westchester County. Studying to be a Speech Therapist. She wants to work with kids. Help 'em talk. She's smart, thoughtful, beautiful, and caring. I know my wife, Vanessa, would be proud of her, and I tell her all the time. She has so many qualities Vanessa had. It's uncanny." Derek's posture stiffened after realizing he referred to Vanessa as his wife. *What is she exactly? My dead wife? She died a lifetime ago.*

"She sounds like a terrific girl. Does she live around here?"

Derek poured more paint into the shallow tray. "She does for now.

She lives with me, but will move into her apartment in August. Maybe you'll meet her. She sometimes grabs lunch from Phil's and brings it to the site to surprise me." Derek looked around the hallway, admiring their work. They were practically done. The old floral wallpaper was gone, and a fresh coat of Gray Heron covered the walls. "This looks great, Crystal. You like it?"

Crystal stepped back, and her shoulder brushed Derek's upper arm. Another jolt of electricity traveled throughout his body, and he rubbed the back of his neck. He stepped to the side to give her more room, and she scanned the hallway, grinning.

"This is perfect. It's on-trend, screams farmhouse, and is neutral enough for any buyer. I love it." They covered the paint cans and moved them to the doorway of her bedroom. "Hey, I meant to ask, can we paint in here?" She nodded toward her bedroom. "And would you be willing to build me a small walk-in closet?" Her pleading eyes taunted Derek and he followed her into the bedroom. "I think we should do a lighter gray for all the bedrooms. I know it's small, but don't most buyers want a large closet?"

Her bare torso peeked over the edge of her overall pants, and he fought a desire to touch her bare skin again. He cleared his throat and perused the room. He caught sight of a bright pink bra hanging off the bed from the corner of his eyes. *Don't focus on that.* He imagined Crystal wearing it and shook his head in disbelief. *What am I doing? Keep your eyes on the project.* "Yeah, we can build a closet here. You would lose the wall space between the window and the corner of the room and about four feet of floor space, but we can do it."

"Great! I'll work on removing all this wallpaper. It reminds me of my grandmother, which is not what people want or need. I need this room to be fresh, hip, and appealing, so it'll sell."

Derek watched Crystal scurry around the room, shoving undergarments of various colors into her top dresser drawer. "Sorry, but I didn't have time to fold my laundry."

Derek felt the sexual tension grow as she moved around the cramped space. He imagined her walking toward him in her pink bra and shook his head in disdain. Thoughts of desire, betrayal, and animalistic tendencies flooded him. He needed air and an escape from her bare midriff, smooth skin, and coconutty shampoo. He walked up to her and hesitated, imagining pushing her onto the bed and kissing her soft belly. He held his breath, willing is brain to control his body.

Crystal looked up at him, tilting her chin. She pulled the bandana off her head, shook her hair out, and touched his beard softly with her fingertips.

Derek's body shivered and he drew in a sharp breath. Alarm bells rang in his ears, warning him not to get involved, but he was almost sure she wanted him too.

Crystal half-smiled with one corner of her lips rising. "Sorry. You had a fuzzy." She turned on her heel and exited the room, leaving him stranded and more confused than ever.

CHAPTER 11: CRYSTAL

T he next day, Derek and Crystal tackled the upstairs bathroom. When Derek told her the bathroom was habitable, he meant the downstairs bathroom with its cramped stand-up shower. The upstairs bathroom was a total gut job because the galvanized steel pipes had failed. Crystal's father built the second bathroom downstairs when Crystal was a teenager, and thankfully that one only needed a makeover.

"Derek, did you get the tile? I think I can put it in if you show me how." Crystal looked at him with dead certainty that she could do it.

Derek chuckled. "I'll do the flooring. Maybe you can paint? We're putting in the original clawfoot tub this afternoon, but you probably want the wall behind the tub to be one color."

Crystal saluted him. "Sure thing, Captain. You're the boss." She marched over to the can of white paint and shook it up. "Are you sure we can do this at the same time?"

"Yeah, you paint over there, and I'll start the floor over here. Once we have the walls painted and the flooring done, you'll be good to go."

They worked diligently, and both focused on their own project. Crystal taped the ceiling and started painting.

"Don't worry if you get paint on the floor," Derek said. "The tiles and baseboard will cover it."

When Crystal and Derek finished, and the tub was installed, Crystal's stomach grumbled for dinner. "I didn't realize I was hungry, but I haven't eaten all day. Do you want some food?"

"Nah, I have to check on the guys. They're probably all packing up by now. Molly's cooking me dinner tonight, and I told her I'd be home at six. I won't be here tomorrow. I'm assisting another job in Saratoga for one of the guys. Another bathroom, if you can believe it. I haven't renovated a bathroom in about three years, and now I have two in two days." Derek patted his back pocket and his keys jangled.

The clawfoot tub rested beautifully along the far wall, and the water ran clear. "This looks great," Crystal said, rubbing her hands along the new pedestal sink. "I love the checkered tile we decided on, and the blue hexagons pop against the white walls." Crystal headed downstairs.

Derek's heavy footsteps followed her into the kitchen. She leaned against the counter, pulled off her bandana, and threw it between a tall red toolbox and the overflowing trash can. "So, what do you need me to do tomorrow?"

Derek looked around. "I don't know. The bathroom's done. Maybe you can decorate it? New shower curtain, bathmats, whatever you want to feel more at home."

Crystal gave water to Derek and the three contractors as a thank you and watched them file out of her mother's broken-down home. Instead of devastation, growing merriment spread throughout the rooms and into her jittery limbs. If she used her imagination, it almost felt like a new home. Almost.

She hummed to herself as she pulled jelly out of the refrigerator and peanut butter and bread out of the new pantry. The disappointing memories from her childhood slipped away, and dreams of the future in her old home crept across her mind. *No, I can't do that. I have a job and a son to consider—a son who needs stability. Plus, our life is three hours away.* She finished her sandwich and decided it was time to get out of her filthy clothes and into something more comfortable.

The wooden floorboards creaked as she walked upstairs and into her bedroom. She gathered her pajamas and a clean towel from the messy pile on the floor and turned on the tub. The bathroom sparkled, and Crystal looked in awe. The bright overhead light illuminated the chrome faucet she and Derek picked out and installed together. This masterpiece was her work. She closed her eyes and pretended she was in a five-star hotel.

She didn't have a shower curtain yet, and the floor didn't have any bathmats, but the glistening new tub invited her to enjoy the night and relax her aching muscles. Crystal imagined herself in the hotel bathroom with a glass of wine in one hand, and a book in the other. She looked around the room and realized that if she had a glass of wine, there was nowhere to put it. *I'll have to ask Derek to build me a shelf on that wall.*

She dragged a folding chair from her bedroom into the bathroom and rummaged through the kitchen for a disposable cup to fill with wine. She carried it upstairs and set the cup on an old phone book she found in the kitchen. The flimsy chair rocked from side to side, and the red liquid sloshed up and down, creating rhythmic ripples in her pretend wineglass.

Crystal turned on the hot water and listened to it drumming against the porcelain basin. She put in her earbuds, lowered herself into the deep tub, and watched steam rise above her head. She breathed in deeply, feeling the hot stickiness coat her lungs, and her body tingled and burned.

Ah, this is the life. My bones and muscles ache. She lowered herself further under the water until her shoulders skimmed below the surface. She listened to acoustic rock music through her earbuds and closed her eyes. *This is precisely what I needed.*

She thought about Mason and hoped he was happy at camp. Jeremy hadn't called for parenting guidance or assistance, so things must be okay. Her mind traveled to the kiss a few days before, and she wondered what it meant. *Was that a platonic kiss, or was there more to it? Do I even want it to mean more?*

She thought about her life with Jeremy and how young and naïve she had been. She had trusted him, and he shattered her heart with a one-night stand. It may have been more, or there may have been more than one woman, but her heart splintered regardless of the details.

Stop it. Stop thinking. Feel the water, feel the steam, and enjoy the quiet. The only sounds she heard were an acoustic guitar and sensual lyrics that carried her back to her teens and twenties. She savored the wine and focused on the liquid dripping down her throat, eventually loosening her muscles and making her sleepy.

Crystal released the drain and stood in the tub. The now-lukewarm water pushed against her ankles, and her body clammed up in the humid air. She looked around for her towel and saw the corner peek out from under her dirty jeans. *Crap.* Crystal shook her body, and wrang out her hair, hoping to get as much water off her skin as possible. Eddie Vedder's throaty growl sang in her ears.

Crystal stepped out of the tub, and turned toward the towel on the floor. "Ah!" she screamed in panic, covering her breasts and nether region with her hands. Adrenaline shot through her body, her fingers went numb, and the room started to spin. She crouched down to hide, her heart racing against her chest and her body tightened. A man stood before her, staring wide-eyed, mouth dropped open, and a cell phone in his hand.

"Derek!"

CHAPTER 12: DEREK

D erek opened the bathroom door with one quick swoop, heard a kerfuffle, and dropped his keys on the wooden floor. His eyes focused on the naked woman crouched on the floor in front of him. "Crystal, I'm so sorry. Shit! I didn't know you were in here." He covered his eyes with his hands and turned around, feeling his way into the hallway.

"Close the door!" she shrieked after him.

Derek reached backward and grabbed the crystal door knob, pulling it sharply shut behind him.

"What are you doing here?" Her voice carried a mixture of astonishment and shock as it floated through the closed door. He listened to objects clatter and the occasional item bouncing off the new tile floor. Crystal mumbled to herself but Derek couldn't make out the words this time.

"I'm sorry, I forgot my mixing paddle in there, and I need it for tomorrow."

"You should have knocked. Or called." Her voice barely carried through the door.

Derek ran his hand through his hair and smiled. He felt like such an idiot for walking in on her, but he wasn't complaining. He stifled a laugh and relaxed his face, shaking his head and looking at the ceiling with a smirk on his lips. He inhaled deeply and steadied his voice. "I did, but no one answered. I let myself in with my key to grab my paddle. I swear. Do you see a paddle in there? I need it."

"Ugh! Let me look."

Derek heard objects tossed around, the door slowly creaked open a smidge, and the paddle appeared between the door jamb and the door.

"Here. This it?" It was like her wrinkled fingers were speaking to him.

Derek took it out of her hand, and their fingers touched. His heart pounded, and the smell and feel of heat tiptoed through the cracked door.

The door opened further, and Crystal emerged with a towel around her head. Her sweatpants hung around her hips, and her tank top stuck to her body. Her erect nipples poked against the cotton fibers.

Feeling like he had to do something, he shoved his empty hand in his pocket. "Thank you." He raised the paddle to his chin. "For this. I'm sorry for walking in on you. I honestly didn't think you were in the bathroom. It was quiet when I came upstairs. Scout's honor." He held up three fingers and smiled like a loyal boy scout.

She rolled her neck and shoulders. "It's fine." She dragged out the words and spoke like each word was its own sentence. She looked down at her prune-like fingers and slowly up again. Her wet eyelashes made her look like she had just applied mascara. "You didn't see anything, did you?" She bit her lip.

Derek hesitated, not sure how best to respond. "Nothing I haven't seen before."

Crystal grinned and smacked him on the arm. "Ha!" she said.

He followed her down the stairs into the kitchen.

"How was dinner?" She pulled the towel off her head, and her wet, dark hair fell to her shoulders. Her bangs draped over one eye, and she brushed them to the side.

Derek tapped the counter with his fingers. "It was delicious. Molly cooked Chicken Parmigiana with angel hair pasta. She found a new recipe online, and I think she's practicing for when she has to cook for herself and her roommates next year. It was good. If I ordered it at a restaurant, I would order it again." Derek grinned and Crystal returned the expression.

"I love Italian food," she said.

Derek heard a faint *plink* and his head shot to the left. "Wait." He stared into the distance; his body frozen to prevent any sound from disrupting his attention. The two stood like statues. "Did you hear that?"

Crystal frowned and furrowed her brow. "Hear what?"

Plink!

"That." Derek's ears were like a hound's nose. He investigated the kitchen, stopping now and then to listen intently. "I keep hearing it." He roamed around the kitchen and dining room like a bat using sonar.

Crystal followed behind, looking for something out of the ordinary.

He stopped, and Crystal crashed into him from behind. "Oh no," he said, pointing to the room's far corner. A small puddle sat on the subfloor of the what-used-to-be dining room.

Crystal walked over and eyed it. "What is that?"

"Crystal, what room is above us?" Derek pointed to the ceiling.

"I don't know. Bathroom?" Her eyes widened, like a lightbulb had gone off over her head.

"Yes, bathroom. Something's wrong. The tub's draining, and it's leaking through the ceiling. We gotta get a plumber in here tomorrow. Don't use the tub again." He ran into the kitchen and grabbed a cardboard box, securing a trash bag around the edges. "In the meantime, this'll catch the water."

Crystal looked up at the ceiling, and a slow drip of water fell into the cardboard bucket. "Look at that." She pointed at the corner above them. "A heart." The water stain created a narrow heart about the size of his palm.

"Look at that. Could it be your mom sending you a message?"

Crystal leaned against the wall, her jutted hip accentuating her curves. "Could be. Or maybe it's Vanessa."

Derek's heart stopped and skidded in his chest like a car slamming on its brakes. Hearing his wife's name on another woman's lips, and not just any woman, but a woman that made his heart flutter and his palms sweat, triggered his protective side to erupt like a volcano. His body chilled and his lips curled. He stiffened and straightened his back with narrowed eyes and retracted shoulders. "I got stuff to do. I'll have the plumber come by tomorrow."

He stomped to the front door, the empty dining and living room embracing the force of his feet. The antique chandelier jangled with every step.

He was out the door before Crystal could say goodbye or ask when he'd return.

CHAPTER 13: CRYSTAL

"Naked! I was mortified." Crystal held her cell phone against her ear and rummaged through the kitchen drawer for silverware. She pulled out a bronze-tinted spoon and stirred her travel coffee mug. It was the following day, and Crystal was chatting with her closest cousin, Melanie. They had been writing letters since the fifth grade, which eventually turned into emails in the middle of the night and phone calls over coffee in the morning.

"No! Did he see your hoo-ha?" It was just like Melanie to rip the band-aid off and say it like it was.

"I don't know. I couldn't look to see where he was looking, and I was too preoccupied with covering myself." Crystal laughed. "It was so awkward."

"What's he look like? Like Jeremy?"

Crystal thought carefully before responding. "Not at all. Do you remember that guy, Shane, that I dated in high school? He looks kind of like him. Rugged, tall, and could probably chop down a tree in three hits if you really needed him to. Total opposite of Jeremy." Crystal nodded to the plumber who entered the kitchen. "Upstairs, first door on the left," she said over the phone's mouthpiece, directing him to the bathroom.

"I remember Shane. He was cute. It's probably too soon to know, but it sounds like you might have a story for me by the end of the summer." She chuckled into the phone. "How's the house?"

Crystal stared at her hands, and her shoulders slumped. "It was awful when I got here, but it's slowly coming around. I need to organize that memorial for my mother, but I can't have family over with the house looking so neglected. I'm embarrassed for my mom, and I know she's rolling over in her grave at the state it's in now."

"Don't worry, Crystal. There's only a handful of us within driving distance. Maybe you can plan on October. Maybe Columbus Day weekend? Or, I have an idea. How about one last Thanksgiving at the old farmhouse before you sell it? That could be fun. Your mom always hosted Thanksgiving, so we can honor and celebrate her life then."

Crystal's eyes perked up. "Melanie, you're brilliant! What a great idea. Yes, the house should be finished by then, so we'll have one last party. Will you help me plan it?" Crystal paced the kitchen, searching for a pen and paper.

"I'd love to. If nothing else, my family will be there. I'll tell my sisters, mom, dad, Auntie Jan, and Uncle Mitch. You can probably count on at least ten people...I think everyone else lives too far. Regardless of who comes, it'll be great."

Crystal bounced from one foot to the next. "Thank you, Melanie." She felt renewed pride, knowing her mom deserved one last Thanksgiving, despite their personal difficulties. Once the celebration was over, Crystal could finally say goodbye to the house.

The plumber reentered the kitchen, and Crystal quickly hung up the phone. She felt a pit in her stomach grow with anticipated bad news.

"All set," he said.

"All set?" Crystal repeated.

"Yep. Tightened up all the pipes and tested the water. No leak. You're all set. I also finished installing the pipes for the laundry room. Once you get a new washer and dryer, it should be good."

Crystal made the sign of the cross and looked up at the ceiling. "Thank you." She walked him to the door with light steps and moved upstairs to check out her new soon-to-be laundry room. She wrapped her arms around her torso, giving herself a tight hug, and thought about the paint color she needed to buy.

Her phone buzzed in her pocket with a number she didn't recognize. "Hello?"

"Crystal, it's Derek. Listen, sorry for being so rude yesterday when I left. It had been a long day, and...it doesn't matter, but I wanted you to know I'm sorry for storming out."

She furrowed her brows and bit her lip. She had wondered if she said something hurtful, but nothing she said was intentionally mean or malicious. "No problem." She leaned against the dusty wall and waited for him to continue.

"I don't know if you're busy, but my brother's having a July Fourth party this weekend. Want to come? It might be nice to meet people since you'll be around this summer. I don't know if you have plans or not, but you're welcome to come." Crystal struggled to hear Derek through the background noise of machinery and tools but wondered if he was asking her out on a date. Her heart tingled in her chest, and she swallowed loudly.

"Sure, yeah, I have no plans. It'll be nice to meet people. I haven't exactly kept in touch with anyone since high school, so it's not like I have any other raging parties to attend." She had yet to bump into anyone familiar, or she maybe did, but thirty years apart created a permanent disguise. "That sounds fun."

"It's at the diner. Well, not at the diner, but behind the diner in the field at the back. I'll meet you there around one or so."

Crystal smiled to herself. Maybe she could make her mother's famous Spangled-Spaghetti Salad. She hadn't had it in at least twenty years but could still taste the Italian dressing and sliced tomatoes. Her mouth watered. "Thanks for the invite, Derek. I'll bring a salad."

She hung up the phone, turned on music, and danced in circles around her empty laundry room. *This house is going to look amazing when it sells!* Feelings of excitement mixed with remorse as she thought about Derek. Her dancing ground to a halt and she cursed the universe for another chapter of bad timing.

Crystal went up to her bedroom and scanned her suitcase, clothes strewn up and over the sides, and discarded each item, as they all seemed too casual for a public event. *These paint-covered overalls won't cut it.* Crystal grabbed her purse and wallet and set out to get the perfect outfit for her first maybe-date with Derek.

CHAPTER 14: DEREK

"**D**erek, this is Christina." Phil motioned to the petite blonde woman standing next to Amy.

Derek stuck out his hand. "Nice to meet you, Christina." He noticed her deep mocha eyes, thin lips, and arched eyebrows and guessed she was in her mid-thirties. She wore a tight-fitting sundress that clung to her bosom and ended at her knees. Her handshake flopped like a fish out of water, and Derek squeezed and released. He glanced around the field, recognizing almost everyone standing amid the large, flat yard.

Amy leaned between them. "Christina lives in Saratoga and recently got a job at the salon." Derek wondered if Amy knew Phil had warned him that Amy invited Christina to the picnic, but he nodded just the same. He hoped Phil had told Amy he wasn't interested.

Amy hurried away to help Phil set up more chairs, leaving Derek standing with Christina. "Do you want a drink?" she asked, motioning to the array of soda and beer cans floating in the cooler.

"Sure. Thanks."

As he scanned the field, he hoped to see Crystal, but she hadn't appeared yet. Christina handed him a drink, and they stood awkwardly, chatting about Farm Cove.

"So, do you like it here?" Derek cursed the clichéd question, but he could barely pretend interest while thinking about Crystal.

Christina flashed him a bright smile and stepped closer. He shuddered as he felt her breath on his neck and stepped back to get some air. "I do. I've always wanted to live in a rural area where everyone knows everyone. Saratoga's beautiful, but I could do without the gambling crowds in the summer. I live there because I grew up there, but I enjoy working in a small town. Building relationships with all the locals keeps my days interesting." Something about the way she said relationships caused Derek's stomach to churn.

He broke eye contact and looked over her head toward the parking lot. He didn't know why he wanted Crystal to show up so badly, but he hadn't stopped thinking about her since the bathroom incident. Plus, he still felt terrible for storming out. Crystal had asked why he left so abruptly, and he lied, saying he forgot he was meeting Molly, but the real reason was Vanessa. Just thinking about another woman caused feelings of betrayal to creep around him. Phil said that was why none of his relationships since Vanessa had worked out, and he needed to forgive himself.

"Derek, you made it." Margie strolled over, wearing blue jeans and a t-shirt. Her pink nail polish matched her shirt, which matched her shoes, and her curly hair framed her face. "Hi, I'm Margie. I work with Phil. And you are…" She stuck her hand to Christina, and Christina limply shook.

"Christina. I work with Amy. Nice to meet you." Christina and Margie chatted next to Derek, and Derek sidestepped his way to Phil.

"Phil, does she think I'm interested?" Derek took a long swig of beer. "Who?"

"Christina." Derek tilted his head toward the two women.

"I don't know. I told Amy you weren't, but who knows if she relayed the message? For now, just be polite and excuse yourself if she comes on too strong. Or give her a chance. You might like her."

Derek wandered around the field, checking his watch and looking for Crystal. She was twenty minutes late, and unexpected feelings of melancholy settled around him like Pig-Pen's blanket. He spotted Molly carrying a large bowl in the distance and sprang to help her.

"Hey Mols, what'd you bring?" Derek took the bowl out of her hands and maneuvered the tinfoil off to sneak a peek.

"A new recipe I found. It's called Spaghetti Salad and is cold spaghetti mixed with salad dressing, tomatoes, cucumbers, and peppers. I thought it sounded refreshing for a hot, humid day." She followed Derek to the food table, where he set the dish next to the macaroni salad.

"Thanks for making this. Uncle Phil will love it. The more food, the better." He leaned across and kissed his daughter on the forehead.

"Are we having the Home Run Derby later?" Molly asked, looking around the field.

"Yeah, in about two hours. After we eat, I think."

"Did Uncle Phil fill in all those cuts the tractor left?" Molly asked.

Derek scanned the area behind the restaurant where Phil created a community garden. Tractor cuts that traveled from behind the restaurant to the wooded area created a maze hidden in the grass. Walking along the field often felt like riding on a sailboat and Derek knew someone was going to fall before the day was over. "He said he did, but be careful." He looked at Molly's wedged heels. "It's not consistent. Besides, how are you going to play in heels?"

Molly pointed to her bag. "In here. Sneakers. I always come prepared, Dad."

Derek felt a tap on his shoulder from behind. He turned and caught his breath. Crystal stood in front of him, wearing a loose summer skirt, a form-fitting t-shirt, and slip-on sneakers. A delicate pendant necklace hung above the neckline of her shirt. She looked perfect. His skin tingled, and his stomach fluttered. *Why is this happening?* He felt out of control and disoriented. He turned toward Molly, who was staring at him, waiting for an introduction.

"Crystal. Let me take that." Derek reached across and grabbed the bowl from her arms. "What is this?" He shook his head quickly and closed his mouth. "Sorry. I'm being rude again. Crystal, this is my daughter Molly. Molly, this is Crystal. I'm working on her house." The words tumbled out of his mouth like a leaky hose.

Molly gave her a wave and stared at her father with pursed lips and narrowed eyebrows. Derek could tell she thought he was acting weird.

"Nice to meet you. What did you bring today?"

Crystal grinned. "It's a secret family recipe but was my favorite growing up, and it's called Supreme Spaghetti Salad."

Molly's face dropped, and she narrowed her eyes at Crystal. "With Italian dressing?"

Crystal nodded.

"And tomatoes?"

"Yeah, have you had it before?" She scratched her chin. "I thought it would be something fun to eat."

"Yeah, me too," Molly said. "I brought the same salad, and it's over there. I guess we'll have a lot of spaghetti to eat for the next week or so."

Crystal laughed but Molly did not. Crystal ran the necklace chain along her fingers and bit her bottom lip. Derek watched her carry the salad to the table, her body stiff and gait slow.

"Molly," Derek said. "Be nice."

"I am, Dad. I thought I had made this amazing salad, and you know I can't cook! And she did the same thing." Molly threw her hands up in what looked like exasperation. "I bet hers tastes great, and mine tastes like cardboard."

"I'll eat yours, and I'll love it," Derek said, trying to smooth Molly's ruffled feathers. "You should give her a chance. I think you'd like her."

Molly stepped back and froze. "What do you mean? Do *you* like her?"

Derek stumbled over his thoughts which trickled out of his mouth. "I, uh, well, I don't really know her. All I know is that she and I will be working together for the next few weeks fixing the house."

Molly glanced at Crystal, who was still walking toward the food table with her salad. "I don't like her. Someone in their forties should not be wearing a skirt that short." Derek understood the implied message Molly was too polite to say.

"Be nice. Not everyone is as thin as you or your mother."

Derek looked at Crystal from top to bottom to top again. *Short skirt or not, she's got a great butt and the confidence to pull it off.* She was the physical opposite of Vanessa, but Derek still wanted her.

CHAPTER 15: CRYSTAL

Molly's icy stare penetrated Crystal's backside, and Crystal focused on the flowers decorating the food table to shake the uncomfortable feeling. She wished she had come empty-handed to the picnic but she had been trying to be polite. Crystal tucked the salad bowl in the far corner of the table, hidden by the large watermelon basket and cluster of two-liter sodas. For Molly's sake, she almost didn't want anyone to try it.

She slithered away from Molly's gaze and stumbled upon Margie, recognizing her from the diner. "Hi Margie, good to see you again."

Margie did a double-take and looked from Crystal to the petite, blonde woman next to her. "Hello! How are you?"

"Crystal," Crystal said.

"Oh, let me introduce you two. Crystal, this is Christina. She works with Phil's wife, Amy. Christina, this is Crystal. Crystal is renovating her mother's house in town." The women exchanged pleasantries and chatted about simple things, like the weather.

Eventually, the conversation moved to Phil and Derek. Christina asked Margie questions about Derek that Crystal didn't know, so she sat back and listened while observing the group of guys at the grill and the collection of children playing kickball.

Margie pushed back her hair and turned toward Christina. "He's never really gotten over her. She was one of my best friends, so I knew the family well. After Vanessa died, I tried to help Derek raise his little girl. Long story short, he fell into a depression that lasted years. He finally started dating when Molly was in middle school, but they never lasted. This town is so small, everyone within a fifteen-mile radius knew about Vanessa's accident. Plus, it was in all the papers. I think it was too painful for him to talk about it, and it created a wedge between him and everyone else."

Christina tsked, sighed heavily, and covered her mouth with her hand before dropping it to her side. She glanced at Derek, who was now helping Phil grill.

Margie continued. "They could never compare to Vanessa, and poor Derek felt responsible for her death because he asked her to pick up Molly at Girl Scouts that day. Of course, no one came for Molly, and when the leader called, he knew there was a problem. He had heard the sirens fly by his house about twenty minutes before, but hadn't thought anything of it."

Christina put her hand on Margie's arm, and Margie stopped talking. "That's terrible," Christina said.

It really is terrible. Crystal's mouth fell open, placing her hand on her breastbone. Her shoulders dropped, and she shook her head in sadness. She moved away from Margie, feeling the pull to Derek dragging her across the field.

Halfway to Derek, Crystal heard a loud whistle blow, and Phil holler, "Time to eat!" He carried a platter of dogs and hamburgers to the table.

Crystal stepped back and watched everyone congregate around the table like a band of hungry coyotes. *It's so tragic.* She couldn't stop thinking about Derek and now understood why he didn't always smile or make conversation when they worked side by side.

Her heart yearned to be near him, to comfort him, and support him. She held back until she was last in line, her depressing thoughts about history and trauma dampening her mood. Molly and Derek stood about seven people in front of her, and she could make out a few words here and there between the two.

They appeared to have a close relationship based on their body proximity and facial expressions. Crystal understood Molly's disgust toward her. *She probably didn't have a mother to teach her how to cook. This might be the only thing she can make, and here I am, bringing the same salad.* Crystal's stomach clenched and she blinked rapidly, trying to calm her nerves over the Spaghetti Salad misstep.

When she arrived at the table, she noticed that the cover of her salad sat snugly against the perimeter of the bowl, while Molly's salad was nearly gone. Crystal grinned and puffed out her chest, her left hand resting on her hip with confidence. Relief ballooned within her for not messing up Molly's day.

Crystal ate alone under the big oak tree to avoid being immersed in townie gossip. She didn't have a blanket to protect her legs from the bristly grass and tiny bugs, and rested her plate and cup on the giant tree root. She moved her legs back and forth like scissors, feeling each blade of grass prick her calves. Crystal closed her eyes and listened to the chatter of the townspeople and the birds above her. *Maybe coming here was a bad idea.*

"Hey Crystal, you want to join us?" She opened her eyes and saw a towering man standing over her. She smiled at Derek, still content that no one had eaten her salad.

"No thanks, I'm happy here. Just me and the birds. I think I might head out shortly. Thank you for inviting me."

Derek's face dropped, and he rubbed the back of his neck. "Really? You're not going to stay for Home Run Derby? That's the best part, I promise."

Crystal hesitated. She never enjoyed baseball and probably only hit a ball once in her life. "Eh, I'll watch, but I won't play. I'm terrible at hitting balls." Her cheeks reddened at the verbal innuendo, and Derek grinned.

He clapped his hands. "I'm hoping to extend my title for one more year, and you can be my good luck charm."

Crystal giggled and took another bite of food. "Sounds fun."

Derek returned to his table, and Crystal continued to think about him and Molly and their complicated story. There was a depth to him she wasn't sure she was ready to investigate, but she knew that the next two weeks of working closely with him would reveal his strengths and flaws.

An hour later, Crystal sat in a lawn chair behind home plate. Phil pitched the baseball repeatedly, the ball slowing down with each subsequent throw. Amy, Christina, and Margie sat next to Crystal, and Molly stood behind Derek, both waiting for their turn. They were fourth and fifth in line to show their batting skills.

Margie gave the play-by-play of each person up at bat. She explained to Christina who was who, who they were married to, who their kids were, and where they worked.

Crystal didn't engage, but she learned a lot about the townsfolk. She was surprised she hadn't recognized anyone from her past, but she had graduated high school almost thirty years before. She left after graduation and never looked back. Perhaps everyone she knew had left too.

By the time Derek was up to bat, the number to beat was four. He shook his shoulders, tapped the bat on the ground a few times, and pulled it into position. One run, two runs, three runs, four runs.... Crystal's heart beat out of her chest, and her hands dripped with sweat. She couldn't help but smile at his concentration as he zeroed in on the ball. His calf muscles flexed, and his butt pushed out as he bent his knees to get ready for another pitch. *He looks good.* Crystal licked her lips and pressed them into a thin line. *Please get another run.*

Slam! The ball flew back toward the trees. Crystal cheered, but not too loudly because she didn't want to draw attention. Christina jumped up and down, clapping her hands above her head. The next pitch flew down the first base line. His run was done.

Derek had hit six home runs and currently led the leaderboard. He walked toward Crystal to watch Molly hit. Margie slid toward Crystal, and Derek squeezed in between Christina and Margie. Crystal leaned forward to eavesdrop on their conversation.

"Oh, Derek, you did great," Christina cooed. Her sing-song voice irritated Crystal's core. "When did you learn to play baseball so well?"

Crystal rolled her eyes and stared at her hands as she listened to them talk and cheer as Molly hit her first home run.

"Derek, I'd love to get to know you better." Crystal glanced past Margie and saw Derek turn toward Christina. "Do you want to go out for coffee sometime?" she asked.

Coffee. Would that be after a fun night in bed? Crystal, stop. You're barely friends with him. You live three hours away. It would never work. Jealousy boiled within her, and Crystal pulled back at the familiar feeling.

Crack! Crystal heard the bat and ball connect but couldn't entirely take her eyes off Derek and Christina. Instead of hearing cheers, she heard yells, but couldn't interpret the concern within the dissonance. Margie jumped from her seat and interrupted Crystal's view of Derek and Christina. Her eyes followed Margie as Margie tipped the baseball, using her pocketbook as a shield, but didn't quite bat it out of the way.

The next thing Crystal saw was spinning stars and white puffy clouds meandering through the blue sky, then darkness.

CHAPTER 16: DEREK

Derek's head whipped around when he heard the metal beach chair thump to the ground. He ran to Crystal, who lay on her back with her legs up and over the edge of the over-turned chair and her forehead turning a beautiful shade of purple. Her mid-length flared skirt, which Derek had been admiring earlier, haphazardly rested along her hips. Smooth thigh and yellow underwear peeked out at him as he gently tugged her skirt down to avoid others from seeing.

"Crystal, you okay?" She looked up at him and smiled. Her mouth pulled into a grimace and her eyes closed when she touched her forehead. "Careful. You're going to have quite the egg." He pulled her to a sitting position.

"Thank you. I'm fine. Just embarrassed." She checked herself for bruises and lay back on the ground.

"I'm getting an ice pack. Don't move." Derek exited the crowd and rummaged through the freezer, pulling out half-melted ice cubes. He wrapped a handful in a paper towel and nudged his way back through the small group surrounding Crystal.

"Dad, I'm so sorry," Molly said. "I don't know what happened." She made a face at Crystal's forehead. "Do you think she has a concussion?"

Derek chuckled. "Nah, it wasn't a direct hit. She'll be fine." *But what if she wasn't?*

Crystal took the ice out of Derek's hand and placed it on her forehead. "Thanks again. I think I'll lay under the shade back here for the rest of the game." She meandered to the tree where Derek saw her earlier and lay at the base of the trunk.

I shouldn't have asked her to stay. Guilt settled on his shoulders, and he slumped forward. "Molly, she'll be fine." Margie, Christina, and Amy returned to their seats. "Why don't you finish your run?" He nodded toward home plate.

"Nah, I'm good. Do you need anything?"

Derek shook his head and eyed Crystal, whose head was resting against the thick, rough trunk. Her closed eyes and still body soaked up the comfort of the ice cubes, which balanced precariously on her forehead. Derek tiptoed over and eyed the rising mountain. "Hey, can I take you home? I would feel better driving you. The party's wrapping up, anyway."

Crystal opened her eyes, and Derek saw a single tear slip down her cheek. He crouched down to look at her directly.

"What's wrong?" He wanted to reach out and touch her but didn't want to make a scene.

"I feel like such an idiot. First the Spaghetti Salad, then the ball. I never thought your daughter wouldn't like me."

Derek touched her forearm with his left hand and readjusted the makeshift ice pack with his other. "She feels terrible for what happened, and don't worry about the salad. Really. Can I drive you home?" he asked again.

Crystal nodded. She retrieved her purse from Christina's chair and returned to Derek.

Derek nudged Molly's elbow. "Molly, I'm bringing her home. I'll be back in about an hour."

Molly hugged Derek and half embraced Crystal. "I'm so sorry. I hope you feel better." Derek saw Crystal's eyes glaze over, and she nodded with a sad grin.

Derek adjusted the air conditioning and turned down the radio in his rumbling truck. "Thanks for coming today. I'm sorry I didn't get to spend more time with you. I hope you didn't feel uncomfortable." The truck trotted out of the gravel parking lot.

Crystal leaned her head against the closed window and stared straight ahead. "It's fine. It was nice meeting everyone."

A few minutes later he pulled down her driveway and helped her to the front door. She rested her weight against his soft torso, and he hugged her close. His anxiety about her accident overpowered his growing desire for her.

Lulu barked from the top of the stairs. He led Crystal to her bedroom and went to make her a cup of tea. By the time he returned, Lulu had nestled in the crook of Crystal's bent legs and was snoring softly. "You know, I would feel better not leaving you alone. That bump is big, but it looks like the swelling is going down." He touched it, and Crystal's eyes teared up.

"It doesn't feel great, and I have a small headache, but I'll be fine. Promise."

Derek thought about his options. His decision twelve years ago led to Vanessa's death; there was nothing he could have done to stop it. He would also hate himself if something happened to Crystal because he left her alone. "I'm going to go home for a few hours and check in with Molly. I know it's kind of forward, but would you be comfortable if I spent the night? I have an air mattress in my truck, and I'll sleep on the floor. I want to be here if you need someone."

Crystal closed her eyes and hesitated before replying. "Sure." She didn't elaborate, and Derek wondered if he was overstepping.

"I'm afraid something will happen in the middle of the night. I don't think you should be alone."

Her eyes shot open. "It's fine." Her voice carried an edginess that Derek hadn't heard before.

He sat with her in silence until she fell asleep. After an hour of watching her, he left for home to check in with Molly and pack an overnight bag.

Molly sat at the kitchen table reading a tabloid magazine. "Is she okay?" she asked as he walked through the door, continuing to flip the pages.

"Yeah, just a big goose egg. She'll be fine, but I don't want her to be alone tonight. You never know." He knew Molly knew that life could change in an instant, so she didn't argue or question him.

"Sure, that makes sense." It may not make sense to anyone else, but the two carried an air of caution everywhere they went.

"What do you think of her?" Derek asked. He still wasn't sure what he thought, but the pull to be with her tonight clouded his thoughts.

Molly tilted her head from side to side. "She's nice. She's pretty. She seems like a decent person, but I don't have a real opinion yet."

Derek looked into his daughter's eyes, and the untruths about her statement reflected at him. The way she glanced to the ground from the left corners of her eyes told him she did have an opinion. He was grateful she didn't share, because he wanted to create his own judgement. He decided not to ask again.

Derek pulled together an overnight bag and kissed Molly on the cheek. "I'll be working on the farmhouse tomorrow, so I won't be home until dinner."

Molly closed and locked the back door behind him, and he drove to Crystal's, wondering if it was peculiar that he felt so comfortable letting himself in with his work key.

CHAPTER 17: CRYSTAL

T he following day, Crystal woke to a house full of contractors. Her head ached, and the pain reminded her of the previous twenty-four hours. She stumbled to the bathroom and gazed at her face, grimacing at the reddish-purple bump that stood out against her pale skin. She grabbed her compact powder and dabbed the lump, hoping to hide it, but no matter how much powder she applied, she couldn't hide the shadows and discoloration. Sighing heavily, Crystal rummaged through her luggage and squeezed her baseball cap over her head, hiding her forehead.

She threw on her paint-stained jeans and ventured downstairs. Derek stood at the circular saw, cutting wood beams to frame the new dining room. His body bobbed to the music blaring through the house. Familiarity washed over her as she caught his eye and waved.

"How do you feel?" he asked, eyeing her baseball hat.

Crystal raised her shoulders. "The best I could feel. Nothing a little coffee couldn't fix. Do you want some?"

Derek shook his head. "I've already had three cups. If I have another, I'll be swinging from the rafters." He pulled at his toolbelt, and Crystal's eyes dropped to his hips, where the belt rested with a slant. She raised her eyes again and strutted into the kitchen.

A group of contractors stood outside, replacing the single pane, wood-weighted windows with something energy efficient. The breeze whipped through the kitchen window over the sink, and Crystal shivered.

She returned to Derek and took a sip. "What do you need me to do today?"

"Nothing too crazy. You should take it easy." He kept his eyes on the wood gliding across the saw.

"Nonsense, I'm fine." Crystal threw her hands up and pulled her cap further down, fighting the dull ache throbbing throughout her forehead. "Really."

"Okay. How about some more painting? You can paint the laundry room. The washer and dryer should be installed tomorrow or the next day."

After breakfast and coffee, Crystal headed to the new laundry room. She cranked up her music, taped the edges, and glided the roller up and down the walls. She didn't mind painting and knew it saved her hundreds of dollars.

A few hours later, Crystal had all four walls done and was finishing the trim. She heard the door creak and found Derek leaning against the door frame, his left foot crossed in front of his right. His toolbelt hung halfway to his knees, and sawdust coated his pants.

"Oh, you scared me." Crystal jumped and placed her hand over her heart. "What do you think?" She motioned toward the walls like Vanna White.

"It looks great, but I must say, your singing is even better." He chuckled and held her gaze a moment or two longer than was necessary, and Crystal's heart jumped to her throat. "I wanted to talk to you about something."

She dropped the paintbrush and turned off the music, sensing a shift in the tone of their conversation.

"Thank you for helping and everything. The house is really coming together. The living room and dining room walls are up and ready to be primed and painted, the windows on the first floor will be done today, and we're going to start on landscaping next week. I've appreciated everything you've done."

Crystal smiled. "I have the time, and every little bit helps. The sooner we can get the house on the market, the better." Thanksgiving flashed through her mind, and she quickly pushed it away.

Derek's face dropped. "Yeah, we're right on track, so you may have it listed by Halloween."

Crystal picked up her paintbrush to touch up the trim but couldn't reach the top. She felt Derek's heat behind her before she realized he had moved. His hand grabbed her wrist, and she turned to face him. He was inches from her lips, and she could feel his minty breath on her. Her heart pounded with desire and electric shocks traveled up her legs, making them tremble.

She tried to break free from his grip but instead found herself moving into him. He closed the final gap between them and his lips met hers. Fireworks exploded behind her eyes. His lips were unexpectedly soft, such a contrast from the feel of his rough beard, and Crystal leaned into him for deeper pressure.

Like a film reel, memories of her past flipped through her mind at high speed, and she could barely make out the images. Her mother gardening, her father drinking coffee, the summer she lost her virginity, and the day she graduated from college sped through her mind. Jeremy proposing on the banks of Niagara Falls and the joy and pure delight she felt in that moment, making love that night, and then standing beside him on their wedding day. She saw herself holding Mason with joy and wonder, then fighting, then lipstick, and then the final fight when she threw Jeremy out of the house. Images of isolation and abandonment, losing her mother to a devastating illness, saying goodbye, and stumbling back to this house. The last image was Derek kissing her. The film reel flipped faster through her mind on a continuous loop.

She pushed him away, fear replacing lust. "I can't do this."

He stepped back immediately, his lips pressed together and his eyes pleading.

"I live three hours away, Derek. My life is not here, and I'm leaving to go home in a week and a half. I'm selling the house and saying goodbye to Farm Cove. For good."

Hands shaking, she grabbed her phone off the sink and squeezed between him and the door frame. She dashed into the kitchen, grabbed her keys and purse, and ran to the door, looking at the empty, broken driveway. *Shit.* She wanted to leave but was stuck. *My car's still at the diner.*

Instead of going upstairs, Crystal sat at the table with hot tea and stared blankly, blinking back tears. She replayed the feelings of worthiness that Derek transmitted to her with his kiss and how they had pushed out feelings of abandonment and pitifulness her mother and Jeremy had fostered. Her brain and heart were at odds, but her rational brain had to take the lead.

When Derek entered the kitchen, Crystal wiped her eyes and smiled, pretending nothing happened. Like she hadn't run away from him or reject his advances. Like they were strictly co-workers. The other contractors milled about the house, commenting on dimensions and projects, unaware of the turmoil inside Crystal. She readjusted her hat and looked up at him from under the brim.

"I need some time to think. Would you mind driving me to my car?"

Derek and Crystal climbed into his truck and quietly drove to the diner.

"Thanks for the ride," Crystal said, opening and closing the door before he could say goodbye. She felt his stare as she walked away, and she willed her eyes to stop the tears from falling.

CHAPTER 18: DEREK

D erek tiptoed around Crystal for the rest of the week, careful not to be alone with her in the same part of the house. He put on his contractor hat and sent her to areas he wouldn't need to enter. He couldn't read her, and that nagging feeling of doing something wrong prickled his skin.

Her body quivered, and she pushed into me. She looked at me with those mesmerizing eyes, opening her soul. She trembled at my touch. He shook his head, refusing to waste more time on the what-ifs.

A few days of walking on eggshells was too much for Derek. His jumbled mind bounced images of Crystal and Vanessa like a tennis match, and he couldn't concentrate or work as fast as needed.

The following weekend, he slumped into the dining room chair and poured himself some brandy.

"Gee, Dad, what's up? You haven't pulled out that bottle since Grandpa died."

Derek looked at Molly and raised his glass to her. "I've got a lot on my mind." He rubbed his eyes and rested his forehead on his fisted hand.

Molly sat at the table beside him and stacked the mail. "Are you okay? Do you want to talk?"

Derek shook his head, conflicted by Molly's nurturing gaze and the demons fighting within his heart. "I'm okay." He sighed deeply and took a swig. The burn trailing down his throat comforted him.

"Is it the house?" Molly asked.

A slow grin penetrated Derek's mouth. "What house?" He had three projects running simultaneously and didn't feel he was doing a great job on any of them, but he couldn't risk screwing up because Molly needed him.

"I don't know—any of the houses. I haven't seen you in about two weeks. Are you okay? How's your life?" Molly leaned into him and gave him her full attention, just like Vanessa used to do. He took another sip.

"Yeah, two weeks. I've been busy. How's everything going with the big move next month?"

"So far so good." Molly's voice sped up, and her smile broadened. Derek's heart swelled, knowing at least one of them was happy. She filled him in on the layout of their apartment, her bedroom, and what bars and restaurants were within walking distance. "I need first, last, and security by August first. It's two thousand dollars." Molly played with her fingers and spun her ring around her knuckle. "I have half."

Derek stirred his drink and watched the center create a tornado. "August first? I'll have it for you."

She wrapped her arms around his neck and squeezed. "Thank you, Daddy." She pulled away from him quickly and looked into his eyes. "Are you sure you're okay? Do you want to talk?"

"I'm great." He threw his glass back and finished the last cognac sip.

Molly eyed him, and grabbed her keys. "I'm heading out, but I'll be home later." The door slammed shut, and Derek sat in the silence.

It was too quiet. Quiet was when all the memories flooded back. Derek wasn't ready to pick up his sword and fight his demons. Instead, he picked up his phone and scanned through his contacts.

The phone rang twice before a familiar woman said, "Hi, Derek."

Derek leaned forward and hesitated.

"Derek?"

"Hi, Amy. Is Phil there?" He stood up and paced the dining room.

"Hey, Derek. What's up?" Phil's voice bounced into Derek's ear.

"You know that brandy we got at Dad's funeral?"

A moment of silence passed. "From Uncle Micky?"

"Yeah. I haven't had it since Dad died, and I dove into it today. It's gone now." Derek turned the bottle upside down and one final drop fell into his glass. "I've got a lot on my mind. Can I come over?"

"Sure," Phil answered a little too quickly. "I'll pick you up in ten minutes."

Derek cringed, embarrassed that he was too intoxicated to drive. "Thanks, man. I'll see you soon."

Derek stumbled around the house, searching for his shoes and keys, then he waited on the porch for Phil's headlights to swing into his driveway. He didn't want to be alone. His mind was dangerous, and he nudged open the door to his nightmares with that first sip of brandy.

He climbed into Phil's car. "Thanks, man. Molly left, and it got too quiet. I didn't want to keep drinking."

Phil glanced over as he pulled onto the main road. "Anytime. Do you want to talk?"

The shadows of the trees whipped by, and Derek focused on the black clouds. "Same as always. I kissed Crystal, she pulled away, and now Vanessa is haunting me for betraying her. I keep having those nightmares, and I don't want to go to sleep because I wake up tired, sad, and guilty as hell."

"Why do you feel guilty?" Phil asked.

"Because I really like Crystal. She's different, and she's beautiful, funny, and nice." The compliments rolled off his tongue like a rolling snowball picking up speed. "I feel good when I'm around her and want to be with her when I'm not."

"All Vanessa ever wanted was for you to be happy," Phil mumbled. Derek barely heard him over the hum of the engine.

"I know. She's always looking out for me. Crystal's selling the house and lives three hours away. There's no way it could work, so why bother?" Derek's heart shuddered, threatening to fracture.

"Because life is about living and loving hard. You know better than anyone that each day is a blessing, and tomorrow may never come. If she makes you feel good, why fight it? You deserve to feel good, too." Phil turned into his driveway; his three-story colonial lit up. Derek saw shadows move around the first floor and noticed an extra car in the driveway.

"Who's that?" He nodded toward the shadowed SUV.

"That? Christina."

Derek threw an annoyed glance, his eyes settling on the car roof. "Why didn't you tell me?" He threw his hands in his lap and scrunched up his face. "She's the last thing I need after I've had a few too many drinks." He couldn't think straight, but his body got hot, his heart raced, and his hands tightened into fists.

"They're doing work stuff. It's fine. We'll sneak into the den, and she won't even know you're here."

Derek opened and closed the door with a quiet click, then followed Phil, careful not to make any noise. He floated into the kitchen and almost made it to the den when a high-pitched squeal broke the silence.

"Derek!"

"Christina, hi." He leaned against the wall. *Pull yourself together.*

"I didn't know you'd be here." She approached him in three steps, and stood directly in front of him. Derek felt the space between them shrink. She flipped her now-auburn hair over her shoulder and tilted her head to the left.

"Yeah, just for a little while." Derek looked behind him, wondering where Phil went.

"Hi, Derek." Amy's voice carried through the kitchen.

"Hey, Amy." He wanted to escape from Christina, but his mind went blank. Her dark brown eyes shimmered behind her dark eyeliner, and he recognized curiosity and desire.

He thought about what Phil said and felt his body pulling toward Christina's petite frame. He stumbled forward and grinned. "You look beautiful."

Christina kissed his cheek and touched his lips with her smooth thumb.

Fireworks exploded inside his chest and his eyes rested on her plump lips. The alcohol made everything warm and fuzzy.

"You're too sweet." She tilted her head to the right and whispered, "so, are you up for a nightcap at my place later tonight?"

It felt good to be wanted. Derek nodded, his body pulsing.

She kissed him on the other cheek and whispered, "I'll drive you home."

CHAPTER 19: CRYSTAL

The scent of coffee wafted up the stairs and woke Crystal. She hummed and rolled, stretching her short arms and legs toward the head and foot of the bed. The rhythmic hum of a vacuum cleaner below echoed up the stairs. Instead of music and yelling, she heard the birds chirping through the open window over her head.

Crystal wasn't sure who was working on the house today, but the inside was nearly done. Painted walls, a finished laundry room, and a designated dining and living room transformed her home from a broken box of disappointment to an empty photo album waiting to be filled. Crystal closed her eyes and shook her head, reminding herself she needed to sell to make ends meet for her and Mason. If she didn't sell, she'd go into foreclosure for not paying the renovation debt.

She threw on her bathrobe and shuffled downstairs, hoping to sneak into the kitchen without being seen. It had been days since she and Derek spoke, and Crystal needed more time to process her thoughts about the kiss.

The floorboard creaked, and Crystal froze. The vacuum cleaner continued. Lulu looked at Crystal with caramel doe eyes urging her to move forward. She tapped her leg and continued to the kitchen, where Lulu ate breakfast.

Her parents' old kitchen looked reborn, fresh, and modern. She never imagined a chic kitchen in this old farmhouse but knew it would draw buyers. A dozen men were hard at work transforming her outdoor space just beyond the kitchen window. Derek wasn't there.

She leaned in closer, her nose touching the pane, and squinted her eyes. *What in the world?*

A small woman in tight jeans, heeled boots, and a white tank top strutted through her yard. Her heels stuck into the mud like molasses, and she flung up dirt with every step.

Who is that? Crystal recognized her face but couldn't place her name. The men ignored her as she marched to the house with a swift cadence.

"Lulu, come on, girl." Crystal hooked the leash on Lulu's collar and stepped outside.

The woman approached and removed her sunglasses. "Crystal." Her smile looked more like an unfriendly sneer, and her eyes flared with mischief.

Crystal smiled hello as scenes from the picnic flashed through her mind.

"Christina. From the picnic. Your forehead is turning green," she said, pointing at Crystal's face.

Crystal's eyes thinned like frisbees. She touched her forehead, having forgotten to put on her hat. She hadn't recognized Christina with her new hair color.

"I have something for Derek. Is he inside?" Christina smiled like she had a secret and was dying to tell. She pushed her hands into her tight pockets, and puffed out her chest, accentuating her perky breasts to make room for her hands. "He left it at my house last night."

Crystal's heart sank and she tried not to react as she looked back at the house and then around the yard. "Honestly, I don't know. I haven't seen him."

"Well, can I go in and look?"

Tears burned behind Crystal's eyes. She nodded and turned her attention to Lulu, pulling her to the back trees. *Last night, huh?*

"Oh, and Crystal, I like your bathrobe. Pink looks good on you." Christina smiled, with superiority flashing behind her straight posture and pink lipstick, as she marched past Crystal into the house.

Crystal's cheeks flushed, and her lips tightened to a scowl. "Lulu, come on," she said, dragging Lulu toward the house. She waited outside the door and counted to twenty, not wanting Derek or Christina to know she was inside.

She creaked open the door and slipped into the kitchen, tiptoeing toward the dining room. She spied Derek and Christina in the far corner of the living room near the front door, huddled together and whispering. Crystal couldn't make out what they were saying, but Christina's face was in clear view. Her pouty, pink lips leaned toward his cheek. He said something, and she threw her head back in laughter. Crystal felt like a voyeur and pulled herself back into the kitchen.

It's none of my business what he does. She seethed inside, anger bubbling into her heart and red clouding her vision. *I turned him down.* Crystal busied herself with the dishes, slamming silverware into the drawer. She picked up the saucepan on the drying rack and threw it into the cabinet, where it clattered to the floor with metallic reverberations. Lulu froze in the corner and seemed to wait for Crystal to say everything was okay.

She looked toward the door and saw Derek with Christina directly behind him. "Are you okay?" he asked. His gaze flitted around the room, searching for the noise's origin.

Her body melted against the counter like marshmallows over a fire, and her lip curled up on one side. She glared at Christina. "I'm fine."

Derek picked up the saucepan and placed it in the sink with

slow movements that guaranteed distance between them. Christina watched from the outskirts of the room.

"You sure?"

"What's she doing here?" Crystal tilted her head in Christina's direction, and her sugary voice hid the hatred and envy brewing inside.

"Nothing. I left my wallet at her house yesterday—"

"Last night," Christina said.

Derek raised his eyes to the ceiling. "Last night."

Crystal grabbed her coffee. "I'm getting dressed. I'm going out, and I want to return to an empty house." Her voice cracked as memories of Jeremy came crashing down on her.

Am I overreacting? She didn't care. She needed to get away and clear her head before she did something she would regret.

CHAPTER 20: DEREK

She stormed out of the room and was gone less than five minutes later. The engine revved as he watched her car speed out of the long driveway. A large dust cloud blocked his view, and he didn't know if she turned left toward town or right toward the highway.

He felt a sharp tug on the hem of his t-shirt and he turned his attention away from the window. Christina stood close enough to smell her perfume. She rubbed his arms up and down, and instead of feeling consoled, he felt trapped. His chest tightened, and each breath consumed less and less air. His toolbelt suddenly felt like it was made of iron, and he needed to free himself of the weight. His arms yanked out of her bony grasp, and he pulled away from her. His shaking fingers fumbled with the toolbelt and dropped it to the ground. "Jesus, Christina. What was that all about?" Before she could respond, he stormed out of the room to grab his phone and wallet.

Christina followed him, staying at least three steps behind, until he reached the kitchen. She approached with narrowed eyes and pursed lips. "What was what?" She touched his arm, and he jerked away from her.

"Last night was nothing, and you made it seem like we slept together." His heavy work boots stomped through the messy home as he searched for his keys. He refused to look at her and instead scanned each room, finally spotting them in the dining room. "I have to get out of here."

He snatched his keys and wallet and held open the door for Christina. "Get out. Now."

She stepped outside, and Derek slammed and locked the door behind her. *Please, Crystal. I need to talk to you.* He texted, asking her to meet, but she never replied. His jumbled mind and rapid heartbeat made him wonder if he was going crazy or having a heart attack. He climbed into his truck and—*Bam! Bam! Bam!*—his fists met the seat and steering wheel. "Damnit!" The ignition turned with a black cloud of smoke exiting the tailpipe, and the intense music muffled his thoughts. The truck sped in reverse, leaving a cloud of dust in the broken driveway.

He racked his brain for places she might go, and the first place that popped into his head was the diner. *Would she really go to the only place directly connected to me?* He couldn't imagine her wanting to see Margie.

Instead, he drove around the small town looking for her car.

He searched for two hours before convincing himself that she had returned to Rochester and back to her old life. He pulled into his driveway and saw Molly's car. The last thing he wanted was to talk with her, and he fought the urge to turn around and exit their driveway. He pulled himself out of the car, one heavy limb at a time, and trudged into the house.

He greeted Molly with a wide grin. "Hey, kiddo."

She closed the dishwasher and pressed start. "Dad? Why are you home? It's not even two." He noticed Molly look at his slumped posture, and he straightened his back.

"Oh, just home for lunch, and I thought maybe we could eat together since you're leaving in a month." *Lies.*

"You should've called first. I already ate, but I can make you a sandwich."

Derek didn't want one but needed an excuse to be home. He accepted her sandwich and sat at the table, avoiding eye contact. It tasted like beeswax, and he washed it down with a can of Coke.

"You sure you're okay? You're never home for lunch." Molly tapped a pen against the table and waited for a response. Derek slowed his chewing and gulped what remained in the soda can.

"I'm good, just a little stressed."

"Is it the money, Dad? Because I can work something out if you can't come up with the money."

Gratitude toward her generosity washed over him until he realized he was, in fact, the one being generous by agreeing to pay half. "Not the money. Don't worry. All I want is for you to be happy, and I know your mother would want that too." Tears stung behind his eyes as images of Vanessa flashed before him. Time went by too fast, and Derek couldn't believe he only had a few weeks left before Molly left him for her new life.

Molly looked at him and waited for him to continue, but he had nothing to say. He widened his eyes and raised his shoulders as if to say, *what do you want from me?*

Molly changed the subject. "Dad, how's Crystal's farmhouse coming along?"

Derek's eyes shot up from his plate and his neck and shoulders tightened. He rolled them out, hoping she hadn't noticed. "It's coming. The inside is practically finished. Now we have the outside, which is most of the big-ticket items. I think she'll be able to make some cash off it."

"After she pays you?" Molly said.

"Yeah, even after she pays me and I pay all the guys."

"So, what's her story?" Molly knew how to poke Derek until he almost broke.

He folded his hands. "What do you mean?"

Molly raised her eyebrows. "Like, her story. Her past. Does she have kids? Is she married?"

"Her husband cheated on her, and now they're divorced. She lives in Rochester with her ten-year-old son. Her mom died, and Crystal inherited the house. She's here for another ten days to help renovate and will head back to Rochester then." He took another bite of his sandwich to show he was finished talking.

"And? What do you think of her?" Molly hadn't removed her eyes from Derek's face, and Derek squirmed in his seat, his foot tapping against the leg of the chair.

"I like her."

"Like, like-her like her? Or just like her?"

Derek's heart sped up at the memory of Crystal with paint on her face, watching her sleep, the bump on her head, and the nakedness in the bathroom. He blushed under his beard and cleared his throat. "I like-her like her, and I think she's great. Do you like her?"

Molly thought before responding. "I do, and I feel awful that I hit her with the baseball." She grinned at the memory. "It was totally an accident, but I still feel bad. She hid her salad to save my feelings, and I like that you like her. I don't remember the last time you liked a woman. Like, liked-her liked her."

"Molly, it's been years." Derek sat back in his seat and crossed his leg over his knee.

"Whatever you do, I approve—not that you need my approval, Dad, but I don't want you worrying about me."

Derek smiled and nodded.

"And Dad?"

He looked up and saw a small tear fall from the corner of her eye.

"If you like-her like her, Mom would like her too."

93

Derek swallowed the lump in his throat and hugged her. "Thanks, Mols."

CHAPTER 21: CRYSTAL

She drove out of town with no clear direction, traveling Interstate 87 North, past Saratoga and into Lake George. The contents of her emergency overnight bag were scattered across the back seat and Lulu sat beside her, her fluffy head peeking over the edge of the window.

About fifteen minutes into the ride, she felt her heartbeat slow to normal, her hands relax, and her inner voice calm. Thirty minutes in, she leaned back in her seat, her shoulders comfortable, and her brain singing to the radio. By the time she got to Lake George, she had talked herself off the ledge, questioning her reaction. *Maybe it was nothing.*

Crystal pulled into a gas station to fill up, get coffee, and call Melanie. Reception on the lake could be spotty, and Crystal needed to talk to someone. She sat in her stuffy car with the windows rolled down. The heat made her lungs burst and scorching sunbeams penetrated her left arm. *Come on, Melanie, pick up.* It took four rings.

"Hello?"

"Melanie, I'm so glad I caught you. Can you talk? For like, five minutes?"

Crystal brought Melanie up to date with the Derek debacle, from the picnic to the kiss to the unexpected guest and then storming out. Melanie peppered Crystal's story with questions, trying to fill in the blanks when Crystal omitted the essential details.

"So, he kissed you, and you pulled away. Then you found out he spent the night with another woman, and now you're upset? Am I getting this right?" When Melanie said it, it sounded so stupid.

"Yes. But that's putting it simply." Crystal pulled her lips to the side and chewed the inside of her cheek. "Am I a complete idiot?"

"You're not an idiot, Crys, but you are overreacting. He didn't cheat on you. You aren't even together."

Crystal lowered her eyes to her hands and cried, pulling the phone away so Melanie wouldn't hear. "Why did I do that? My jealousy took over like an angry monster. I wanted to kill Derek, but I wanted to kill Christina more."

"Because you like him," Melanie said. "Why'd you pull away from that kiss?"

"Melanie, it was a beautiful kiss. Tender and then rough. Soft and then powerful. My entire life flashed before my eyes while he kissed me."

"Okay, sounds great. What's the problem?" Melanie's logic kept Crystal's emotions in check.

"It's the unknown, and knowing that I'm leaving. It'll never work, and I can't open my heart to have it stomped on for a few weeks of fun." Crystal pulled back her damp hair as sweat droplets appeared on her forehead like morning dew. She took a sip of lemonade and leaned her seat back for a more comfortable conversation. Lulu crawled into her lap and Crystal stroked her soft fur.

The five-minute phone call turned into forty-five, and by the end, Crystal's battery life notified her of its impending demise. She glanced in the rearview mirror and gasped at her purple, clammy face. "Hey,

Melanie, I have to run. I'm overheating here. I think I'll check in at a hotel and enjoy the quiet for the next day or so. There's a lot of thinking I need to do. Thanks for your help."

Crystal hung up the phone, plugged in her charger, and drove through the small towns directly on the lake. She found a small pet-friendly resort with a private beach and booked a room for the night. The price tag scared her, but not as much as admitting to Derek that she had made a mistake.

Crystal and Lulu sat on the soft grass by the beach. The temperature had cooled, and the sun nestled behind the trees. She kicked her feet in the refreshing water and inhaled the clean, crisp air. A few families and couples explored the area, but Crystal felt alone. It was a beautiful experience, but she wished someone was there with her.

She had one text message and one voicemail from Derek that she ignored. Her muddied emotions made it hard to think, and she was never one to admit when she reacted poorly. Her constant suspicion led to the breakdown of her marriage and possibly led to Jeremy's cheating. He might never have sought companionship elsewhere if she had trusted him from the beginning. But every late night at work, business trip, and business dinner pricked her deeper and deeper until her heart was dripping blood. She ignored her animosity and threw her attention to their son, which further deepened the wedge between her and her husband. Looking back, she recognized how her nagging and constant suspicion enabled his behavior.

In the distance, Crystal spotted a young couple sitting side by side on the dock. Their legs kicked free, and the girl leaned into the boy. Both laughed at something funny, and Crystal recalled being young and in love. She remembered Jeremy's charismatic personality, and how he always had something to say to everyone. Crystal had admired his ability to connect with others and often wondered how he did it so effortlessly.

Her thoughts shifted to when she brought him home to meet her mother. Evelyn had seen right through him and even warned Crystal privately, 'Don't let him stray if you're going to keep him.'

Crystal had stood back with her mouth wide open at her mother's rudeness. How could she say something so insulting? And yet she was right. When Crystal told Evelyn about the separation, Evelyn said she saw it in the way he dressed and smiled and agreed with everyone. 'Don't trust him if everyone he meets is his friend,' she had said. *Oh, Mom, if only you could meet Derek and tell me what you think.*

She leaned back and closed her eyes, focusing on her feelings for Derek. His kind face, deep voice, scruffy beard, and round butt elicited a tingling in her chest, a flutter in her stomach, and a knot in her throat. She felt alive again, after years of loneliness and commitment to her son's emotional well-being above her own.

She felt pretty around Derek, despite her round mid-section and mousy hair. His kiss was sweet and lustful, which she hadn't felt in years. Before coming back to Farm Cove, she was a crazed, middle-aged single mother, desperately trying to keep her life afloat for her son.

Now, a silky, but sticky cocoon embraced her, sometimes making it hard to breathe and think, and other times exciting her for the future. It was turning her into a butterfly, where she could erase her past and start again. Perhaps she deserved to focus on her needs and her happiness, even if it was fleeting.

CHAPTER 22: DEREK

I t had been three days, and Derek worked on Crystal's house in isolation. She and Lulu were still missing, but Crystal had replied to Derek's text saying she'd gone away for a few days, so he knew they were safe. He didn't know when she'd return though, so he continued to plug away at the house.

The house had become muted and dim without Crystal there. He missed her constant questioning, enthusiasm, and laughter. He even missed Lulu sleeping on her red and white checkered dog bed. Derek looked at the corner of the room. The dog bed was gone.

He hated when his mind hyper-focused on the past, replaying conversations, words, and actions that he wished he could take back. If he could do it again, he never would have gone back with Christina. He would never have called Phil. He would have stayed alone that night, passing out on the couch and feeling sorry for himself. Now he was in a bind that he didn't think he could stumble out of, and was afraid his words would intensify the situation.

Three days of thinking about Crystal was torturous. He couldn't sleep or eat, and he disengaged from his family. He didn't want to be alone, but he also didn't want to be with anyone who would make him talk.

"Hey," a familiar voice squeaked from behind.

Derek dropped his hammer, and the impact against the wooden floor reverberated throughout the room. His heart dropped to his stomach, and his body jerked like a marionette. He wanted to smile when he saw her, but it required too much energy. "Hi." Instead of smiling, he half-waved, intending to protect his heart.

She looked beautiful. Her oversized sunglasses sat on her head, holding her hair away from her face. Her skin glowed from the effects of sunshine, and she radiated into the room. She placed Lulu on the floor, and Derek peeked at her cleavage, falling out of her tight tank top. She stood upright, and his cheeks flushed, holding onto the image of her body.

He approached her and pulled up one side of his mouth. "How've you been? I thought you went home to Rochester." He chuckled, but he didn't find it funny. He needed to ease any tension that was building in the room.

"I went up to Lake George for a few days because I needed a break from everything going on here. I'm glad you're here, though. I wanted to talk to you. Do you want to grab some coffee?"

Derek held up his empty mug and glanced at the bottom of the cup. "Sure, I'll go make some." He ambled into the kitchen, and she followed, resting at the old kitchen table. He fumbled around pouring coffee grounds and water into the machine, and they listened to the coffee drip into the carafe. After a few moments, Derek broke the silence. "Is everything okay?"

Crystal cleared her throat and organized the tools Derek had splayed on the table. She placed all the nails in a pile, lined up the screwdrivers and hammer by size, and spread the paint samples to create a rainbow. She looked at him and he held her gaze; her eyes were hypnotizing. "I'm sorry. About the other day. I shouldn't have reacted the way I did."

Derek poured the steaming brown liquid into a mug and handed it to her. "Here's the cream and sugar." He sat beside her instead of across to give her his full attention. "It wasn't what you think."

Crystal leaned forward. "What do you think I think?"

"That I slept with her. I didn't, Crystal. I was drunk at Phil's, and she drove me home. We stopped at her house because she wanted something to happen, but nothing did. I promise. By the time we got to her house, I was sober but didn't have my car and still needed a ride. She drove me home about twenty minutes later once she realized I wasn't interested. I left my wallet in her kitchen." The words tumbled out of his mouth like an avalanche. He needed to get it all out before Crystal interrupted and stopped the words from flowing.

Her hand rested on Derek's knee, and fireworks shot from inside his stomach up to his neck. "It's none of my business what you do with your time. I shouldn't have gotten upset or jealous. We aren't together. We shared one kiss, and I pulled away. It's none of my business what you do." She pulled her hand off his knee and looked at her fingers.

Derek grabbed her hand and held it between his palms. "We had one kiss, Crystal, and I felt something that scared me. I know it scared you too. I felt a pull toward you that I haven't allowed myself to feel in years. You are beautiful."

Her eyes welled, and one tear fell. Derek wiped it away with his thumb. He cupped her chin in his hand and turned her face to him. His lips pressed against hers, and time stopped. He didn't care that he was on the job or that other contractors would see him through the window. Nothing mattered except him and Crystal.

A warmth traveled throughout his body, and he pulled away, looking tenderly into her eyes. "Was that okay?"

She nodded, grinning like the Cheshire Cat, and took a sip of coffee. "That was nice. I liked that." She rubbed her foot against his shin, and his body erupted with desire. He kissed her again, this time harder, pouring his soul out of his mouth and into hers. When he pulled away, he was speechless, his brain and body not working as one.

"I like you," he repeated.

"Derek, I like you too. But I'm leaving in a few days. What are we doing?" She tilted her head and squeezed her eyebrows.

Derek's shoulders slumped forward, and he grabbed her hands again. "I know you're leaving, but let's see what happens. Let's take it slow. I'm still working on the house, so we'll be in touch. And maybe we can make plans to see each other again. Let's take it one day at a time. While you're gone, let's become friends. I like learning about you, hearing you laugh, and spending time with you. Let's enjoy the rest of the time we have together."

She nibbled on her bottom lip and then clapped her hands and kissed him hard.

Lights flashed behind his eyes.

"You're right. We deserve to feel good. Let's enjoy the next four days and see what happens," she said.

Derek hooked his long pinky finger around Crystal's. "I pinky promise to enjoy the next four days." He kissed her knuckle. "And hopefully more days after that."

CHAPTER 23: CRYSTAL

D erek's lips tasted like peppermint. Instead of pulling away, Crystal melted against him and embraced his thick torso. He smelled like crisp snow and fire on a cold winter night. She breathed in his scent and felt anticipation race through her veins.

For the last few years, she had been stumbling through life, her heart taking a nap and her head leading the way. She changed the batteries in the dusty flashlight hiding behind her heart and shined the light directly on Derek. She no longer felt lost in the shadows of her overwhelming life.

Her electrified stomach zapped random parts of her body with every move. His long arms and broad shoulders wrapped around her like a blanket, and she found her feet up off the floor as he pressed her body against him. It felt too good to be true.

Crystal pulled away then kissed him on the lips to reaffirm her excitement. "We have four days until I have to pick up Mason. Do you have any plans? Are you working?" She looked around the house, taking a mental inventory of everything that still needed to be completed.

Derek stood up and leaned against the refrigerator, folding his arms across his chest. His assertive stance made him look like he lived there. Almost. "Nah, nothing that's pressing. Do you want to go on a date?"

Crystal's heart fluttered against her shirt. "Sure."

"Tonight, let me take you to dinner and a movie. We'll go on a real date and get to know each other."

Crystal couldn't stop grinning. She had no idea how her life had shifted so quickly, and she knew it wouldn't last, but she wasn't about to stop. He leaned down and kissed her with soft, gentle lips. "Is it a date?"

Crystal nodded, her lips still pushing against his. "Mm-hmm," she mumbled.

"Hey, Derek!" Nicky, the contractor Derek hired, stuck his head through the door.

Crystal jumped back and rubbed the edge of her bottom lip with her fingers.

"Oh, sorry, man, but we need your help."

Derek slid past Crystal, dragging his hand along her hip. "We'll pick this up tonight," he whispered.

Crystal melted at the thought of their date. She pranced upstairs, humming to herself. She grabbed her wallet, sunglasses, and keys, leaving Derek to work on the house while she shopped for a sexy outfit for their first official date.

* * *

Crystal blow-dried her damp hair and applied eyeshadow, mascara, and lipstick to her round face. She slinked into her new sundress, the halter top highlighting her broad shoulders from years of swimming. Two wooden bracelets jangled against each other on her wrist as she pulled her peep-toed slingbacks over her newly manicured toes. She lathered lotion on her smooth legs, and squirted a floral perfume on her wrists and collarbone. Confidence and beauty masqueraded around her deeply embedded feelings of inferiority and frumpiness.

Derek picked her up at 6:15 p.m. for dinner. Crystal thought he looked scrumptious with his gelled hair and pressed button-down shirt.

"You look beautiful," he said, looking her up and down.

She smoothed out her dress and spun in a circle, throwing her head back in nervous laughter. Her pumping heart made it hard to hear. "Thank you. You look handsome, too." She blinked her eyes, hoping to magnify her shimmering eyeshadow.

"Thanks." He cleared his throat, looked at his foot, and scraped his shoe against the doormat like he was removing invisible mud. "Molly helped me. I haven't been on an actual date in years. I wish my truck was in better condition. You deserve the best." He glanced back at his truck and shoved his hands in his pockets.

Crystal grinned. "I'm not here to get to know your truck, silly. I want to know you."

They traveled to Saratoga Springs for dinner and a movie. Crystal felt like she was in high school again. Her nerves fired a million times a second, and whenever she initiated conversation, sudden waves of insecurity reminded her that everyone she loved couldn't be trusted. *But he's not Jeremy; give him a chance.*

Halfway into town, Derek asked, "I'm not very good at this, but would you rather decide on a place together, or do you want me to pick the restaurant?" He rubbed his hands on his pants.

"Do you eat meat?" Crystal asked, and Derek nodded.

"Let's go to a burger joint. Fun and casual and less pressure than a stuffy, fancy restaurant."

"I know just the place." He smiled at her, and she wanted to squeeze his cheeks and grab his hair. Instead, she leaned over his arm to change the radio station. She felt his arm stiffen and purposefully dragged her fingers across his wrist and up his forearm. She watched him shiver.

"I love surprises," she said.

He took her to a brewery on Broadway, where they talked and laughed about everything; from living in New York to the latest social media craze. Crystal felt like she was talking to an old friend she hadn't seen in years, but she avoided certain topics, like Vanessa. His warm eyes and broad smile melted her heart and brought the butterflies in her stomach to life, and she didn't want to ruin the moment by asking about the biggest question mark she carried.

When dessert came, she wanted to skip the movie and return to her place to continue their date. *Am I bold enough to ask? Ugh, Crystal, think. What's the worst he could say? No?*

She stared off into space, lost in her fantasy of flowers, candles, and wine. He quietly watched her and then touched her hand. "Crystal?"

She spun her head back to the center of the table and took a sip of wine. "What? Sorry, I was zoning out." She tucked her hair behind her ears and readjusted her bracelets. The questions about his past, her present, and their future confused her. "What'd you say?"

He smiled. "Nothing. I was watching you, and you looked so beautiful. Deep in thought. What were you thinking about?"

Crystal leaned forward and lowered her voice. "You."

Derek's eyes widened, and he pressed his tongue against the gap in his two front teeth. "Me?" he whispered.

She played with him with her eyes. "You. And me." *Come on, Crystal, spit it out.* "How would you feel about skipping the movie theater and watching a movie at my house? In my room? We can have a pajama party." Her heart couldn't possibly beat any faster. She thought she was going to die with anticipation.

Derek's eyes flashed a combination of amusement and desire. "But I don't have my pajamas."

Crystal swirled the wine inside her glass, conjuring up the courage to be bold, brave, and beautiful. "You don't need any."

CHAPTER 24: DEREK

I**s she serious?** His eyes scanned her body, taking in her forward posture, and the crevice of her breasts highlighted by the tightness of her dress. Her fingers brushed the top of his hand, and his skin tingled. Her eyes bore a hole in his heart, inviting him to join her.

Derek pulled at his shirt collar and rolled his neck. "Is it hot in here?" He unbuttoned the top button.

He felt something rub against his shin under the table. Then it trailed up to his knee. He never broke eye contact, and his body wanted to jump over the table and take her home. He wanted to taste her mouth again but the intensity of his urges terrified him. *Vanessa, give me a sign. Let me know if it's okay.* His body responded to her touch, and he willed his brain to think about anything except the restaurant, the pajama party, and Crystal's beautiful, soft body.

He broke eye contact and stood quickly. "Excuse me. I'm going to use the bathroom before we go." He felt her watch him as he maneuvered between the square pub tables and booths to the bathroom. Water splashed on his face, and he pulled his hands down. *This is what you wanted, Derek. You kissed her first. Well, this is it. She wants you too and you deserve to have some fun.*

He yanked open the door and marched back to the table. "Let's do it," he announced. Crystal beamed back at him, her eyes crinkling with excitement.

The waitress dropped the black checkbook next to Derek, and he picked it up to insert his card. He stopped and stared at the lyrical, swirly purple ink on the check. *'Thank you! Vanessa,'* it read. A large-inked heart stared at him from next to her name.

Derek looked up at the ceiling and swallowed the lump that grew in his throat. *Thank you, Vanessa.*

Crystal touched his hand. "You okay?"

Derek blinked back the tears and regained his breathing. "Yeah, I'm ready to go."

He gave Vanessa, their waitress, an extra-large tip and wrote "Thank you!" at the bottom of the slip. He looked at the ceiling and thanked his wife again for sending a sign.

Derek grabbed Crystal's hand and led her out of the restaurant. He remained quiet as they drove back to the farmhouse, imagining her naked body next to his.

As they stumbled into her bedroom, the awkwardness grew and then melted away with each dropped piece of clothing. After he made love to her, a wave of satisfaction and tranquility washed over him, and he slept like a baby.

* * *

Derek rolled on his side the following morning and stared into Crystal's opened eyes. The sheet wrapped under her armpits, and her nakedness excited him. "Hi," he whispered, nuzzling his head next to hers.

"Morning. Have you been up for a while?" Her hair smelled like coconut, and her skin smelled like sweat. He inhaled and rubbed his nose against her.

"Yeah, just watching you sleep." She pulled away from him and kissed their intertwined fingers.

"I had a great time last night."

A slow grin spread across his face, and he kissed her chin, nose, and lips. "Me too."

They lay like that for a while, enjoying each other's physicality and remembering the personal fireworks that went off the night before. Derek's body still tingled, and he felt like the world had stopped to witness their evolving attraction.

A loud rap on the bedroom door pulled him away from his fantasy.

"Oh, shit." Crystal said, jumping up and grabbing her pajamas.

"Hey Crystal, we ran into a slight problem outside." A male voice carried through the door. "Is Derek here? I saw his truck in your driveway."

Crystal's head whipped toward Derek, her eyes bulging like she was trying to communicate a secret message. Derek raised his finger to his lips and shook his head no. He was trying to rebuild relationships with all the guys, and the last thing he needed was them knowing he was mingling with the clients.

"No, I haven't seen him. He must be somewhere. I'll be right down."

They listened to the heavy footsteps trail to the first floor, and Crystal threw Derek's clothes at him. All he had was the nice dress shirt from the night before, but maybe he could sneak out and come back in his dirty jeans and t-shirt.

"Okay, this is what we're gonna do," Derek whispered. Crystal stared at him without blinking. He could tell he had her full attention. "You go out in the back and talk to the guys. I don't know what the problem is but talk to them. Ask questions, even if you know the answer. I'm going to sneak out the front, drive home and change, and then come back."

Crystal nodded and bit her bottom lip.

"Can I take your car? My truck is too loud."

"Sure." She glanced at him and narrowed her eyes. "Why are we so secretive?"

Derek sighed, and his shoulders slumped. "Because I want to maintain a professional relationship with them. I need them to trust me, and if they think I'm sleeping with the client, they may not ask me to help with future projects." He felt like an asshole for referring to their lovemaking as sleeping together. It minimized the beauty of last night and he immediately regretted his word choice. Crystal's face dropped, her chin trembled, and when she raised her eyes at him, they were wet. "That's not what I meant." He embraced her and stroked her hair. "What we experienced was incredible, but I'm not ready to share what we shared with anyone else."

Crystal's rigid body tossed her keys to him and she gently kissed him on the cheek. "Good luck."

CHAPTER 25: CRYSTAL

H ow did I not think about this morning? Of course, people are milling about the house. She threw a sweatshirt over her t-shirt and marched downstairs. Hopefully, I can stall them so Derek can get out unscathed. She understood why he was concerned about people knowing, but it bothered her. She wondered if there were other women he kept secret. Crystal shook her head, trying to shake her suspicions, and reminded herself to relax.

When she got outside, she found a cluster of men around the old barn that her father and uncle had refurbished about thirty-five years prior. The original cathedral-ceiling barn was built in the late eighteen hundreds, but her father and uncle repainted the outside and built a usable second floor for storage. The red paint disappeared into the wood, and the exterior seemed to rest against a large maple tree. They looked up and down the structure, pointing to the base of the building.

"What's going on?" Crystal asked no one in particular.

"This barn." Nicky nodded toward the faded red building. "Is this something you want to keep?"

Crystal squinted her eyes, trying to block out the early morning sun. "Why? My dad built it, and I didn't expect to knock it down, but we can if we have to." She shielded her eyes with her hands.

"The wood planks are completely rotted with termite damage along the bottom. It's on its last leg, and the new owners would have to knock it down for safety reasons. We can knock it down and rebuild, or we can knock it down and lay sod. Or grass seed if you want the cheaper alternative."

Numbers rolled through Crystal's head as yet another expense piled on top of all the others so far. She was running out of money since the estate was still in limbo. "Knock it down, clear it, and lay grass seed."

She roamed around the property, examining the house and reflecting on all the changes made over the past month. It took Evelyn's death for this house to shine again, and the guilt crawled back into Crystal's core.

Crystal returned to the barn. Her father and uncle had built it the summer Crystal was seven. She recalled standing in that spot watching them haul wood, and Crystal could see them working, laughing, and drinking beer. She had painted the rock pile outside the barn and created a colorful rock garden. Crystal had shown Evelyn, and Evelyn scolded her for getting her new shoes dirty.

The barn became a storage shed to hold their lawnmower and gardening tools. Her parents used the second floor to store old furniture that needed to be tossed when they couldn't get to the dump. Currently, the barn was a treasure trove of her past.

"Wait!" she yelled to Nicky. "When will you tear it down?"

"We need to secure the equipment and dumpster, so probably not 'til next week."

"Hey guys," Derek said from behind her.

Crystal turned, and her heart stuttered. Her breath caught in her throat, and she grinned. Although he wore jeans and t-shirts daily, he looked sexier than usual. *It must be the hair, still pushed back from last night.* Crystal blushed at the memories.

"Where have you been?" Nicky called. "We got another project." He jerked his head toward the barn. "This thing has to come down."

"I'll catch up with you tonight," Derek said, walking past Crystal and squeezing her upper arm.

Her face flushed and she dashed to the house to feed Lulu and get dressed. Heading back to the barn, she strutted past Derek, wearing the shortest shorts she'd brought. She climbed up the rickety staircase and scanned the mess. The damp boxes, decrepit furniture, and moldy aroma overwhelmed her. No one would want their trash, and she didn't have time to commit to organizing everything.

She dug through the piles, careful not to rip the old cardboard holding her parents' history.

"What are you doing up here?" Crystal turned to see Derek standing at the top of the stairs.

"Oh, nothing. I didn't want to throw away anything important, so I thought I'd poke around." She continued to rummage through the boxes, unsure what she was looking for or what she hoped to find.

"Need some help?"

Crystal looked up, and her chest tightened. "Sure. You have nothing else to do?"

"Nah, the guys are taking off soon."

Derek sat beside her and watched. "What are you looking for?"

"I don't know. It seems like my parents used this as their personal dumpster. Did I ever tell you about my mom?" Crystal kept her eyes down.

"No. What was she like?"

"She was tougher than my dad. Nothing I did was good enough for her and she was terrible at hiding her disappointment. It got worse when I got married because she didn't like Jeremy. Said she didn't trust him. My dad never had a problem with him, but my mom ruled the house. It put a huge wedge in our relationship because I confided in

Jeremy about how my mom treated me. He openly disliked her, and she openly disliked him. The wedge grew between my mother and I, but also Jeremy and I. Eventually, she stopped inviting us over for holidays, and by then, we had Mason, so it was easier to stay home. We all pretended it was normal to ignore each other. And then I caught him cheating, and of course, my self-righteous mother had no problem telling me, 'I told you so.'"

"Is that why the house got so bad?" he asked, stroking her thumb.

A tear dripped down Crystal's cheek. "Yeah, I got a phone call a few years ago when she wandered away. I knew she had dementia but didn't know how bad. I put her in the nursing home and never saw her again." Crystal looked up. "I thought the house was taken care of. I did."

Derek wiped her cheek.

"Turns out Mr. Dole, our neighbor, died and no one told me. Am I a horrible person?"

"Nah. Not at all. You did what you thought was best. It's what we all do." He kissed her forehead. "Can I tell you something?"

His magnetic eyes held her gaze.

"Vanessa and I used to drive around looking for our dream home, and this house was the house we fell in love with. We dreamed about what it would be like to live here."

Crystal jerked her head toward him. "Really?"

"Really. When you called me that first day, I knew it was a sign." He leaned toward her, and the butterflies in her stomach took flight. His soft lips pressed against hers and her tongue snuck into his mouth, tracing the bottom of his upper teeth.

"Let's go inside. Sneak away and lock ourselves in my room." She traced her finger along his collarbone, and his body trembled under her touch.

They snuck out of the barn and back to her bedroom, where she forgot about her smug mother, cheating ex-husband, and stressful life back home. She let go, escaping from her past and dreaming about her future.

CHAPTER 26: DEREK

T he rest of the week rained a deluge, and work on the house stalled. Derek had a handful of other jobs pending and in progress, but his time with Crystal was ticking down. He needed to see her as much as possible, so he welcomed Mother Nature's cancellation, and the chance to spend his time wrapped up in Crystal's life.

They spent the next three days and two nights like two people sharing one body. Derek's mind couldn't concentrate on anything other than Crystal, and he spent his time memorizing the curves and crevices of her beautiful face and stunning body.

When he had first met her she was all-work and no-play; wearing her business suit and holding her briefcase. Now she was carefree, laughing at all his silly jokes and touching his bare skin incessantly. She wasn't like Vanessa, but maybe he needed someone completely different.

Derek kissed Crystal on the neck, wrapping his arms around her from behind. She stood at the edge of her bed, loading her overnight bag. "I can't get everything to fit. I think I shopped too much." She turned around, splayed her arms around his shoulders, and pulled his head closer.

"Maybe you should leave some clothes here? In case you come back to visit?"

Crystal dropped her arms and sat on her bed. "Derek, I never imagined the past three weeks would happen. I came home to take care of my mother's house, not to find a man. I'm going home today to my other life. Work starts in a few weeks." She looked down at her bag and fought with the zipper. "Was this a fling, or will I hear from you again?" She didn't raise her eyes.

Derek sat beside her, taking her smooth hand in his. "I want to see you again, and I want to talk to you every day. I want to know what makes Crystal Whitman tick, what makes her cry, and what makes her laugh until her belly hurts." He traced her arm with his fingers, and her shoulders shivered.

"So, does that mean I'll hear from you? I like you." Her voice caught in her throat.

Derek pressed his lips against hers and tugged on her hair. The world stopped, and he felt her fall onto his lips. "I'll call you tonight."

They stayed on her bed, looking at each other, and awaiting the inevitable. Her phone buzzed on the bedspread, pulling him out of his daze.

"Hi, Jeremy," Crystal said into her phone.

Derek watched her and listened.

"Yeah, I'm heading out soon. I know, I know. I should have called last night to say good night to Mason...I was busy...No, not too busy for my son, but a lot is going on over here." She glanced at Derek and walked into the narrow hallway. He didn't follow, but moved to the wall so he could hear her side of the conversation.

"Can I talk to him? Oh, well, tell him I'll be there by four...Yes, Jeremy, four. That was the time we decided on...Are you serious? Okay, I'm on my way. I'll be there before two." She stomped back into the bedroom. "Oh! You scared me." She placed her hand over her heart.

Derek stood by the door, wondering what their conversation was about. Crystal seemed concerned and surprised. "Is everything okay?"

"I have to go." She picked up her luggage and walked downstairs.

"You do?" Derek followed with quick steps. He figured that's what she was going to say, but he didn't realize how sad he would feel when the time came to say goodbye.

"Jeremy's going out to dinner tonight. He said he texted me asking if I could come earlier but I never got it. He said Mason misses me, and I miss him too." Her voice cracked and she swallowed.

Derek placed his thumb on her lip. "We knew you were leaving today. It's time for you to see your boy. Here, let me help you load your car." He plodded out the house, his heavy shoes keeping his feet hostage. He leaned on the edge of the car and gazed at her.

"Thank you for everything. I'll call you when I get home." She kissed him gently, and he kissed her back three more times.

"I'll miss you."

He climbed into his truck and drove out of her driveway with her car trailing. He saw Lulu's small body pressed against the window and Crystal petting her head as she backed out to the main road. Derek's body filled with heat, making it hard to breathe. He grabbed his water and took a sip, hoping to relieve the sawdust settling in his mouth. Everything felt terrible and uncertain, and he wondered if opening his heart had been a mistake.

He drove home and took a hot shower, scalding his body to impair his nagging thoughts. When he emerged from the steamy bathroom, the damp air shot at him like a cannon, and the dismal cloudiness surrounding him cleared.

Despite feeling sad, he was excited about his future with Crystal, even if it didn't guarantee happiness. Vanessa would have liked Crystal,

Molly had said, and he deserved to try.

Derek checked his phone every few minutes, hoping Crystal would text to say hello or that she was thinking of him. Waiting was killing him, and he paced his house and stared out the window. He tried to watch television, but nothing kept his interest.

After dinner, his phone rang, and his heart skipped a beat. He fumbled with the phone, finding the answer button. "Hello?"

Crystal's flushed face filled his screen. "Hi, I'm so sorry I didn't call earlier. It's been a day, and Mason's in the shower, so I have some time to talk." She smiled, but Derek knew she was distracted by other things in her house. It was the way she only held his gaze for one or two seconds, or asked him to repeat himself, or how the background constantly changed with her movement.

"I didn't know if I'd hear from you tonight. How was the drive?"

They talked for the next twenty minutes. Crystal showed Derek her house, and Derek showed Crystal his. It was strange that he hadn't taken her to his home, but it felt too soon. The only woman who'd ever accompanied him into his house was Vanessa. She was his queen and always would be. He couldn't betray her. At least not yet. When he did bring a woman home, he needed to be sure.

That was how they survived for the next week. Chaotic twenty-minute phone calls embedded into their regular lives. Derek kept working, focusing on the farmhouse and the other small jobs, saving money for Molly. He had the initial deposit for her but needed Crystal's payments to start. He knew the estate hadn't been settled, but he had to keep the other guys happy.

It was going to be an uncomfortable conversation, and dating the client definitely complicated things, but he needed to say something to Crystal soon.

* * *

August fifteenth came quickly, and Molly and Derek climbed into the small U-Haul for the long drive to Westchester County. The warm sun and cloudless sky made for an enjoyable drive, so they sat against the soft seats and sang to the radio.

"This music is ancient," Molly said, scanning the radio stations.

"Turn it off. This may be our last face-to-face conversation in months."

Molly sighed and turned the small knob until it clicked. "I'm gonna miss you, Dad," Molly said. "Are you sure you're going to be okay?" Her mascara-coated eyes looked at him, and he smiled.

"I'll be fine, Molly. Crystal and I have been talking every day, and I'm getting used to having another friend to lean on. You're in college, which are the best years, so don't worry about me. Promise me you'll enjoy it."

"Thanks, Dad. And you'll deposit money into my account every month? For rent?"

Derek nodded. "Yep. Every month." He didn't know how, but he'd figure it out.

They traveled in silence for the last hour. Derek lost himself in worries about Molly's apartment, Crystal's life away from him, and work. The house still needed some attention, but soon it would be on the market. The driveway and the barn were the next significant expenses, but they were necessary. He figured it would be ready by Labor Day.

He spent the day lugging heavy boxes and simple furniture into Molly's new apartment. There was no traffic on his drive home, and when he hit the Thruway, he was tempted to head west and drive to Rochester. He watched the exit ramp pass on his right, and a melancholy mood encased him.

When he got home, he collapsed on the couch, wondering how he'd adjust to an empty house and an empty life, again.

CHAPTER 27: CRYSTAL

A few days after Crystal returned home from Farm Cove, Jeremy called and said they needed to talk. Immediately put on the defensive, Crystal prepared herself to say no, to whatever he wanted.

"I want Mason to move in with me," Jeremy blurted out.

Crystal scoffed. "No. Not happening. I am his mother. He needs his mother." She plopped into a chair and rubbed her hairline.

"Crystal, he needs to be in a place that will set him up for success. You live in a city. There are so many kids in his class. He needs to be in a place that's smaller, more intimate, and able to individualize his education. You know that."

Crystal shook her head. *Well, well, well, it looks like Jeremy has actually been listening to me all these years.* She was too tired to fight. "We'll talk about it later. I need to think about it."

After sleepless nights and the countdown to school hitting single digits, Crystal felt trapped. She had to give Mason the opportunity to shine. Maybe Jeremy was right.

A week before school started, Crystal and Mason traveled to Jeremy's house for one last goodbye. Her heart broke on the drive home. If she was good at one thing in her life, it was being a mother, and now Jeremy had managed to take that away from her too.

She worried about Mason and his transition to middle school, and wondered daily how he was doing. Sometimes it hit her at 9 a.m., other times at 9 p.m., but she texted Jeremy for an update every day.

Crystal missed seeing his shaggy hair, sleepy eyes, and wrinkled clothes every morning. She missed yelling at him to clean his room and making him a kid-friendly dinner. Everything felt strange, like she was watching someone else's life unfold. She had lost control, and no one seemed to mind.

Three days into the school year, Crystal felt like she'd been tossed overboard, attached to the weight of the thirty jackets hung up in their cubbies in her classroom. She might be able to tread water the first week of school, but eventually the jackets would become waterlogged and she would be dragged under.

She gazed out her bedroom window, analyzing the dusty trampoline and the oak tree leaves of rust and pumpkin hanging over the neglected swing set. Mason had moved out last week, and the quietness of her new life surprised her. She dug through her purse and pulled out her phone, pressing Jeremy's face.

"Hi, Mom." Mason's enormous head filled the screen, and he pulled the phone closer. One blurry eyebrow occupied the screen's top half, and a distorted brown eye peeked at her. Crystal smiled at his goofiness.

"Hi, Mase. How are you?" Crystal's shoulders slumped, and a heaviness filled her limbs, but she smiled just the same. "I miss you."

They talked about his room, school, and life with Jeremy. Mason bounced around the apartment, showing Crystal the pet lizard Jeremy had bought him as a homecoming gift.

"Will you pick me up on Friday?" Mason asked.

Tears welled behind Crystal's eyes. She had always been Mason's primary caregiver, and the discomfort and constant questioning kept her up at night. *Is this the right decision?*

"You know it. I'll leave straight from work and be there for five." She crossed her fingers and held them up to the camera. "Hopefully, no traffic."

Crystal and Mason hung up, and Crystal's body stilled. She could never understand how a mother could give up custody until now, and the lines blurred between what was suitable for her and what was right for Mason. Crystal knew a smaller town with smaller classes and more individual attention from teachers would put Mason on the right track. City living was too risky for a boy with learning needs. Crystal worked with those kids every day, and she knew the consequences.

Crystal hung up with Mason and she immediately called Melanie. *No answer.* She needed to talk to someone and automatically dialed Derek. She missed him and needed a familiar voice to quell her guilt. They had been texting daily over the past few weeks, mainly regarding the house.

"Hey Derek. How are you? How's the house?" Crystal turned on the dishwasher and scrubbed the counters. She needed to stay busy to keep her mind off the current state of her life.

"It looks great." Derek's deep voice echoed in her ear. "I sent you pictures of the yard. Did you get them?"

Crystal threw the dishcloth in the sink and pulled up the last email from Derek. "Yes, everything looks amazing. You would never know there used to be a barn in that back corner. And the driveway is perfect. That's something buyers need, especially with all the snow, so thank you. Is there anything else that needs to be done?"

"Nothing at all." Derek's rate of speech quickened. "Once you pay your balance, you can put it on the market."

Crystal's heart rate sped, and a marble emerged in her throat, growing into a grape. "I have an appointment with my mother's lawyer next week. Hopefully, I'll have a date for when her estate will be finalized." Crystal didn't know what the holdup was, but there was a different excuse every time she contacted Mr. Meyers. She battled with him, trying to get the cash promised to her in her mother's will. At this point, it wasn't much, but it was enough to pay Derek. "I feel terrible that I haven't paid you yet." She placed her head in her hands and stared into the distance.

"Do you have an expected timeline? The guys have been asking." Crystal heard Derek's voice shake.

"Hopefully, by the end of the month. I already paid half, right?" She knew he was doing her a favor by being patient, but she had no control of Evelyn's estate. With Mason, a new school year, and Jeremy, Evelyn's house was the last thing she needed. Her brain couldn't handle one more ball to juggle.

Derek paused, and Crystal heard papers shuffling. "The balance right now is about twenty-thousand dollars."

That's a lot of money. Crystal's chest tightened, and she struggled to fill her lungs with air. *What if the money never comes?* She tapped her pen against her notebook and her foot against the cupboard. The pen trembled in her fingers. "No problem, Derek. I'll call my lawyer, Mr. Meyers, right away. I'll call you as soon as I hear from him."

Please, Mom, please come through for me.

All Crystal did over the next five days was worry, leave messages for Mr. Meyers, and avoid calls from Derek.

CHAPTER 28: DEREK

⬥

Crystal's house was done. Derek drove the long way to the diner to get a glimpse of the farmhouse during sunrise. The orange sun slowly peeked over the hill just behind the house, and the sunbeams highlighted the beige paint that now coated the exterior wood siding. Drops of dew glistened in the newly mowed grass, sunflowers and dahlias decorated below the front windows, and a fall-themed wreath adorned the mahogany door. The house looked beautiful. Warm, inviting, and precisely what he and Vanessa imagined. He took a photo and tucked his phone into his front pocket.

The house sat empty, so Derek let himself into the basement every few days to empty the dehumidifier. *Crystal spent so much money; it would be a shame if the scent of mildew chased potential buyers away...if the house ever goes on the market, and if, of course, I get paid.*

He and Crystal texted back and forth at least three times a day, but phone calls were few. Crystal seemed distracted whenever he called, so he stopped, and she didn't call him. He wanted to see her, but the situation with Mason was complicated, and he didn't want to push himself into a fragile component of her life.

Derek climbed out of his truck and sauntered into Phil's for breakfast.

"Hey, Margie." He nodded and gave a little wave before seating himself at an empty stool at the counter.

"Hey, Derek. How's everything going? You want some coffee?"

Derek placed the menu at the edge of the counter. "Just coffee today. I have a busy day ahead of me." Since Crystal seemed to be avoiding him, Molly needed money, and he needed a distraction, he filled his calendar with jobs around the county. Nicky's lead man was out with a broken leg, so Derek had about eight weeks of consistent work which would pay Molly's rent through December.

Margie poured the steaming hot liquid into his cup, and Derek dumped all the sugar packets from the caddy into his mug and stirred. "Thanks." He wiped the sugar granules that spilled in front of him into a tidy pile.

"How's Crystal? Enjoying her life back home?"

Derek looked down and played with the edge of his placemat. "She's good. I miss her."

"When will you see her again?"

Derek shrugged. "Not sure. It's complicated."

Margie rocked back and forward from her heels to her toes and back again. "House for sale yet?"

Derek shook his head. "Not yet."

"It looks stunning. You did a great job." She pushed her pencil behind her ear and tucked her receipt book into her apron pocket.

"Thanks." He didn't want to talk about Crystal or the house. Crystal owed him money, and not knowing when he was getting paid was fueling his insecurities about whether or not he deserved to take over his father's business. He could feel the weight of his father's disappointment sitting beside him at the counter.

"You should go see her. She's a nice girl, and I like her." After a pause, Margie added, "Coffee's on the house."

Derek sat alone with his thoughts, not sure what to make of Crystal.

He liked her, but it seemed long distance wouldn't work. He glanced at his watch. She was probably getting ready for work, so he texted her a smile emoji, a morning greeting, and a picture of the magnificent sunrise. If Crystal didn't respond, he'd give up. If she did, he'd drive out and see her.

Three seconds later, a heart emoji popped up on his phone.

Derek took a breath and held it. He typed: **I want to see you. What are you doing tomorrow night?**

His phone rang, and he answered the call before the first ring stopped. "Hi, Crystal." He felt breathless.

"Hi. Tomorrow night? Nothing, but I work tomorrow and Thursday." Her work schedule reminded him that summer was over, and real life had kicked in and left him in the breakdown lane without a tow.

"Can I come over? I want to take you out to dinner on a real date." He imagined her pacing her kitchen, which he'd only seen through video chat. He counted to five before she responded.

"That would be wonderful. Should I plan on you spending the night?"

Derek's limbs tingled. "I don't know, maybe. Only if you want me to."

Crystal laughed. "Pack a bag. As long as you promise you won't keep me up all night, you can stay until the morning."

Derek's heart fluttered against his chest. His intense smile hurt his face.

"Perfect. Let's have another pajama party." He saw Margie snap her head toward him, giving him the thumbs-up sign with raised eyebrows and shoulders. Derek returned the hand motion, and Margie continued down the counter with her coffeepot.

Crystal giggled, and warmth flowed within Derek. "I'll text you my address. Unfortunately, I have to go. I have to finish getting ready because I have eighteen six-year-olds to wrangle for the next seven hours."

Derek leaned forward and lowered his voice, keeping his eyes on Margie. "I'm looking forward to seeing you tomorrow. Have a great day."

Derek disengaged the phone call and gulped the rest of his coffee. He quickly texted Nicky, saying he wouldn't be in the next day. He threw down a dollar, grabbed his keys, and pranced out of the diner.

CHAPTER 29: CRYSTAL

❧⊰⊱❧

T raffic was atrocious. Crystal knew Derek was arriving around five and she needed to get as much work done as possible, so she stayed in her classroom until half past four. The class was still learning how to sit at a table and listen to the teacher, so she didn't have a lot of new material to prep, but open house was coming up, and she needed to plan her presentation.

She drove out of the city in bumper-to-bumper traffic. On a good day, it took twenty minutes to get from her school to her home, but now with rush-hour starting it looked like she'd be meeting Derek in her driveway.

She looked at her eyes in her rearview mirror and noticed the straggly hair growing around her previously waxed arch. Her eyes shot to the roof, annoyed that she didn't take care of herself earlier. *Oh well. I guess he'll see me in my natural form.* She didn't want to be bothered by her unkept hair and messy eyebrows but they gave her anxiety just the same.

It started when she was twelve, and Evelyn told her that no boy would want to date a girl who didn't know how to apply makeup or dress for a date. Evelyn's disappointment overcame the constant pressure to look perfect, and Crystal stamped it out like a burned-down cigarette. Even now, thirty years later, the embers sometimes reignited within her and the overbearing inadequacy squashed her poise.

She cranked up eighties metal music and weaved in and out of traffic until her exit appeared. She was finally home and only three minutes late.

Derek's old truck already sat in the driveway, with 'Fischer Home Services,' spelled across the side.

Crystal climbed out of her car and slowly approached. "Hi, sorry I'm late. I love the signage on your truck." Her hands juggled her pocketbooks, backpack, and work bag, so she nodded in his direction.

The truck door slammed, and Crystal took in his work boots, flannel shirt, and jeans. He looked like he'd just come from a busy day of work. "You look different," she said.

He grinned, and the space between his two front teeth sent the butterflies on a journey. "So do you. And now that I'm working a lot, I thought it might be good to advertise the business. Molly designed it." In three steps, he was directly in front of her and she smelled the coffee that lingered on his breath. "Let me take something." He reached out to her, and she handed over her work bag.

Nerves shook her hands as she struggled to get the key into the lock. It was one thing to see Derek at the farmhouse and another to have him in her personal space. She fumbled with her bags and pushed the door open with her hip. "Come on in."

They hadn't even touched yet, and she wondered if Derek was just as nervous to see her. *I hope he isn't mad at me.* She hadn't returned his calls or texts as she imagined she should have, but life without Mason kept her thoughts busy.

"Welcome to my home," she said, dropping her bags and kicking off her shoes at the door. "If you don't mind, could you take off your boots?" Lulu ran over, and Crystal scratched behind her soft ears.

Derek bent down to unlace his boots, and she explained, "I don't have time to vacuum, so I try to be smart about how we live." She walked him through the house's main rooms and pointed out the pantry. "In case you get hungry."

Standing in the long hallway, he touched her hand, and she froze.

Turning toward him, she gulped and looked into his searching eyes. "Is everything okay?" His husky voice made her knees weak.

She nodded, unable to speak.

"Can I kiss you?"

Her body tensed and relaxed, and she nodded again.

His lips brushed against hers like a fluttering leaf in the wind. Her body melted against him and she pulled the back of his neck toward her, feeling every curve of his lips fit against hers. The stress from the past few weeks flew away and she floated closer. Nothing else mattered except for being in his arms where he would protect her.

Crystal pulled away and touched her bottom lip and then his. "I've missed you." She grabbed his hand and led him down the hall. "Let me show you my bedroom."

An hour later, they emerged from her room.

"Are you hungry?" Derek asked.

"I was hungry for you," Crystal purred. She felt her face get hot and giggled.

Derek laughed. "I hope you worked up an appetite. I'm taking you out for dinner."

Crystal hadn't felt this sexy in years. Jeremy never made her feel like a queen in the bedroom, but Derek gave her complete control. It empowered her and made her want him even more. "Dinner sounds great, but let's have dessert here." She sashayed to the fridge, pulled out the whipped cream can and squirted a white dollop on her finger. She licked the sticky vanilla topping and whispered, "I make a mean sundae. Do you want one?"

Derek grinned and leaned across the counter. He placed his chin in his hand and pulled at the neckline of his t-shirt. "I'll take dessert over dinner any day."

CHAPTER 30: DEREK

T hey never made it to dinner. Instead, Derek ordered pizza and salad from Crystal's favorite pizza place. He usually only ate cheese or pepperoni, but he couldn't say no when Crystal suggested a Meat Supreme pizza.

Crystal excused herself before, during, and after dinner to check in with Mason, Jeremy, or work, but Derek wasn't offended. He knew he was infringing on her life, house, and routine, and he felt lucky just being there.

"Everything okay?" he asked while Crystal settled herself on the couch next to him. She pulled the fleece blanket up over her waist and snuggled against him.

"Yeah, fine. It's a big week for Mason. He started his new school and is having trouble adjusting to life with Jeremy. In the past, I was the enforcer, and Jeremy was the fun parent, but now things have switched, and Mason doesn't quite know what to do with all the new rules."

Derek touched her hand. "You'll get through it. I dealt with the same transition with Molly, except that her mom was dead." Derek's voice shook on the word *dead,* and Crystal pulled away to look at him head-on.

"I'm sorry. I can't imagine what that was like for you or her."

Derek rubbed her hand in between his, comforted by her smooth skin. "It was the darkest time in my life. She was a teacher, just like you, and she loved kids. She was a great mom, and when she left, Molly and I were broken."

Crystal's body tensed, and silence pitter-pattered between them.

He continued. "Our families tried to be there for us, but everyone lived in different states except for Phil and my dad. Besides a quick visit or phone calls here or there, we were alone. We felt alone. For a long time, Margie filled in as Molly's second mom. She was Vanessa's best friend and always wanted to be a mother."

Crystal smiled. "I can see that. She seems like she'd be easy to talk to."

"She is. And when she saw us drowning, she swooped in and saved us. She was the one Molly went to when she got her period for the first time, who helped pick out her dress for her first formal, and who talked some sense into me when I couldn't get out of my way." Derek dropped Crystal's hand and placed it on the armrest. He tried to lounge back against the couch cushions, but the couch was slightly too short for his tall frame. He scooted back, trying to get more comfortable.

"Random question, but did you ever date her? It seems like she really cares for you."

Derek chuckled. "No, never. She was like a sister to me, and I would never do that to Vanessa. Not to mention, Margie has a girlfriend."

Crystal gulped her water. "She does? I never realized."

"Yeah, you know—small town. I don't think she advertises it. Last I knew, her girlfriend lives in Albany, and Margie goes to see her on her days off."

"I won't say a word," Crystal said.

"I knew only because she and Vanessa were so close. I don't even think Phil knows. But now you know." *Stupid, Derek. Why'd you say that?* He crammed a chip in his mouth to prevent him from saying more.

"Our little secret." Crystal hooked her pinky into his and squeezed.

Tears welled behind his eyes, and his mouth tasted like sandpaper. His jumbled thoughts made it difficult to respond. He hadn't spoken about Vanessa to a stranger in a long time, and his feelings vacillated between worry and hope. *Can I trust her with my broken self? Will Vanessa forgive me?* It was too much, and he hesitated before responding, "I have to use the bathroom."

Her eyes followed him out the room and down the hallway. *Even if Vanessa doesn't forgive me, it's too late. We already slept together, and I'm falling hard.*

* * *

That night he couldn't sleep a wink. He lay beside her, feeling the heat of her body and woven blankets under his hands. The matching jersey sheets rubbed against his bare skin, and thoughts of Vanessa, Crystal, his company, and Molly raced through his head like a hamster on a metal wheel. Derek stared at the ceiling and listened to the clock tick, willing his brain to shut down for the night.

Five-thirty came quick, and the loud buzzing of Crystal's phone pulled him out of his half-slumber. "Morning." She leaned over and kissed him on the cheek. "I have to brush my teeth." She rolled out of bed and walked to the bathroom. *She looks beautiful.* Derek admired her messy hair and askew pajamas, and memories from the day before tumbled back to him.

He pulled his clothes on and shuffled to the kitchen to make coffee for himself and Crystal. He rummaged through her cabinets, looking for coffee, sugar, mugs, and filters, and placed them in front of the coffee maker. His coffee-making skills were rusty because Margie or

Molly made him a cup each morning, but he did his best.

While the coffee brewed, he pulled out two Capital Region Apple and Wine Festival tickets from his wallet and tucked them inside Crystal's empty mug. Phil sponsored the festival on his menu, so he received complimentary tickets and gave them out freely to his customers.

After opening and closing three drawers, Derek gave up the search for a notebook and settled on a paper towel. He scribbled a note, careful not to rip the towel and wrapped it around the tickets. **Thank you for a great night. I'd love to see you again, and I'd love to meet Mason.** He debated if he should mention that the two tickets were for Crystal and Mason, not Crystal and Derek, or if he should say that he would only go if she wanted. All those words felt too complicated, so he quickly signed, **Love, Derek.**

He looked around the kitchen, grabbed a fake flower from a ceramic pot sitting on the side table in her living room, and tucked the flower into the mug. It looked unusual with the extra-long stem extending well beyond the mug's rim, but it felt appropriate for his impromptu gesture.

Derek heard the water shut off, and a few minutes later, Crystal hurried into the kitchen, pushing earrings through her earlobes. "Morning!" She placed her work bag on the kitchen chair.

"Coffee?" Derek asked.

Crystal nodded. "And lots of sugar."

Derek placed the mug in front of her. "This is for you."

Her head snapped toward him, her hand still against her earlobe. "What's this?" She took the flower out of the mug, removed the note, and read it aloud. "Aww, this is so sweet! Are these for us?" Her speech slowed, and she waved the two tickets in front of him.

"No, those are for you and Mason. I do want to meet him, but I don't want to intrude on your time together, nor do I want to overwhelm him by being around." Derek poured coffee three-quarters of the way to the top of his cup to allow plenty of room to stir. "The festival's next weekend."

He placed the pot back in the machine, and Crystal threw her arms around his neck, squeezing and pressing her breasts and hips against him. "You are so sweet," she repeated. They stayed like that for a few moments, swaying in the kitchen, and he breathed in the coconut aroma from her hair.

"The house is done, so you guys can stay there. I don't have to come—unless you want me to."

Crystal kissed him, and he tasted cherry ChapStick. "Thank you. I'll talk to Mason this weekend and let you know."

They sat at the table, drinking almost identical cups of coffee, and talked about everything except the house, the money, and the dreaded For Sale sign.

CHAPTER 31: CRYSTAL

C rystal pulled into Jeremy's apartment complex and parked the car in the furthest spot from his door. There had been less traffic than usual and she had arrived too early, so she walked Lulu around the sparse greenery surrounding the pavement while she waited. The crisp air and colorful carpet of leaves on the ground reminded her that winter was coming, and she wrapped herself tighter in her coat for warmth.

Jeremy's SUV pulled into the spot next to her, and Mason waved enthusiastically. Crystal's heart beat fast, and she scrambled over to them, embracing her son. "Mason! Look at you. You've grown this week." His eyes lined up with the bridge of her nose, and his pants were an inch too short.

"Hi, Mom." He bent down and picked up Lulu, caressing her soft fur.

Crystal didn't know how he would respond to this change, and she had worried the entire month. It wasn't just a change in schools; it was a change in parents, houses, and routine too. Based on his grin he seemed okay, but she knew he might open up to her on the drive home, so she bit her tongue to prevent questions from escaping her mouth.

"Jeremy." Her serious tone communicated that she was here for Mason and nothing more.

He gave her an appraising glance. "Crystal."

She broke his gaze and brought her hands together with a loud clap. "Okay, Mason, shall we get your stuff?" They walked toward the entrance, with Mason and Lulu ahead and Crystal and Jeremy behind.

"So, what are your plans for this weekend?" Jeremy asked.

Crystal didn't have to tell him— she was no longer his wife and she didn't owe him anything—but she decided to be cordial, for Mason's sake. "Going to the farmhouse. It's done, so I want to ensure everything is ready for the listing. A friend of mine gave me tickets to the Apple and Wine Festival, so Mason and I will go for a few hours tomorrow." *Stop talking, Crystal.* She had said more than she intended. "How has your week been?"

Jeremy unlocked the door to his apartment, and they entered. It was tidier than Crystal had ever kept their house when they were married. Jeremy used to comment on her messiness, but she needed mess because it was entrenched in her personality. Chaos comforted her. "The apartment looks great," she commented.

"Thanks. The week's been busy. I've been ducking out of work early every day to get home, cook Mason dinner, and help with his homework. Although he hasn't had any yet, it's good to get into a routine."

"Any behaviors at school I should know about?"

Jeremy shook his head. "None."

Crystal checked her watch. "Mason, you ready? We have to get going to avoid traffic."

Mason and Lulu strode out of his bedroom. "Ready."

"Give your father a kiss and say goodbye." Crystal took his backpack and the leash. "Make sure you have everything and use the bathroom before we go."

Mason dropped his stuff and disappeared down the hall.

"Thank you again." She wanted to say more to Jeremy, but the words stuck in her throat.

Jeremy leaned in to kiss her, and Crystal pulled back like his lips contained poison. She crossed her arms and widened her stance. "Jeremy, stop. We're not married."

He narrowed his eyes at her. "Right, but you're still the mother of my child, and I'm being polite."

"Stop. Kissing me is not polite Jeremy, and it's not good for Mason to get mixed signals. Either we're together, or we're not; and we're not, and we won't be. Plus," she shrugged, "I'm seeing someone." His face dropped and she saw a flash of confusion before he sneered at her. "Don't be so surprised, Jeremy." She lowered her voice. "You could have a fling on the side, and I can't have a boyfriend? Please. Don't be so self-righteous. And stop kissing me."

Lulu ran out of the bathroom and waited at Crystal's feet. "Time to go, Mason." She spun on her heel and walked out of the apartment with Mason and Lulu trailing after her, leaving Jeremy speechless in her assertiveness.

The ride back to the farmhouse was quicker than Crystal expected. Mason was quiet during the ride, talking more to Lulu than he did to Crystal. She let it slide, reminding herself that things were different.

"Are you excited about the festival tomorrow?" Crystal asked.

"Yeah."

Mason loved animals, rides, and carnival food, but at that pre-teen age, any interruption in his day was a hassle. The hum of the engine filled the car, and Crystal changed the subject. "The farmhouse looks great. You probably don't remember it; it was so long ago that I brought you."

Mason didn't respond, so Crystal rerouted their conversation to school. "How was your second week? Do you like it?"

Mason shrugged. "It's okay. I like my teacher."

After another pause, Crystal asked, "And what about Dad? Has it been okay living there?" Crystal wanted to know if there were any women in Jeremy's life, but she didn't want to use Mason as a ping-pong ball in their messy relationship.

"He's been good."

Crystal wanted Mason to tell her it was okay, that she made the right decision sending him there, but that was too much to ask a child. She wouldn't know if she made the right decision until they passed this phase in their lives.

They traveled the rest of the way in comfortable silence. Crystal pressed her shoulders against the seat and settled in. She focused on the music and wondered what she was doing with her life.

Darkness overcame the sunset, and the lit farmhouse pulled Crystal out of her insecure thoughts. "Mason, look."

The welcoming house sparkled like a perfectly wrapped Christmas gift. She drove down the curvy, smooth driveway, admiring the change. The pruned trees and recently mowed grass created a painting against the backdrop of gray, blue, and purple sky. Two exterior lights illuminated the mahogany door, contrasting perfectly with the black shutters. Flowers decorated the front of the house, and the moonbeams floated through the background's red, orange, and yellow leaves. *Mom would have loved this.*

Memories filtered through Crystal's mind, and her body grew warm with pride. "This is the house, Mason. This is the house from my childhood."

The car doors slammed shut, and Mason, Crystal, and Lulu made their way to the new and improved farmhouse. Images of her mom and dad, the scent of Thanksgiving, and the sound of football on the television brought Crystal back to her childhood. Feelings of home wrapped their arms around her as she walked Mason into the house.

CHAPTER 32: DEREK

T he morning drive to the farmhouse was easy—Derek had
driven here so many times that he could close his eyes and
still arrive safely. He had showered, shaved, and taken special
care in picking out his clothes, settling on a clean pair of blue jeans
and a long-sleeved t-shirt with a flannel jacket.

Derek only had the morning to make an impression because Crystal
and Mason were leaving for the fair around lunchtime. He needed an
excuse to visit unexpectedly, so he had purchased flowers and bulbs
the day before.

Derek texted Crystal to ensure they were up and offered to bring
breakfast. Before pulling into the driveway, he adjusted the box of
donuts so it wouldn't slide when he made the final turn.

He sat in his car for a few moments, twisting his watch and fiddling
with the radio knobs, before grabbing the donuts and coffee, and
pushing his way out of the truck. The walk to the front door was slow,
and he was careful not to step on any of the newly planted flowers.

Crystal opted for a knocker over a doorbell, so he grabbed the cast
iron ring in the majestic lion's mouth. With three loud thuds, the door
flung open. Derek's mouth dropped, and he immediately smiled. She

wore a knee-length hunter-green dress that squeezed her torso and flared at the waist.

"You look beautiful," he whispered, looking to see if any small eyes were peeking around the corner. He handed her the donut box and followed her into the kitchen. "What do you think of the house?"

Her eyes sparkled, and her smile reached her ears. "It's beautiful. It looks different from the hell-hole I walked into a few months ago. I love it." Crystal spun around to take in the house, and her skirt flared. She stumbled back on her high heels and giggled.

He followed her through the empty living room and dining room into the kitchen. He handed her the disposable coffee cup, and she slurped the rim. An imprint of her lipstick remained on the white plastic.

Mason raced into the room wearing gym shorts and a button-down shirt wide open. "Mom, I need help. I can't get the buttons right. Oh, hi." His attention turned toward Derek and then back toward Crystal.

Derek held out his hand. "Hi, I'm Derek. I worked on the house."

Mason eyed Derek's outstretched arm and gave him an awkward high-five. His short, chubby fingers pushed against Derek's stiff palm. "Hi." He turned away from Derek. "Mom, I need help."

Crystal crouched down, her calf muscles tensing, and fastened the buttons. "You look handsome. Is this what you're wearing?"

"Yeah, casual on the bottom and nice on the top. I'm wearing the Mets hat Dad bought me and my new school sneakers."

"You look great."

"Mason, I like your style. Do you want a donut?" Derek held out the open container, and Mason grabbed two.

"Thanks." He sat at the table and began doodling in a notebook.

Derek turned his attention to Crystal. "So, I brought some tulip bulbs of various colors. I wasn't sure if you wanted to plant them near the top of the driveway around the mailbox?" Of course, Derek bought the tulips to have an excuse to see Crystal and meet Mason. If Crystal wasn't into it, that was fine; he'd plant them at his house.

"Oh!" Crystal seemed surprised. "Sure. Mason, do you want to help me plant these bulbs?"

Mason didn't look up. "Not really."

"Okay, I'll be right back," Crystal said.

Derek followed her out of the house and admired her backside. His body got hot, and his mouth went dry. He didn't realize how much he had missed her. *She's got curves for days.* Crystal looked like a woman. A desirable, exquisite woman. A deep sense of gratitude spread over Derek.

"Do you want me to dig? I don't want your dress to get dirty," he said.

Crystal crouched down, and the hem of her dress rested on the grass. "We can do it together. How about you dig and I drop them in?"

Derek dug six holes around the mailbox post. He felt Crystal's eyes scanning his body and tried to keep the grunting to a minimum. The packed dirt flung over Derek's shoes like confetti pouring out of a pinata.

Crystal dropped the bulbs in the narrow holes and asked, "Oh shoot, what colors were those?"

Derek had purchased four sets of six, but they sat in a pile at Crystal's feet. "Good question. I guess it'll be a surprise."

"When do tulips bloom?" Crystal asked.

"Around April." She touched his arm, and electric jolts raced to his shoulder. "Maybe one day we can drive by and see."

Her face dropped, and she stared at the piles of dirt covering the bulbs. Derek touched her hand, and she didn't respond. After a moment, she turned her head.

"We'll drive by together," he said. He sensed her disappointment and squeezed her hand. "Look, we have all these extras." He dropped the

145

extra bulbs into his open palm. "I'll take some, and you take some, and we'll have the same surprise at your house and mine. Just because you won't live here doesn't mean you can't enjoy the beauty."

Crystal held out her hand and accepted five bulbs. "Thank you." She hugged him and quickly pulled away. "I have to get ready for the fair. Thank you so much for the tickets. And the flowers. And the coffee. And everything."

Even though she couldn't kiss him, he knew she was falling in love.

"Text me tonight when you get home."

"I promise." She held up her pinky, cradled the bulbs against her abdomen, and trotted to the house.

Derek looked around, and for the first time, he didn't see himself and Vanessa dancing within the house. He saw Crystal.

CHAPTER 33: CRYSTAL

"Mason, did you have a good weekend?" Crystal gripped the steering wheel and slowed her speed. The tumultuous rain pelted the roof and windshield, and the wipers couldn't keep up. Traffic was slow, and a sea of brake lights filled her vision. She hated driving in the rain but she couldn't let Mason see her discomfort.

He bounced in the backseat with Lulu. Snacks, books, and toys filled the surrounding seats, and he leaned against his stuffed animal and pillow. "It was fun."

Crystal paused and asked, "What did you think of Derek?" She squeezed the wheel and leaned forward. The black sky in the rearview mirror contrasted with the light gray sky in front of her.

"He's nice."

Crystal wished Mason shared more, but he was only a child. Any sexual tension or shift in body language between her and Derek floated above him. *Nice is good.* She inhaled the warm air from the heater vents and exhaled. "He is nice, and I like him."

"Yeah."

"I'd like to see more of him. Would you be okay with that?" She glanced in the rearview mirror and met Mason's gaze.

"Sure."

Crystal stopped peppering Mason with questions and accepted his approval. "Thanks, Mase, because I really like him."

The rest of the drive to Jeremy's was wet; the rain slowed down but never stopped. Crystal dreaded Sundays, and the emotional rainstorm fit her mood. Leaving Mason felt like abandonment, and she never wanted to be that type of mother. But here she was, juggling a divorce, co-parenting drama, and a boyfriend.

She stood in Jeremy's parking lot and kissed and hugged Mason. "You be good for Dad," she said into his hair-covered ear. She pulled away and looked deep into his innocent eyes. "Listen to Dad and your teachers. I'll call later to say goodnight. I love you."

"Love you too, Mom. See you Friday."

Crystal plodded to her car, the weight of parenthood sitting on her shoulders. Heaviness dropped on her as she watched Jeremy usher Mason into the building. Tears flowed freely down her cheeks, and Lulu licked her hand as if saying, 'it's okay.' Crystal pulled Lulu to her chest and rubbed her face in Lulu's long, soft fur. The dog licked her cheeks, and Crystal half-smiled. She took five deep breaths and pulled out of the parking lot. *Five days. I can make it five days.*

She listened to downhearted music for the second leg of her drive, reflecting on her weekend. Even though she didn't see Derek as much as she had hoped, she considered it a step in the right direction. Mason approved, which gave Crystal confidence that any effort she put in would be worth the time and possible heartbreak. *Do long-distance relationships even work?* They both carried heavy baggage, and sometimes it felt easier to stay home.

When Crystal got home, she collapsed on the couch and poured herself a glass of wine. Excitement and opportunity crept around her with every new school year, and she pulled out her planner. She called

Mason to remind him that she was there, even if she was over an hour away, and climbed into bed, dreaming about the life she had imagined for herself twenty years before.

* * *

September turned to October, and the leaves transitioned to a muted cornucopia. Derek and Crystal texted or talked every night, slowly learning about each other. When Crystal had Mason she focused on him, which Derek understood. Crystal freely talked about Derek when Mason was around because she needed him to feel comfortable with Crystal's new friend.

Crystal's phone chimed, and she looked down. She answered the phone with a smile on her face. "Hey, Derek!"

"Hey. Can you talk?" Derek asked. His gruff voice was sharper than usual.

"Yeah, what's up?" Crystal put down her fork and listened.

"I was wondering if you spoke to your lawyer yet? It's been a few weeks, and we need to finish the job. It's a lot of money, Crystal, and I'm relying on that money to pay my guys and help Molly with her rent."

Crystal swallowed and coughed. "Yes, sorry. I met with my lawyer yesterday, and I have an appointment with him next week to review the final papers." This was the third scheduled appointment, and each time he had postponed it because of some unforeseen circumstance.

Derek sighed. "If I knew the money wasn't in place, I wouldn't have taken on the job."

Crystal felt a knife pierce her heart. *Is he saying I purposefully deceived him?* "Derek, I swear, I was told it wouldn't be long. It's out of my control."

"It's been four months, Crystal. I feel like I've been patient."

Crystal's shoulders slumped, and she leaned her head against her fist. Her eyes narrowed, and her voice sharpened. "I don't know what the holdup is, but when I meet with him next week I'll see if I can get a portion to pay you." Her teacher-voice kicked in, and she felt her blood pressure rise. "I get it. I owe you money, but I promise, it's coming."

His voice softened. "Please, Crystal. Molly's counting on me. I've been working my ass off, waiting for you to come through, but I feel like it's never coming."

Crystal straightened her body and leaned back into the dining chair. "It's coming, Derek. I promise."

"Don't you want to sell the house?"

"Of course, I want to sell the house. It doesn't do me any good, just sitting there." Her concrete arms and legs wouldn't move, and her muscles ached from the tension holding her.

"I'm sorry if I sound like a jerk, Crystal, but this is business. It's my business, and I can't jeopardize my company or my relationship with my daughter because I can't come through. You get it, right?"

Crystal rolled her eyes. He sounded like her father, scolding her for staying out too late. "Yes, dad, I get it. I'll report to you on Tuesday after meeting with the lawyer. I'll send him an email ahead of time saying that I must sign the documents to finalize the estate. Okay?" She was denying him what was rightfully his, but it wasn't her fault.

"Thank you." After an awkward silence, he continued, "I gotta go. I have a lot of work to do. I'll talk to you tomorrow." His sentences were short and to the point.

"Derek, please." Her voice wavered. "I called and emailed my lawyer, but every time there's something holding up the transaction. I will go to the bank and see if I can take out a loan. I'll ask my ex-husband if I can borrow some money. I know I owe you, and I promise I am working on it."

He didn't respond and Crystal pulled her phone away from her ear to see if the call had been disconnected. It hadn't. "Derek?"

"Crystal, I have to go. I hope the next time I hear from you, you have a check for me."

"Okay." She swallowed the lump in her throat. "Bye." She hit the red end button and placed her phone face down on the table. She stomped through the house, transported her dirty dishes into the dishwasher, and climbed into bed.

Things between her and Derek seemed to have taken a turn for the worse. Crystal had never seen him so stern or demanding, and his verbal attack surprised her. She hoped it was strictly business, because she couldn't stand the idea of losing him.

CHAPTER 34: DEREK

erek's hand shook, and his body jerked as he dropped the phone on the table—he felt like such an asshole. He hadn't said a word to Crystal about the money for the entire month of September, thinking she would surprise him with a check, but she never did.

Derek had confided in Phil because he needed five-hundred bucks to send to Molly for October's rent. Memories of his father's harsh words traveled through his brain. *You'll amount to nothing, and you'll never get a job. Don't come asking me for money.* His father had always compared him to Phil; the responsible son who had a clear vision for the future. Even when Derek's father had expressed disappointment that Phil didn't want to join the construction business, he supported Phil's decision to go to culinary school. He had allowed Phil to carve his own path, while Derek struggled to carve his own trail.

When Derek took Phil out for dinner to catch up, he didn't know how to approach the subject without just blurting it out. It wasn't the best approach, but it was all Derek could do.

"I can't believe I'm asking, but I need to borrow some money."

Phil stared at him. "What for?" He leaned forward, concern crossing his knitted brows and surrounding the deep lines shaping his mouth.

"Molly. I had agreed to pay half her bills, but I don't have the money this month." Derek crossed his arms and leaned back.

Phil rubbed his forehead. "But you've been working so much and just finished that old farmhouse."

"Yeah. Well. I haven't gotten paid yet." Derek wanted to drop his eyes but held tight onto Phil's almost-black pupils.

Phil dropped his fork, and it clattered against the ceramic plate. "What? It's been over a month."

Derek pulled a slight smile. "Yeah, I never said I was a good businessman. I assumed she had the money and never reviewed payment guidance. I hadn't had a big job in so long that I wrote a quick contract. All it had listed was the total cost, not the due dates for when she needed to pay. She's waiting on her mother's estate to be settled." Derek rubbed his neck. "I'm an idiot."

"Jesus, Derek. What's wrong with you? Contract writing is in Business 101." Phil took three large gulps of water. "How much does she owe you?"

Derek sighed, and his shoulders hunched over the table. "Over twenty grand."

Phil's eyes popped and he shook his head in disappointment. "You need to get that money. Without a contract, you don't have a leg to stand on."

Derek tapped his fork on the table. The last thing he wanted to do was take Crystal to court. He liked her and found himself thinking about her all day long. "I know, I know. Can I borrow the money for Molly or not?"

Phil's slit eyes lasered into Derek's. "Fine. But you better get that money."

Practicing the conversation he needed to have with Crystal was like prepping for a root canal. He dreaded it up until the moment it was happening, and it hurt after, but he was glad it was over. He needed that money.

Derek drove to the liquor store to get a case of beer. He needed something to take the edge off. He had a busy week ahead of him and refused to spend any more time thinking about Crystal or the money.

Browsing the aisles, Derek pulled a six-pack of Blue Moon from the shelf. Between the rift with Crystal and conversation with Phil, his mind was all over the place, and he didn't see the petite, black-haired woman in front of him. She had her back to him, and Derek reached around to grab the bottle of whiskey to quiet his inner voice.

"Ow," the woman said, readjusting the heel of her shoe.

"Sorry," Derek mumbled, stepping back.

She spun around and glared before hiding her discontent with excitement. "Derek, hi!"

He hadn't seen Christina since that day in the old farmhouse. She looked different with her dark hair, but her aggressive facial features were the same. "Hi, Christina. What are you doing here?" He wasn't in the mood to talk, so he slid around her to pay.

"I just got out of work and thought I'd swing by for some wine before the store closed." She held up a pink bottle, proving that she didn't bump into him on purpose. "I see you're done with that farmhouse. It looks great." The dimples in her cheeks smiled at him.

"Thanks."

"Is anyone living there?" Christina asked.

"Nah, I think it might be on the market soon if you know anyone." He placed the beer and whiskey on the conveyor belt.

"Oh, I've been looking for a place in town. Maybe living in the country would be good for my soul."

She stood too close, and Derek smelled her floral perfume. It reminded him of his mother. Her long, red fingernails wrapped around the bottle.

"Are you saying you'd want to buy the place?" He put his card in the machine and waited for it to beep in approval.

"Well, if you worked on it, I know the bones are good." She raised her head, and her neck lengthened. Her collarbone stood out above her low-cut blouse. Her hand crept toward his on the counter, and Derek recoiled, planting it in his pocket.

"Good luck, Christina." He hurried outside and climbed into his truck before she could sneak up on him again.

She's not getting that place—over my dead body.

CHAPTER 35: CRYSTAL

Mason spent Halloween weekend with Jeremy because a new school friend invited him Trick-or-Treating. Crystal took advantage of the unexpected time off and returned to Farm Cove. She told herself she needed to check the pipes, but giddiness filled her at the hope of surprising Derek. They still communicated about the house, but nothing more profound than that.

Mr. Meyers had finally called Crystal with good news. "The estate is settled," he had said, and Crystal dropped the phone in disbelief. She drove into Saratoga the day before Halloween with a mixture of dread and relief. *It's almost over.* She climbed out of her car, yanked up her pantyhose, and smoothed her black skirt.

Inside Mr. Meyers' office, she saw a short, round man with wire-rimmed spectacles. "Hello, Mr. Meyers." She nodded in his direction and shook his hand with vigor. "Nice to see you." She sat in the stuffed leather chair facing his desk. His office overlooked Broadway, and the street traffic shook the old windows. The radiator hissed, fighting against the chill, as the clouds outside threatened snow.

Mr. Meyers adjusted his round-wire frames and shuffled a handful of papers. "Thank you for meeting with me. We could have done it over the internet, but I always feel better closing out cases in person."

Crystal nodded. "Of course." She crossed her legs, uncrossed, and then crossed them again. Bad news seemed to follow her every time she interacted with Mr. Meyers, and she didn't have high hopes for today. She rested on the edge of the seat and extended her legs under his desk.

"Everything is all set, Crystal. I just need you to sign a few documents. The money is yours. Your mother left you the house and forty-four thousand dollars." He smiled at her like he was holding the winning lottery ticket.

Crystal's heart palpated and pounded against her chest. *This cannot be real. Forty-four thousand dollars!* She resisted the urge to jump up from her chair, run around Mr. Meyers' wooden desk, and kiss him.

Instead, Crystal sat still as a statue and spoke in her calmest teacher-voice. "Thank you, Mr. Meyers. I'm happy we can finally close this chapter." *It's only been five months.* Derek's beautiful, cheerful face flashed through her mind, and a magnetic pull urged her to see him. She couldn't wait to hand him the check to prove her commitment to him and the work he did.

She scribbled her autograph and initials on all the highlighted lines, took the photocopies, and a check for forty-four thousand dollars. She walked out of his office on a cloud of ecstasy. Her face beamed, she danced in the elevator, and she laughed and squealed all the way to her car.

Her mind raced with thoughts of her future. Paying her debt created more relief than she imagined. It wasn't fair to Derek to deny him the money for almost half a year and she recognized the wedge jammed between them. She missed the old, loving Derek, who had looked at her like she was the most beautiful woman on Earth. The old Derek who had treated her like a queen. She hadn't seen that Derek since

Rochester, before their interactions became business-only. She missed him.

She wanted to fill her hands with sugar, confetti, or glitter and throw it in the air in celebration. The glowing check sat next to her, and the sheer intensity of that small piece of paper scared her. *What if I lose it?* Her neck bent, allowing her peripheral vision to spy the check while remaining attentive to the road. She stepped on the gas and sped to Farm Cove.

Stopping at a local bank, she danced inside, her sweaty palm dampening the check. She sat in the stiff chair outside the customer service offices, her heart thumping rhythmically with the background music.

"Hi, can I help you?" A familiar-looking man with short, cropped hair and a clean-shaven face greeted her. His long eyelashes highlighted his hazel eyes.

Crystal jumped. "Yes, I need to open a bank account." *I need to get this check out of my possession.* She followed him into the small office and placed the check on the crowded desk. "And I need to deposit this check."

He picked up the check and looked Crystal up and down. "Crystal? Oh my God, how long has it been? Twenty-five years? You look great!"

Crystal half-smiled and looked around. Her eyes focused on the name placard. "Shane?" He looked completely different. This professional businessman sitting across from her used to be her rugged, carefree high school boyfriend. *What happened to you?* "No way." She jumped up from her chair and hugged him.

"Yes, wow, it's so great to see you." He held the check in his hand. "You want to deposit this?"

Crystal smoothed her skirt, sat back down, and nodded. She needed to explain herself. "My mom passed away a few months ago."

Shane nodded. "I heard. I'm so sorry. I would have reached out, but I didn't know how to find you." He was polite, but Crystal knew it wasn't true. He could have looked on social media if he wanted to reach out. She wasn't hard to find.

"Thanks. This is from her estate."

He nodded in understanding. "Sure, but I need proof of identity and proof of residency. Do you, by any chance, have anything?"

Crystal's eyes widened, and she cringed. "I have my license and an e-bill. Can I forward it to you? Will that work?"

Shane nodded. "Sure."

Twenty minutes later, Shane handed Crystal an envelope of temporary checks.

"Oh, Shane, how long before all this clears? I have to pay a contractor for some work on my mom's house."

"It'll be a few days. Probably Monday."

Crystal fast-forwarded to Monday when she would be home in Rochester. She needed to pay Derek this weekend. "Can I use this temporary check for a large check amount? Like over twenty thousand dollars large?"

Shane tilted his head, thinking. "You should probably get a certified check, just in case something goes wrong. Come back Monday morning, and we'll take care of you."

Crystal nodded and bit her thumbnail. Her principal barely approved today's personal day, and another day off could jeopardize her job and her students' learning. "Okay, thanks. I'll be here." *Oh well. Derek's more important than saving a sick day.*

She gathered all her documents and drove to the farmhouse. Crystal pulled into the driveway, and her stomach dropped to the floor of her car. She checked her hair in the rearview mirror and reapplied her lipstick. A busted-up twenty-year-old truck greeted her.

CHAPTER 36: DEREK

erek never heard Crystal's car pull into the driveway. He continued to walk around the house, pointing out the new windows, refurbished floors, and updated layout. A younger version of Vanessa followed three steps behind, mumbling agreement and asking questions. He walked upstairs and pointed out the bedroom and renovated bathroom. Crystal's naked body flashed through his mind, and warmth swelled inside him.

"What do you think?" he asked her.

She smiled and hugged him. "It looks great. I can't believe the transformation."

He kissed her forehead and squeezed her shoulder. "I'm so happy you're back."

She flipped her hair behind her shoulder. "Only until Sunday, and then I have to go back."

A car door slammed, and he glanced out the front-facing window. His chest tightened and then immediately floated away. His fingers squeezed the windowsill and his nose pressed against the glass. "Crystal?"

Dread mixed with excitement as he bounded down the stairs and stopped at the closed door. He should have called or texted to ask if he could use the house, but he didn't expect to see her. She hadn't been back since the apple festival, and besides, it was mid-day on a Friday. *Doesn't she work?*

"Stay here," he said. "Be right back." He swung open the door and sped to her car like a freight train.

She stood between her car and his truck and gazed at him with a relaxed smile crossing her face. She puffed out her chest and readjusted her pocketbook, which hung loosely on her shoulder. She laughed under her breath and clapped her hands.

"Derek! What are you doing here?" she called, waving high above her head. She stumbled over to him and wrapped her arms around his neck. Lulu ran in circles around their feet. "I can't believe you're here. What are you doing here?"

Derek couldn't tell her; she would think he was crazy, and maybe he was. His mind raced through a Rolodex of excuses before settling on one. "I needed to check your dehumidifier. It's been a few days, and I didn't want the mustiness to creep up to the first floor."

Crystal kissed his lips, bouncing lightly in place. "I'm so happy you're here. I have news for you. Let's go inside."

Derek paused, glanced at the house, and back to Crystal. He had already told one lie, so what was his excuse for the other visitor? "Let's go," he said, grabbing her hand.

He walked through the red door and stomped his feet, shaking off the excess dirt and grime from the almost-winter weather. "Crystal." He placed his hands on her shoulders and held her still. His eyes penetrated hers, and she stepped back, tilting her head. Temptation told him to lean down, press his lips into hers, and feel her body melt into his, but he couldn't. They had an audience.

Curious eyes looked at him from the far corner of the room.

Derek glanced up and then down again. "Crystal," he repeated,

"Molly's here."

Crystal spun around, scanning the room. "Molly?"

Molly stuck her head out from the kitchen doorway and waved. "Hi Crystal. House looks great. Hi, Lulu."

Lulu scampered into the kitchen, and the two of them disappeared.

Crystal walked into the house and removed her jacket, revealing the curves hiding underneath. Derek's heart skipped a beat, and he scanned her body from her toes to her head.

"You look beautiful," he said. It had been over a month since he felt her skin against his and his body missed her. He wrapped his arms around her and nuzzled his face in her hair. "I've missed you so much."

Crystal pulled back and searched his eyes. "Do you forgive me?"

He clasped his rough hand over hers. "I was never mad at you, just frustrated with the situation."

A slight smile pulled at her lips and she led him into the kitchen. "Hi, Molly. You're home from school?"

Molly nodded. "Just today and tomorrow. I have to go back Sunday. Dad wanted to show me the house—I can't believe the difference."

Crystal's face ballooned with pride. "It looks beautiful and so homey. I think my mom would have loved it."

"Dad? I have to get going. Would you mind driving me home? I'm meeting some friends for dinner tonight and have some homework." Molly pulled on her peacoat and secured her beanie.

"Sure." Derek turned toward Crystal. "Will you be here when I get back?"

"Absolutely. I'm here until Monday."

Derek kissed her gently. "Be right back, don't go anywhere."

He grabbed his keys and followed Molly out. The heavy truck doors slammed, and the heat blasted at their feet. "You like the house?" he asked her again, turning onto the main road.

"I love it, Dad."

"Did you know that your mother and I used to dream about that house?"

Molly's big blue eyes looked at him. "No, what do you mean?"

"Before you were born we drove around looking for our dream house, and that was it."

"Sounds like karma, or the universe, or something."

Derek pulled his shoulders back and rested on the seat. "Yeah, something like that."

He dropped off Molly, kissed her on the cheek, and said, "Be safe tonight. I'll see you tomorrow." His vague statement could mean she was staying out all night, or he was; it was open to interpretation.

He sped back to the farmhouse, the fallen leaves kicking up behind his wheels in a cloud of color. He threw his truck in park and hopped out, and was inside in the blink of an eye. "Crystal?"

He found her at the kitchen table, clutching a thick envelope in her hand. Two almost-full wine glasses sat in the middle of the table.

He glanced at his watch. It wasn't even three o'clock. "Wine?"

"We're celebrating. Sit." She patted the table across from her and placed the envelope between the two wine glasses.

Derek did as she commanded and looked across at her exhilarated face. Her eyes crinkled in the corners, and her smile touched her ears. She hadn't stopped smiling since she arrived, and Derek wondered what the special occasion was.

"What's up?" He took a sip of wine to quiet his nerves. His knees jangled under the table, and he traced the base of the wine glass with his finger.

"I just came from the lawyer's office." She stopped and took a sip of wine.

Derek leaned forward, waiting. "Oh yeah?"

"And everything is finished." She jumped up from the table and ran to the other side, wrapping her arms around Derek's neck and sitting on his lap.

He rubbed her waist. "Everything?" Memories of the last time they saw each other reignited his senses.

"Everything." She kissed his eyebrows, nose, the crevice above and below his lips, and then just below the ear. His body trembled beneath her, and he squeezed her against him.

"Mmmm," he moaned.

"I'll have your money on Monday." Her breath grazed his ear, and he shivered.

"Monday. That means I have three days with you."

She kissed under his chin and up and down his neck. His body grew hot, and his breathing slowed. "Three days."

At three o'clock on a Friday, with red wine running through his veins, he gave himself to Crystal in the new farmhouse. After, he lay in her bed, naked and warm. He traced his finger up and down the silhouette of her smooth body. *Something brought me back here.* He felt alive for the first time since before Vanessa died. *Thank you, Vanessa.* He kissed his index and middle finger and held them up to the ceiling in honor of his wife. He knew he had her blessing.

CHAPTER 37: CRYSTAL

T he weekend was a whirlwind. Crystal and Mason talked daily, especially with the build-up toward Halloween on Sunday.

"Mom, are you going to get any trick or treaters?"

Crystal hadn't thought about Halloween at the farmhouse. She was supposed to have been home on Sunday, and the bag of miniature chocolate bars sat in the plastic grocery bag on the floor of her foyer. "Gee, Mase, I don't know. It's a really long driveway. I doubt anyone will come, even if I have the light on."

"I miss you, Mom."

"I miss you too, and so does Lulu. Be sure to send us lots of pictures. I'll stop by after school on Monday on my way home."

Crystal hung up the phone and returned to Derek. The house was still empty, so there was little to do besides stream movies on their phones and make out like teenagers. She curled against his warm body, and Lulu wedged herself in the crevice of Crystal's bent knees.

"Derek, now that the house is done and you're about to be paid, I think I need to put it on the market."

Derek's eyebrows scrunched together, and he pulled his lips tight. "Are you sure you want to sell it?"

165

Crystal sat up, disturbing Lulu, who jumped to the floor. "I have to. My life and job are three hours away. I can't afford to keep this house, especially after I just paid you an enormous sum. I need to sell it to feel comfortable again. Comfortable financially, I mean."

Derek nodded, but stayed silent.

"I love this house now, but it carries a lot of mixed emotions for me." She felt she needed to justify her decision because the invisible string she felt tethering her to the house was tightening. She tried to break free but struggled, and it seemed her heart and head were fighting again.

"I can help you with whatever you need." Derek traced her arm from her shoulder to her wrist.

"Do you know any realtors?"

"Not really, but I bet Margie does. She knows everyone."

Crystal pulled herself out of bed and grabbed her sweatshirt.

Derek sat up and paused the movie. "Where are you going?"

Crystal wrapped her scarf around her neck. "To Phil's. I only have two more days here, and I gotta get the ball rolling."

Derek climbed out of bed and pulled on his socks and boots. "I'll drive."

* * *

The diner was empty except for one table. Margie sat at the counter, rolling silverware into paper napkins. She looked up when the bell dinged and smiled.

"Hi, Margie," Derek said. He sat across from her at the counter.

Margie held up one finger to cue them to wait, and transferred the silverware into the basket. Derek and Crystal froze until Margie made eye contact. "Crystal, hi! Nice seeing you again."

Crystal smiled and removed her hat and gloves.

"Can I get you guys anything?"

"I need a realtor. Do you know of any?" Crystal asked.

Margie filled the sugar caddies with multiple colors of sweetener packets. "Why? You selling?"

Crystal nodded. "I'm hoping to have it sold by Christmas."

"Just so happens, my neighbor's cousin's best friend is a realtor, and she handles all the small towns in Saratoga County. Do you want her number?"

Crystal's eyes sparkled at the thought of being done with the house. "Please."

"When I get home, I'll text Derek the number. I gotta ask my neighbor for it first."

Margie continued finishing her side work and clearing the last table in the diner.

"Well, well, well," a deep voice bellowed. "Look who it is." Phil emerged from the kitchen wearing an orange-stained apron, and Crystal wasn't sure if the stains were from today or years of restaurant abuse. "Haven't seen you in a while," Phil said to Derek.

Derek's body stiffened, and he stretched his neck. "Phil. How's it going?"

"Good, good. Hi, Crystal." He turned back to Derek. "November first is rolling around, and I haven't heard from you. Are you good?"

Crystal looked back and forth between the two men, seeing defeat on one and disappointment on the other. Phil scratched his neck and pulled at his ear before releasing a breath. Derek crossed his arms over his chest and stood at the counter.

"Yeah, good. Everything's fine." His voice sounded thick and hairy. "Thanks for the help, Margie. See you later, Phil. Let's go, Crystal."

Before Crystal picked up her purse, Derek was out the front door. She trotted to catch up with him.

His face remained stony for the drive back to the farmhouse. She touched his arm, and he flinched. "Are you okay?"

Derek snapped his head around to look at her. "Yeah, fine. I'm fine. Hey, what time do you think you're going to the bank on Monday?"

Crystal narrowed her eyes at him, trying to figure out what crucial nonverbal cue she had missed at the diner. "Um, I don't know, probably nine? I need to be on the road by lunchtime."

"I have to work, but I'll swing by at eleven-thirty to say goodbye." Crystal noticed his white knuckles gripping the steering wheel.

The rest of the day felt off. There seemed to be a disconnect that had started at the diner, but Crystal still wasn't sure what caused it. It seemed Derek tried to remain enthusiastic, but their conversations fell flat, and he lost his sense of humor.

At dinner that night, his phone beeped. "I got the number for the realtor. You should call her first thing Monday morning," Derek said. He jotted down the digits in a notebook and adhered the ripped paper to the refrigerator. "Tell her you got her number from Margie."

After dinner, he kissed her goodbye. "I've gotta go take care of some things, but I'll see you in the morning."

Crystal's face crumbled. She couldn't help but feel responsible for the swift change in tone and increased tension between her and Derek. She felt like she was fighting a battle with her eyes closed. Nothing seemed out of the ordinary until the diner, but nothing about their stop there seemed unusual. She racked her brain for anything that could explain his sudden mood swing.

Crystal climbed into her bed with Lulu by her side and snuggled into Lulu's neck. Like a waterfall, Crystal cried herself to sleep, blaming herself for being too something. Too needy, too controlling, too emotional...too much of something Derek didn't want.

Why did everything go so wrong so quickly? What did I do? Crystal barely slept a wink that night. When her eyes opened the following day, she was alone in bed. Even Lulu had left her.

CHAPTER 38: DEREK

Derek drove home from Crystal's in a daze. He kept his eyes on the road, but his mind was distracted. He turned up the music, hoping to tune out his inner critic, but feelings of worthlessness ebbed and flowed as his father's constant nagging and lectures floated around Derek's brain, interspersed with images of Phil's concerned expression.

He wallowed in self-pity at home for exactly one hour before pulling out a notebook, pen, and laptop. Molly was out again, and the house was quiet except for the occasional drip from the kitchen sink. The sound echoed in his ears, and he gathered everything and went in search of a more tranquil place to work.

He walked into the living room, dropping everything on the kidney-shaped coffee table Vanessa's parents had bought them as a wedding gift. The scratched top reminded him of the time Molly did her homework without a book underneath her paper. The water rings reminded him of all the coffees he and Vanessa had drank on Sunday mornings. This table held a window to their past, and he wondered if he was ready to let go.

He pulled up his bank account, analyzing the numbers. He compared his business account to his personal account and hypothetically moved things around, drawing various number combinations in his notebook. It was difficult to predict the future and whether his father's business would flourish, but Derek projected the next twelve months' income. Best case scenario would give him enough to survive, and the worst-case scenario would force him to renege on his deal with Molly.

Derek owed Phil and Molly money. It wasn't his fault, but he should have been more careful. He was so wrapped up in the farmhouse that he didn't think of the consequences. He tried to remain angry at Crystal, but he couldn't. He was so close to getting the money he deserved.

He needed time away from her to organize his thoughts and figure out his future. *What would Vanessa do?* He heard her laugh in his head: the belly laugh, the giggle, and the chuckle. They were all so different but encompassed her personality. He fell in love with her spontaneity on their first date, when he loosely planned dinner and a movie. Somehow, she convinced him to take her to the city for a Broadway show. Derek had never seen a professional theatrical production, nor did he want to, but the way her eyes lit up and her lips pouted…he would have done anything to make her happy.

They had boarded the train into New York, found day-of tickets at a discount, and took the last train back to Albany after the show. His fifty-dollar date had more than quadrupled, but it didn't matter. He had the best date of his life.

He had fallen in love with her on that train, riding into an unfamiliar city with a mystery woman. He couldn't help but wonder what he was doing with this exquisite woman with a contagious laugh, bubbly personality, and carefree attitude. Derek hadn't felt worthy of her love or attention.

But, for whatever reason, they worked. And now he had Molly, who carried some of Vanessa's most remarkable qualities: her kindness, compassion, and gratitude. Derek loved that Molly had inherited some of the best parts of Vanessa.

He knew Vanessa would tell him to go for it.

He continued working all night, coming up with a plan. It was risky, but Vanessa taught him that risks were one hundred percent guaranteed success. 'Either you get the outcome you want, or you learn a lesson, which makes the risk worthwhile,' she always said. Derek still heard her voice in his head.

He texted Margie and texted Phil. He didn't want their approval or opinion, but needed them to know he would be okay, regardless of the outcome.

He pulled up the text from Margie, googling the realtor's name. Her office was the first one listed on the internet search. Derek clicked on her website, read her bio, and clicked on her email. He introduced himself, explained his situation, and asked for her to call him at her earliest convenience. He hit send, tipped his head back, and closed his eyes. Goosebumps appeared on his arm, and he rubbed vigorously. His heart raced, and a feeling of invincibility overwhelmed him. He lifted his beer bottle and clinked it with Vanessa's invisible glass, imagining her smiling at him from across the table. It was happening.

Derek called Crystal late that night, and her phone went straight to voicemail. "Crystal, hey, it's me. Listen, I'm sorry for leaving like that. I had a lot on my mind and needed to get home to do some thinking. I'll be over in the morning with breakfast. Good night."

Derek lay in bed, his mind racing, when he was hit with a thought. The euphoria dissipated, and he wrinkled his forehead. His breathing slowed, and his chest tightened.

Molly's going to kill me.

CHAPTER 39: CRYSTAL

Sunday morning came too fast, and Crystal's puffy eyes and streaked cheeks taunted her in the bathroom mirror. *Stupid. Why'd you let a man hurt you again?* Memories of Jeremy stormed through her mind. She saw the texts he disguised as "Mr. Lyons" and the way her face had distort into agony when she realized that Mr. Lyons wasn't a mister at all. A quick Google search revealed that Mr. Lyons didn't even work at Jeremy's company. It had been a farce, and Crystal had fallen for it.

She had picked up his phone and smashed it outside their house. Their new stamped concrete steps took the blow; the only evidence was the shards of glass smattering the path.

"Crystal!" Jeremy had grabbed her arm and yanked her back to face him. "What the fuck is wrong with you?" He squeezed her arm, embedding his fingernails into her pale skin. Daggers shot out of his eyes like laser beams. Inside, she hadn't felt a thing.

She didn't feel anything that Sunday morning after Derek's quick departure the night before, either. She washed her face in the newly renovated bathroom and removed the mascara sliding down her cheeks. *Derek could be over any minute.* Her queasy stomach slid around like a yacht in a storm. The waves pushed up and out, drowning her breaths. *Why do I feel so sick? So scared?* She still couldn't place it, but something felt off.

Crystal slowly padded downstairs and let out Lulu, who lunged for a squirrel racing across the crinkly, brown fallen leaves. "Lulu, come." Crystal didn't have the energy to chase after her, so she ushered Lulu back inside and scolded her. "Next time, don't chase the squirrels. You'll be out longer." Lulu pushed her ears back and narrowed her eyebrows. Her sad, stooped posture made Crystal feel like a lousy dog-mom, so she bent down and petted her head. "I'm sorry," she mumbled.

Crystal slumped at the table and poured herself a cup of coffee. Besides removing her makeup, she hadn't done anything to prepare for Derek's arrival. Her wrinkled pajamas hung snug against her round body, and her hair was probably all over the place. She considered changing and freshening up, but decided coffee was more important. She'd rather be awake to face whatever turmoil was coming her way than appear to have her life together.

A knock rapped on the door, and Crystal pushed herself up from the chair to open it. She didn't smile but said hello. Before Derek could respond, she sat at the table again. "Coffee?" she asked.

He moved quickly. "Sure. I can get it." His steps carried an airiness that Crystal wasn't expecting, and his happy mood confused her. "Did you get my message?"

"Yep."

Derek sat across from her and poured in the sugar. "I'm sorry, Crystal. I shouldn't have just left like that."

She looked past his right shoulder. "It's fine." She needed to protect her heart against being stepped on, especially since she had lowered her walls to him.

As the day progressed, her forced abrasiveness waned. She wanted to show him how much his abandonment hurt her, but being angry all day zapped her energy. His front-tooth gap, wavy hair, and goofiness made her smile, so whatever residual anger she had turned inwards.

Over dinner, she grasped enough nerve to ask him about the day prior. "What happened, anyway?"

Derek placed his fork on his plate and sipped his water. "What do you mean?"

Crystal's eyes bulged. "Derek. You left me. You got upset and left. What did I do?" Her voice rose and cracked. Tears formed behind her eyes, and she squeezed them back.

"Nothing, I swear. I was overwhelmed seeing you here, and I needed to think. That's all. I'm sorry if I hurt you. I didn't leave you on purpose; I needed to leave for me." She stared into his convincing eyes, searching for the truth.

She listened to his excuse and didn't ask further questions. She slurped her spaghetti, wiping her chin after every swallow. After clearing her plate, she cleared her throat and spoke. "Do you want to go to the movies? Let's go on a date."

There wasn't anything playing that Crystal especially wanted to see, but Derek jumped at the idea. Crystal needed to break up the tension that hung within the farmhouse walls.

"How about that new action movie about space invaders?" Derek asked.

Crystal hated those types of movies, but she agreed. She looked up the times online. "Next one is a little after eight. Want to go?" They had about an hour, but the ride into Saratoga would take at least twenty minutes.

Derek cleaned up the kitchen while Crystal got ready. She changed into her favorite jeans and a tunic that hit just below her butt. She pulled on her black leather boots with the two-inch heels. The leather toes squeezed her feet and she questioned whether or not she should switch her cotton socks to trouser socks to give herself some extra room. She rummaged through her drawer and didn't find anything thinner.

Crystal spun around in the full-length mirror, admiring her curvy hips and additional height from the shoes, and applied a coat of pink lipstick. She practiced walking in the uncomfortable boots, gingerly stepping from one side of the room to the other. *It's just one night. You'll be fine.* Every now and then her toes pinched and her ankle swayed as she tried to compensate for the pain.

She stepped downstairs, grabbed her purse, and kissed Derek as a peace offering. "I'm ready," she said.

The movie itself was unremarkable. Crystal wanted Derek to stay the night but not enough to ask him. They walked out of the dark theater into the bright lobby, and Crystal's eyes blurred.

Derek stood before her, and she followed his tall body through the crowd. "Hey Derek, I have to use the bathroom." She separated from him and came out a few moments later. Three steps into the lobby and she stopped, before slowly sneaking toward him. He was talking to a petite woman with black hair and big boobs. Crystal knew who it was without even properly seeing her.

She leaned against the wall, partially hidden behind the trash can, and watched.

Christina leaned into Derek and placed her hand on his chest. She smiled and stepped forward, so their bodies were practically touching.

From behind him, Crystal couldn't decide if he was pleased to see her or annoyed, but she did notice that he didn't step away from her. Crystal traveled the wall's perimeter until she stood about four feet behind Derek, with the crowds of people in line for popcorn blocking her view.

She tiptoed closer, trying to eavesdrop without being obvious. She didn't think Christina saw her, but she was ready to throw on a smile

175

and a cheerful greeting as soon as they made eye contact.

Christina held Derek's gaze for way too long. She laughed and rubbed her hand up his arm. Crystal flared her nostrils, and her muscles burned with tension. Derek stepped back and looked around. Crystal pushed her chin forward, took a deep breath, and marched toward him.

The tile floor transitioned to a carpeted step-up, but Crystal focused on Christina's full lips and white teeth. Her hands remained on him, and smoke billowed out of Crystal's eyes. "Oh, no, you don't," Crystal murmured under her breath. Her fists hung at her waist, and she couldn't breathe.

She practically ran toward them, and her ankle buckled just as she approached Derek. Her arms flailed and her body swayed, reaching out to anything that could break her fall.

She grabbed Derek's forearm on the way down, and braced herself with her free hand. His torso splayed across her chest, and Crystal gasped for breath. She stared up at the ceiling and burst out laughing. Derek guffawed and rolled off her.

Christina looked at the tangled mess on the floor and stepped back. "Crystal, nice to see you again." She didn't offer help, and Derek limped up first. He extended his hand and pulled Crystal beside him.

"Hi, Christina." She smiled brightly and hooked her arm through his, throwing a side-eye dagger at her. "Did you just come from a movie?"

"Yeah, but I'm on my way out."

"Did you come alone?"

"No, but they're in the bathroom."

Bullshit. I was just in there, and I was alone. Crystal grinned and squeezed Derek's arm with her free hand. She lowered her hand and interlaced her fingers through his. "It was good seeing you, Christina. Are you ready to go, Derek?" She turned toward Derek and rubbed her breasts against his forearm, making it look like a hug to any observer in the lobby.

"See ya, Christina," Derek said. He led Crystal toward the entrance.

"I'll call you," she called to Derek.

Crystal's blood went cold and then burned through her veins.

Derek didn't respond and kept walking.

They didn't talk for the entire car ride back to the farmhouse.

Derek pulled into the driveway and said, "I have to work tomorrow, but I'll be over before lunch to say goodbye." He leaned over, and his lips brushed her cheek. Their passion from earlier disappeared, and her head raced with images of him and Christina.

She wanted to know why Christina would call him but was too afraid to ask.

"Good night."

She climbed out of the car and fell into her bed. Like always, Lulu was there to pick up the pieces of her fractured heart.

CHAPTER 40: DEREK

The next day Derek sat across from Crystal at the kitchen table, looking at the check in her hand. The paper shook and waved like a flag blowing in the breeze. "Here." She placed it on the table upside down. "It's my balance."

Derek's heart pumped, and his arms and legs wanted to dance, but the atmosphere didn't elicit joy. There was more tension today than yesterday, and Derek wasn't sure what had happened. *Was it Christina?*

He took the check, reviewed the total, and folded it into his wallet. "Thanks. I'll send you the final payment receipt today when I get back to the office." He let out a huge breath that he didn't know he was holding. *Phil will be thrilled to get this.*

"Let's talk about the realtor. I left a voicemail with Tamara but haven't heard anything back yet. I don't think I am coming back soon, so would you feel comfortable walking through the house with her? You can be my eyes and ears." Crystal's back remained erect and her shoulders straight. She tucked her hair behind her ear and folded her hands on the table in front of her. She resembled a librarian.

Derek nodded. "Of course." He didn't tell her he reached out to the realtor a few days ago and had already been in communication.

Tamara had cut her hours to part-time and couldn't take his request, so she passed him on to another realtor in the office. He already had an appointment for Wednesday but didn't want to tell that to Crystal just yet.

"I'll be in touch once I hear from her."

Derek looked at her and waited for another item on her to-do list that he needed to complete.

"I think that's it," she said. She stood from the table and hugged him, and her limp arms grasped his shoulders briefly and then fell to her sides.

"Hey, are we okay? You've been weird ever since the movies."

Crystal half-smiled. "You've been weird ever since the diner."

Hurt crossed Derek's face because Crystal seemed to blame him for whatever tension remained between them.

"Yeah, we're good. I've gotta head out because I told Mason I'd be there when the bus dropped him off."

Derek kissed her, and she turned her cheek. His lips brushed against the corner of her mouth. He took her chin in his hand and angled it toward him. His lips touched hers, and fireworks exploded behind his eyes. He knew she felt it, too, by how her knees buckled and her free hand gripped the wall.

She smiled, and her head tilted back. "Thank you."

"You know, I don't know when I will see you again. I'd love a kiss that I can think about when I'm feeling sad and lonely late at night. When I think of us, I think of silliness, kisses, and deep conversation. I want you, Crystal. I want you so badly."

Tears filled behind her eyes and splashed onto her cheekbones.

He gazed into her eyes with tenderness. "Why are you crying?" His voice softened, and he pulled her into a hug.

"I'm scared, Derek. I like you too much. I think about you all the time. I'm scared I'm not good enough. Once you find someone better,

I'll be gone. We live so far away, and I know I can't be with you the way I should. Please promise me you'll be honest with me. If you find someone else or want to date other women, you'll tell me. Please." She spoke into her chest, and he barely understood her muffled words.

He kissed the top of her head. "I promise I will always be honest with you, but you have nothing to worry about. Nothing." He kissed her again and escorted her outside. He loaded her bag into the backseat and lay Lulu's bed on the passenger side. "Call me when you get home."

His truck idled as she backed out of the driveway. He hated himself for lying to her, but didn't see any other option. There was no way she would go along with it.

Instead of going back to the office, Derek returned home and texted Molly. **Hey Mols, call me when you can. I have something I need to talk to you about.** Derek looked at the phone, reading and rereading his message. He willed his finger to press the green arrow, pushed it, and placed his phone upside down on the coffee table. He stared ahead, his thoughts bouncing around like a tennis ball.

Less than ten minutes later, his phone rang. "Hi, Molly. Do you have a second?"

"Sure, Dad. What's up?"

Derek heard cars and trucks whizzing past in the background. "Where are you?"

"I took the train into the city. I wanted to do some shopping, and it's beautiful today. Warm weather, but they're starting to get ready for the holidays. Anyway, what's up?"

Derek cleared his parched throat. He rose from the couch and poured himself a glass of water. "I wanted to talk to you about the house."

"Whose house?"

"Our house, Molly. I told you how your mother and I dreamed of that farmhouse. Well, it's going on the market, and I think I want to buy it." He paused, waiting for a reaction, but Molly remained silent. "Molly?"

"Yeah, Dad. I'm here. What exactly do you want to talk about? Do what you want with it." Derek heard sharpness emerge in Molly's voice. Vanessa used to make him spit out uncomfortable topics, when a little inferencing would connect all the dots. It seemed Molly had the same characteristic.

"How would you feel about that? Our home is just as much your house as mine and your mother's." Derek's voice cracked at the mention of Vanessa. He felt his chest constrict, and his lungs squeezed.

"It makes me sad, Dad, but I get it. Mom's been gone for most of my life. Sometimes you have to move on. And if the farmhouse makes you happy, then go for it." Molly sounded out of breath, and Derek imagined her squeezing between crowds of busy New Yorkers trying to race to their next destination. He couldn't imagine Molly returning to Farm Cove, NY. It was too remote and too much of a dead-end for her personality. She would never want their home once he was gone.

"Thanks, Molly." His voice cracked again as gratitude swept over him. He could swallow again, and his skin no longer felt enflamed. "I love you."

They hung up the phone, and Derek grinned to himself. He climbed into his truck and drove to the office in a daze. With Molly's blessing, he could dream about their future.

CHAPTER 41: CRYSTAL

❧

"How does Thanksgiving sound?" Crystal asked. She held the phone between her shoulder and ear carefully as she scrubbed a large pot. Caked spaghetti sauce covered the sides and had been taking up prime sink space for two days.

"Huh? Can't hear you," Melanie said.

Crystal turned off the running water, dried her hands, and readjusted the phone. "Thanksgiving, Mel. Do you think that will work for the celebration party?"

"Yeah, that'd be perfect. It's a drive, but I know my family will come. Even if it's just us, I think your mom would have loved it. Won't the house be sold by then though?"

It had been almost a week since Crystal last spoke to Derek. She had given Tamara Derek's number to handle the house showing and she electronically signed the paperwork to officially list the house on the market; now she waited.

"Thanksgiving's in three weeks. Even if I get an offer, it's not like the sale will be closed by then." Crystal methodically scrubbed the stove and reorganized her spices.

"True."

"You email your family, and I'll email the rest. All of my parent's friends are dead, so it'll probably be less than twenty of us. We can use Mom's secret turkey recipe, make her chocolate cream pie, and your mom can bring the green bean casserole like she always does. It'll be fun. Small, but nice. I think my parents would like us to have one last Thanksgiving in the house before it moves onto its next owner." Crystal pressed the phone between her shoulder and ear again and threw the laundry into the dryer.

The phone tumbled to the floor, and Crystal strained to hear Melanie. She grabbed the phone and mm-hmm'd, trying to piece together Mel's response.

"I can't believe the house is on the market," Mel said.

"Yeah, it feels weird, but it feels good to be done with it. It's beautiful, Mel. You wouldn't even recognize it. All that nasty wallpaper is gone, the first floor is an open concept, and the updated bathrooms and kitchen are luxurious. It looks like a house I would buy if I had the means. Did I tell you we knocked down my dad's barn too?"

"No, you didn't. I remember playing Hide 'n Seek in there when we were kids. Hey, do you remember when we stumbled on Grandma and Grandpa's wedding photos? What'd you do with all their stuff?"

Crystal bit her lip, ashamed at how easily she discarded their history. "I browsed through all the boxes and kept enough to store in my basement here. The furniture smelled musty so I tossed it. I saved Grandma and Grandpa's photos, though. Maybe we can look through them at Thanksgiving. I bet your mom would like that."

"Am I going to meet Derek?" Melanie's sing-song voice cut through Crystal like a knife.

"We haven't talked since last weekend. Getting the house on the market was my priority, so we never talked about Thanksgiving. I'd like you to meet him, but he doesn't have to meet the whole family. That would be way too weird." Crystal plopped on her sofa, the cushions bouncing and kicked her feet up on the coffee table.

"Maybe the three of us could go out for coffee or something."

Crystal grinned. "Yeah, I know the perfect breakfast place. You'll love it."

After Crystal hung up her phone she called Derek, but it went straight to voicemail. She quickly texted him, asking about his day. She missed talking with him and wondered why he was so busy this week.

Crystal pulled up the farmhouse listing online and read the description. "Adorable farmhouse on 1.2 acres of land. This 3-bedroom, 1.5-bathroom home shines with an updated kitchen, updated bathrooms, and open concept living/dining room. New windows, landscaping, driveway, and roof just completed. Come soak in the clawfoot tub or relax under various flowering trees. Host friends and family in the private backyard. Enjoy small town living at an affordable price. Due to high motivation, the seller will consider all offers." Crystal reviewed the staged photos highlighting the house. It looked beautiful, and Crystal still could not believe this was the broken-down house she had crawled back to five months before.

The scheduled open house was the following day. When she had confirmed the date with Tamara, she had begged Derek to attend. "Derek, pretend you're interested in the house. Comment on things, ask questions, and watch people's reactions," Crystal had said. "Then report back to me."

The house was listed yesterday and already thirteen people hearted it. *How soon before I get an offer?* The financial opportunity excited her, but saying goodbye felt bittersweet. She tried not to think about the fact that she'd never be in that beautiful farmhouse again. *At least I'll have Thanksgiving to say goodbye.*

She closed her laptop and pulled out her work bag. *One more day until I see Mason.*

Her phone buzzed, and Jeremy's face flashed on the screen. Crystal immediately answered, expecting to hear Mason. "Hi!"

"Crystal, we need to talk." Crystal pulled back at Jeremy's harsh voice.

"Everything okay?"

"Not really. Mason got kicked off the bus for a week."

Crystal's mouth dropped open. "For what?"

"Fighting."

* * *

Crystal pulled up against Jeremy's building and sat in the desolate parking lot. The conversation she had the night before with Jeremy and Principal Whaling ticked through her brain. She thought a change in scenery would surely set Mason up for success, but it only took eight weeks for him to fall into his previous ways.

She knew she had to go inside, but her heavy legs prevented her from exiting her car. Her shoulders hunched forward, and her lips dropped into a frown. She had been dreading this day.

Crystal trudged into Jeremy's building and up the narrow stairs. She reminded herself to tread lightly because Jeremy was the primary parent now. She missed the day-to-day affairs and didn't know the entire story.

The loud, buzzing doorbell centered Crystal, and she straightened her shoulders. *You must remain in control.* The door creaked open, and Mason's beautiful face stuck through the crack.

"Hi, Mom." He opened the door wider, and Crystal pushed through. She hugged him tightly and examined his face. Besides a slight scratch on his cheek, he looked like the same loving boy she left on Sunday.

"Where's your dad?" Crystal peeked down the hall.

"Kitchen." Mason led the way to Jeremy.

"Hey, Jer. Smells great in here." Crystal inhaled, soaking up the garlic and onion aroma simmering from the pot on the stove.

"Spaghetti. My friend Amanda's coming over for dinner." He didn't look at her and kept stirring the pot.

Crystal's mouth firmly closed, and her lips sucked into her mouth. *Amanda?* She replayed the word over in her head. *Did I know about this Amanda?* Crystal pretended she didn't hear him.

"Can I talk to you privately?" Crystal eyed Mason and tilted her head toward the hallway. Jeremy set down his spoon and led Crystal to the bathroom.

Crystal looked at the toothpaste-covered sink, overflowing trash can, and mildewy shower curtain and shuddered. Jeremy closed the door, and Crystal stepped back into a pile of dirty clothes. She kicked the shorts out of her way.

"What happened with Mason?" she asked. She searched his eyes and recognized the concern reflecting at her.

"Yeah. He's off the bus for the week. Mason claims it was self-defense, but the school had to suspend him. Zero tolerance." Jeremy crossed his arms and shook his head. "I don't know, Crystal. It's a he-said-she-said situation."

"Are you able to bring him and pick him up? If you need, I can take a few days off work." If Crystal took any more time off she'd probably get fired, but she knew she needed to be a mom first.

"No, it's fine. Amanda's a teacher too, so she can bring him."

Crystal stepped back and leaned against the bathroom door. *Amanda's a teacher, huh?* "Great. Perfect." She turned and exited, calling Mason's name. "Mase, grab your stuff. It's time to go."

The entire ride home, she thought about Amanda. She imagined a twenty-something brand new teacher, with no kids or pets, and free of all responsibility. *Why would Amanda be attracted to Jeremy? And why would he find someone who reminded him of me?*

CHAPTER 42: DEREK

D erek stepped into the kitchen and smelled a mouth-watering combination of sugar and pumpkin spice. A batch of warm cookies sat in the center of the table, and a candle burned on the stove. Derek inhaled, and memories of his grandmother moved around him.

"Hi," he said, stretching out his hand. "I'm Derek. Nice to meet you."

The tall brunette held out her hand. "It's so nice to meet you finally. I'm Tamara Hazelton, and this is Christina Mendez." She pointed at the younger woman beside her.

Christina gave him her card, which he tucked into his back pocket. "You can call me Chrissy. Tamara passed your file onto me." Chrissy glanced at Tamara. "Open house starts in about fifteen minutes. Do you plan on staying here for the entire time?"

Derek shook his head. "No, I just wanted to come in and introduce myself. I haven't seen the house since it's been staged, so I thought I'd hang out for a bit. I won't stay too long. Crystal wants me to get a feel for potential buyers that walk through."

The two women busied themselves, spreading business cards and flyers on the counter. "Chrissy, this is a guest book for people to sign in. This is how you gain potential customers. You can also add them to your newsletter, so if they decide to sell, your name will be fresh in their mind."

Derek looked out the kitchen window and recalled the dilapidated barn that had once stood in the back. Memories of him and Crystal, starting in the barn and ending in the bedroom, fluttered in his stomach and electric waves traveled down his legs. "I'll be outside," he told the two women.

He sat in his truck and rubbed his hands together. He had forgotten his gloves at home, and the clouds threatened snow. He crammed his hands between the seat cushion and the seat of his pants and looked at the house. The front lights welcomed visitors to enter, and the large yard encouraged children and dogs to run and play. He saw future moments of his life emerge against the backdrop of the house.

Quick taps on his window pulled him out of his fantasy and back to his truck. He turned his head and saw Christina smiling broadly. *Crap. I guess she was serious about buying the house.* She waved back and forth. Derek hesitated and then opened his door.

"Fancy seeing you here!" she said.

Derek smiled politely and leaned against the hood of his truck. "Hi, Christina. What are you doing here?"

She rocked on her heels and bounced her knees. Tiny snowflakes dotted her black hat. "Open house, right? The house looks beautiful, and I had to see it in its finished state. I told you I wanted to buy it. What are you doing here?"

Derek looked past her and saw a handful of people enter the front door. "Same as you. Crystal couldn't be here, so I offered to come and talk to the realtor for her."

Christina nudged closer to him. "It's so cold out here." She hooked her arm through his and vigorously rubbed up and down. "So, what's the deal with you two?" She looked past him toward the house.

Derek didn't know. He thought she was his girlfriend, but this long-distance thing was more challenging than he thought. He hadn't spoken to her all week and wasn't sure if she felt the same level of discomfort. "It's complicated," he said.

Christina seemed pleased with his response and squeezed his arm. "I'm going in." She left him at his truck, and he watched her hips jut back and forth as she strutted across the snow-speckled earth.

Derek watched a few more people enter before roaming around the house and entering through the back door. He heard comments such as, "I love these floors", "a clawfoot tub!" and "this yard would be perfect for a trampoline or swing set." It seemed like there could be multiple offers by the end of the day.

As he returned to the kitchen, he saw Christina cozying up to Tamara and Chrissy. All three women smiled, and Christina's eyes sparkled. "I'll be in touch," she said, and she waved to Derek before leaving the house.

Derek approached the two women and ate a cookie off the floral platter. "Any feedback for Crystal?"

Tamara smacked her lips and tapped her fingers on the counter. "Well, Mr. Fischer, everything has been wonderful. I expect at least one offer on the table by the end of the day."

Derek's muscles tightened, and his body got hot. He swallowed the lump in his throat, his Adam's apple feeling sticky. "Great. Any word on my house?"

Tamara looked toward Chrissy for information.

"Oh! Yes, Mr. Fischer. Are you ready for your open house tomorrow? It's a hot market right now, so hopefully, you'll have an offer by the end of the day."

"Great." Derek removed his hat, pushed back his hair, and readjusted his cap, pulling it over his eyes. "Great. I'll see you tomorrow."

Instead of excitement for Crystal and anticipation for tomorrow,

Derek felt like he was losing control. He couldn't allow Christina to buy the farmhouse.

CHAPTER 43: CRYSTAL

❧

"Mel, I haven't talked to Derek in almost two weeks. Should I be worried?" Crystal knew she should be lesson planning, but her mind couldn't shake the feeling that Derek was avoiding her.

"Like, at all?" Melanie asked.

Crystal sat on the couch with a glass of wine and put her phone on speaker. "Well, we text here or there, but nothing substantial. I'm worried. Do you think he found someone else?" She gulped what was left in her glass and poured another. Images of Christina's perky breasts, short skirt, and sexy voice replayed through Crystal's mind. *Was Derek being polite or did he like the attention? Was there something going on?*

"No, Crystal, I don't think so. You said you opened up to him about Jeremy cheating, and he understood. You said he agreed to never lie to you. He wouldn't do that."

Crystal flipped through the television channels. "You're right. He wouldn't." She knew she was obsessing like a high school girl crushing on the football quarterback. Melanie had been her sounding board for at least a month, her frustration and fear growing. She changed the subject to distract herself from Derek. "The party's in a few weeks. How many people from your family are coming? I'm trying to plan the menu." Crystal pulled out a notebook and pen.

"There'll be eight of us. Me, my sisters and their families, and my mom."

"Great. And I also have eight. Aunt Donna can't make it, but her kids are coming. Uncle Mitch and Auntie Jan are coming, but their kids aren't. So, I'll plan on twenty. Thanks for all your help."

"Anytime. What's going on with the house?" Mel asked.

"I didn't tell you?" Crystal doodled flowers and hearts around the guest list.

"You said you had three offers but didn't tell me what you decided."

Crystal pushed back against the sofa and crossed her legs. "I ended up with five offers. I either priced the house just right or below its value. I guess the appraisal will determine that. Anyway, three offers were under the asking price, one offered me five thousand more, and one offered me the asking price, all-cash, as is."

"Really? That sounds too good to be true."

Crystal nodded even though Mel couldn't see her. "Yes, he had me at cash offer. Or she. The only kicker is that it's contingent on them selling their house, so right now, the closing is scheduled for the end of January."

"Can you wait that long?"

Crystal took another sip and her body radiated heat. She ate a cracker to absorb some of the alcohol. "The other offer I considered wanted a sixty-day closing, and waiting another thirty days for cash seemed like a better move. I'm not really in a huge rush."

"Maybe, it's because you aren't ready to part with that house." Melanie's words cut through Crystal, and her body stiffened like Melanie had revealed her deepest secret.

"What do you mean?" Crystal asked.

"I mean, you love that house."

"What? No, I don't. I hate that house. That house seeps bad memories revolving around my adolescence and early adulthood."

"You hated the house it was, but you love the house it is now. You told me that yourself. You said that you see happy memories when you look at it now."

Crystal hated that Melanie was so intuitive. She always said things Crystal wanted to lock down deep inside and ignore until they disappeared. "Maybe, but I have to sell it. I need the money, just in case. Mason's struggling at school. Who knows, the next step may be a private school or tutoring or having him move back home with me. If he moves home with me, I need the money to get him into a better district. I need the money for my family, so even if I love the house now, I can't keep it." Crystal rambled, thinking about her son. Report cards came out a few days ago and Mason managed Bs and Cs, thanks to the school's extra help.

"I totally get it, Crystal. I wasn't attacking you, just mentioning something I noticed." Her quiet words echoed through Crystal's brain.

Crystal and Mel ended their call, and Crystal continued to work on the menu for her mother's party. She picked up her phone and texted Derek: **Hey, we're having a party for my mom on Thanksgiving. I don't know what you're doing, but you and Molly are invited. I get it if it feels weird. My family will be there and my best friend/cousin.** She hit the green arrow and waited.

After a few minutes and no response, Crystal typed more: **Or maybe you can meet Melanie after the party. We'll be around all weekend.** She hit the green arrow again, and again she waited.

Derek texted back a quick **K**, and Crystal wondered what she had done to upset him this time, or if Christina had anything to do with it.

CHAPTER 44: DEREK

Molly sat on the couch with a notebook on her lap and a dinner tray beside her. She folded a floppy slice of pizza in half and took a large bite. "Dad, this is so good. I forgot how much I love Antonio's pizza."

"Can you get pizza like that in New York?" Derek asked, shoving a third of the slice into his cavernous mouth. Remnants of tomato sauce splashed his chin, and he wiped it with a napkin.

"Yes, but I can't afford it. I can barely afford anything beyond pasta and peanut butter."

Derek grinned. "Welcome to living on your own."

Molly placed her glass on the coffee table. "I might have a paid internship for next semester. There's a work program at school that I applied for, and I should know by Christmas if I got in. Maybe then I can buy myself a pizza."

"Good luck. I hope you get it." Derek took a sip of soda and belched under his breath. "Sorry. I forgot what it was like having a lady in the house."

"It doesn't bother me. I don't live here anymore." Molly hiccupped, and her body jerked and straightened. She grabbed her stomach and

194

rolled her head to the top of the couch. "Pizza and soda. It happens every time."

A comfortable silence settled between them. After dinner, Derek cleared the table. "Happy Thanksgiving. I'm glad you made it home." He grabbed her empty plate and walked toward the kitchen.

Molly pushed up her glasses. "Dad. I would never leave you alone on Thanksgiving. What's Crystal up to?"

Derek raised his shoulders. "She and her son are here this weekend, and they're having a family party at the farmhouse in memory of her mom. We're getting together on Saturday after everyone leaves. It's been a crazy month, so I haven't seen or spoken to her as much as I probably should have." Crystal texted daily and Derek always replied, but he was so distracted by the house that he never had time to talk, get deep into life, or ask about hers and Mason's lives.

Now that the winter was approaching, work had slowed considerably, and Molly's financial stress weighed on him. He always had Vanessa's settlement money, but he didn't want to dig into that unless he had to. Vanessa had given her life for that money, and Derek didn't want to spend it unless it were something Vanessa would want. He knew she would have used that money to pay Molly's rent if she were still here, but Derek needed it for something tangible that he could hold. Something that said 'thank you,' to Vanessa for all she had sacrificed.

"What time are we going to Uncle Phil's and Aunt Amy's?" Molly asked. "I still have to make mom's pie."

"One o'clock. I'll help you bake tomorrow."

Molly turned, returned to her notebook, and flipped through her textbook. "I have an exam Tuesday, and I need to study."

Derek left her in the living room and turned on the television in his bedroom. He hadn't seen Molly since August, and she appeared older and more mature. Her hair had grown, her slender figure had softened, and she carried an air of confidence he hadn't seen before.

Maybe I should tell her now. No, tomorrow. I'll tell everyone tomorrow.

He pulled into himself and half-listened to the sitcom coming from his television. *If only life were that easy.* The laugh track painted an alternate reality; Derek sometimes wished he lived in that world. Nothing too heavy, and no stress.

Derek spent the night in his room, lounging in his bed, dreaming about what might be.

* * *

"Molly, welcome home." Amy embraced Molly in a wide hug and held on for a few seconds. She pulled away and held Molly's shoulders. "You look great. Let me take your coat." Molly handed her the pie, which Amy gave to Phil before she turned and pulled Molly's coat from her shoulders.

They walked into the kitchen and saw Margie and Christina. *What's she doing here?* Derek threw Phil a glance and gave Christina a cordial hug. He felt her hands press into his waistband, and his body stiffened.

"Molly, it's great to see you," Margie said. "Did you make your mom's pie?"

Molly smiled. "You know it. We can't have Thanksgiving without Save-A-Trip Pie."

Christina looked over. "Save a trip what? What's that?"

Molly grinned. "It's a variation of pumpkin pie and apple streusel pie. When I was a kid, I only ate pumpkin, but my dad loved apple, and my mom only had so much time to bake, so she combined our favorites and made her own. She called it Save-A-Trip because if you like apple and pumpkin pie, you'd only have to get up once. It's been a holiday tradition ever since."

"And Molly's mastered the recipe," Derek added. "It's a fan favorite."

Christina's blue eyes twinkled. "Looks delicious." She licked her lips for emphasis, but kept her eyes on Derek.

He sidestepped out of her view.

After dinner, he pulled up enough nerve to make his announcement. The desserts lay across the table like a feast, and everyone hung around, eating a smidgin of each sugar-filled happy ending.

"I have to tell you something." He looked at his family and avoided Christina. He wished she wasn't there, but there was nothing he could do.

"I sold the house. My house. Mine, Vanessa and Molly's house." It still felt unusual, and hearing it out loud sent a shiver up his spine. Margie gasped, and Molly smiled.

"You did?" Margie placed her hands on the back of the chair. "Congratulations."

"Are you sure you want to do this?" Phil asked. "Where're you going to go?"

Derek shrugged. "Molly's out of the house, Vanessa's gone. It's just me." He wasn't yet ready to reveal his true intention. "That house is too big for just me. Plus, the business has been slow, and I'd rather have something smaller and more manageable." He looked down and waited.

"Congratulations, Derek," Amy said. She patted him on the shoulder, and Derek stepped back against the counter's edge. "You need to do what's right for you."

"If you need somewhere to stay until you find a place, you know we have room for you," Phil added.

Derek looked at Molly and gave her a quick look. She knew better than to ask questions or comment in front of everyone, so she continued to eat her pie with a knowing smirk on her face.

"When's the closing?" Margie asked.

"Mid-December. I might need a place to crash until January first. I might get an apartment for a year to re-evaluate." That wasn't entirely true either, but it solved the timing problem.

"I can help you move. Just let me know when." Phil collected the dirty dishes and carried them to the kitchen.

Derek followed, carrying the empty glasses. "Thanks, Phil." Whatever animosity had grown between them a few months back had dissipated with the final resolution of Derek's debt.

Confidence grew within Derek, and he ambled back into the dining room. Christina pulled on her coat and hugged Amy. "Thank you, Amy, for having me over. It was wonderful celebrating this holiday with you."

Amy smiled. "Any time."

Christina hugged Molly, shook hands with Phil, and waved to Derek.

"I'll walk you out," said Derek, pulling on his winter hat.

They walked to her sporty two-door coupe, and Christina leaned in to hug him.

"Wait." Derek held up a hand to stop her. "I want to discuss something that's been bothering me for a few months. Christina, I hope I'm not stepping out of turn, but I'm not interested in you. You're a beautiful, nice woman, but my heart belongs to Crystal. So, if I led you on, I'm sorry, but please understand that I'm not interested."

Her face dropped, and her eyes narrowed. "Of course."

He held out his hand. "Friends?"

"Sure." She took his hand and wagged her wrist.

Derek watched her drive away and waved a last goodbye. He felt like a million bucks walking into the house.

He and Molly drove home a few hours later. The snow-covered road created a sparkly blanket, and two tire tracks led the way.

"Dad, you're sure about this?" Molly asked.

Derek didn't have to ask what she meant. "Molly. I'm sure with a hundred percent of my being."

Molly placed her hand on his. "Good luck."

CHAPTER 45: CRYSTAL

❧

C rystal considered Thanksgiving a success. As expected, the farmhouse came to life with a handful of cousins, Auntie Sue, and Auntie Jan and Uncle Mitch. It was advertised as a celebration of Evelyn's life and an honor to the legacy she left behind, so Crystal masked feelings of resentment and anger toward the way Evelyn treated her as a young adult, and smiled as the family told stories and reminisced about Evelyn's life.

Crystal's cousins cleaned the kitchen, while Crystal drank a glass of wine with her aunts. Uncle Mitch drank a beer on the couch, watching football with Mason. Crystal pulled out the boxes of weathered photographs and albums she found in the barn.

"Auntie Jan, I think these were Grammy and Grampy's photos. I don't recognize anyone. Do you want to look?" The stained, damp box sat on the floor next to the dining room table Crystal had used for the open house.

Auntie Jan leaned over and held out her hand. "My memory isn't great, but I'll take a look." Crystal grabbed a handful of loose photographs and scattered them on the brown tablecloth. Auntie Sue picked up a few and flipped through.

"Oh, Crystal, there are so many pictures of your mom here." Auntie Sue held up a photo of a young woman wearing hot pants and a halter top. "This is your mom in the late sixties. See the hair?"

Crystal smiled at the bouffant.

"That was all the rage."

Crystal grabbed the photo from Auntie Sue's hands and held it close to her face. "That's my mom?" Her eyes widened, and a smile spread across her face. "Wow, she was a looker!"

Auntie Jan snatched the photo and studied it. "She sure was. Did you know your mom went to Woodstock?"

Crystal shook her head and sat down between the two older women. "I had no idea. She never talked about her past."

"Oh yeah, your grandparents prohibited her from going because they thought rock and roll would ruin her. They were afraid she'd come home pregnant or not come home at all. Your mom snuck out of the house, met up with friends from school, and drove the three hours to get there." Auntie Jan put down the photo and picked up another.

"No way," Crystal said. Her mother, the prim and proper, tight-lipped woman, would never go to Woodstock. The image refused to form in Crystal's brain.

"No way, what?" Melanie stood in between the dining room and kitchen.

"Mel, check out these photos. They're wild. Auntie Jan and your mom were telling me my mom went to Woodstock. Can you believe it? I can't."

Mel sat down and grabbed a handful of photos.

"I remember that weekend even though I was just a child," Auntie Jan said. "Our parents first got concerned when Evelyn didn't come home that night. They called all the neighbors, and one of the kids said they thought she drove down to Woodstock. When she got back, they kicked her out of the house. It was a terrible night. I was crying,

Evelyn was crying, and our parents were fuming. I never thought I would see her again." She turned toward Auntie Sue. "Where were you that night? I don't remember you being there."

Mel's mom leaned forward. "I was out with my girlfriends at the drive-in. Can't remember the movie. It must not have been that good. But Evelyn was my big sister and I looked up to her like no one else. I came home that night and every light was on in the house. Usually, mom and dad fell asleep early. I knew something was wrong. I shared a room with your mom, and the room was destroyed. It was terrible." Auntie Sue shook her head in disbelief, remembering.

Crystal leaned forward, enthralled by her mother's past. "I never heard this story. What happened next?"

"Well, she left, and I didn't see her for six years. She moved to a commune with her boyfriend. She lived with a bunch of hippies where they worked and grew food together, and lived in harmony." Auntie Jan air-quoted 'in harmony'. She rummaged around for more photos.

Crystal and Melanie's cousin, Jimmy, entered the dining room with a platter of cheese and crackers. "Food will be ready in about an hour," Jimmy said. "What are you guys looking at?"

"Old pictures. You should check these out and take some home with you."

"Hey, guys, old pictures in the dining room," Jimmy hollered into the kitchen. Incoherent chatter traveled throughout the house like an ocean wave cresting.

"Wait, Auntie Jan," Crystal said, "that's not where she met my dad, was it? They told me they met at a disco."

"They did. She broke up with her boyfriend and had to leave the commune. When I was in high school, she came back home. My parents didn't want to take her back. By that point, she was twenty-five years old and a complete disappointment in their eyes, but they needed help to pay the bills. Daddy had just lost his job, so Evelyn

201

moved back in as a tenant. She was desperate to move out again. She met your dad at a disco, just like they told you, and moved in with him a month later. My parents were angry and told her that if she left, that was it. She could never come to them for help again."

Auntie Sue chimed in. "I didn't know where she was. By then, I was married, and living in Massachusetts with your father." She looked at Mel. "And we only had one car and only one of us was working, so I didn't keep in touch much with anyone beyond a phone call here and there. As close as Evelyn and I were growing up, I didn't even know she'd left again."

Melanie looked into her mother's eyes. "Mom, that's so sad. I can't believe Grammy and Grampy did that."

Auntie Jan shrugged. "It was a different time. Evelyn didn't return home for another ten years; when she did, she was married and had a toddler. You." Auntie Jan pointed at Crystal. "I had married by then, and life went on. My parents were still angry, but they were old. I think they realized how much of her life they missed. When they realized there was a child, they put their pride aside and welcomed Evelyn back into their lives."

"Things were different. They would never be the same. Too many past hurts eroded whatever trust they had." Auntie Sue piled the pictures. "But they loved you, Crystal. That was never a doubt in anyone's mind."

Crystal's heart ached for her parents. She couldn't imagine being forced away from her family or having to choose between what her family wanted and what she wanted. Her shoulders slumped and her throat constricted. She had prevented Mason and her parents from having a relationship, but Crystal's parents put their anger aside so Crystal could have a relationship with her grandparents. *No wonder Mom was so hard on me.* Sadness floated around Crystal as the magnitude of her choices crystalized in front of her.

Over dinner, Crystal, Melanie, and their cousins listened to her Auntie Sue and Auntie Jan relay stories about Evelyn's youth. They painted a picture of a woman Crystal never knew. "Remember the time Evelyn tricked Daddy into giving her the car for the night?" Auntie Jan asked Auntie Sue.

"And then she drove it into the tree on Mr. Smith's farm, and when Daddy asked what happened, she refused to admit it was her. I was just a kid, but I remember that night!" Auntie Sue said.

"I remember the night Evelyn babysat us younger kids and her boyfriend snuck in," Auntie Jan cackled. "She gave me bubble gum to keep me quiet." She shook her head at the absurdity of the bribe and laughed. "Mommy and Daddy never found out."

Crystal listened closely, imagining the fun-loving mother she could have had, but didn't. Evelyn was never the cool mom, or the mom her friends ran to when they had a problem. Evelyn mothered Crystal to a fault and meddled in Crystal's life, offering advice when Crystal didn't want it. Evelyn always wanted to help and, eventually, that help led to resentment when Crystal chose a different path. As Crystal became an adolescent, her mother became overly protective, prohibiting Crystal to experience life. Her overprotectiveness became disappointment, and her better-than-thou attitude made Crystal feel like she wasn't good enough.

That was the Evelyn she knew. Crystal couldn't believe this other woman had existed.

They went outside, each holding a candle and sharing their favorite memories of Evelyn. Crystal couldn't believe how this old farmhouse had changed her perspective on her childhood. Even though Evelyn grasped at sand sifting through her fingers, and tried to stop life from being too dangerous and painful, she pushed Crystal away. She sacrificed her own personality to be a 'good mom'...whatever that meant. Her motive to control was brought on by fear of her only daughter leaving her. And ironically, that was exactly what had pushed Crystal away.

Tears formed behind Crystal's eyes, and she looked at Mason. He bounced around the group playing with Lulu. Even if Evelyn wasn't the easiest person to get along with, she still could have taught him something. She knew Mason didn't have a memory to share with the group, but he didn't seem to mind. Even so, she was happy he heard the stories.

The stories traveled around the group and stopped at Crystal. Everyone looked at her, and she hesitated and cleared her throat. "As you all know, my relationship with my mother was rocky. Thank you for teaching me that one side of a person is not all they truly are. My mother was courageous and beautiful, and I'm lucky she was mine."

The guilt Crystal carried for not being with Evelyn when Evelyn couldn't care for herself melted away. If she could do it all again differently, she would have, but it was too late. All she could do now was forgive the past and move on to the future. Crystal promised herself that she'd keep the lines of communication open with Mason, because honesty is how they would learn and grow through their successes and mistakes.

Mel raised her candle. "To Auntie Evelyn, for bringing us all together."

Everyone followed and a web of light sparkled above them against the stars in the sky.

"Thank you, Mom," Crystal whispered. "For doing the best you could and doing what you felt was right." She wiped the tear falling from the corner of her eye and side-hugged her son. She kissed him on the top of his head, smelling his hair and feeling the bristles poke her face. She hoped her story with Mason would be different, but knew she was doing the best she could, just like Evelyn.

* * *

The following day, Crystal and Melanie pulled out all the leftovers from the refrigerator. "Mel, there's so much food here. We have turkey, stuffing, sweet potato casserole, mashed potatoes, green bean casserole, and turnips. Should I heat it all in the oven or microwave it?"

"The oven will fit more. What time's Derek coming over?"

Crystal glanced at the clock. "In forty-five minutes. I know I said we could go out for breakfast, but it seems silly when we have all this food to eat."

"My favorite part of Thanksgiving is eating all the leftovers the next day, so this is perfect."

Crystal nodded. "I'm glad one of us knows how to cook. Thanks for all your help yesterday."

Mel smiled. "You did a great job hosting. I could feel your parents with us; the atmosphere felt so peaceful."

Crystal grinned at her best friend. "You're right. I bet they were here. Thanks for spending the night. It felt like old times when we had sleepovers at Grammy and Grampy's." The night before, after the rest of the family had left, Melanie and Crystal drank a bottle of wine while Mason watched Christmas movies upstairs.

"Are you excited to finally meet Derek?" Crystal asked. Nerves zinged through her body. Her heart rate stuttered, her stomach flopped, and her fingers trembled.

"I'm so excited. I've heard so much about him; I feel like I already know him." Mel leaned against the counter, and Crystal stuffed the food into the oven like a jigsaw puzzle.

They fell into easy conversation about Christmas as they prepared lunch, until Crystal heard three knocks on the door. She dropped her potholders, pulled back her thick hair, and wiped her damp hands on her jeans. "He's here." Before Mel could respond, she hurried to the front door.

She hadn't seen him since Halloween. Her heart practically stopped as she took in his tall, confident frame. He held his shoulders back and his head high. He whipped out a bouquet from behind his back and kissed her. She smiled so hard that her cheeks hurt. She grabbed the flowers and wrapped her arms around his neck. "Derek, I've missed you so much."

He pulled away and she gazed into his eyes. "Happy Thanksgiving."

"You look great. I love your coat. Is that new?" He wore a heavy fleece-lined flannel that hung to his hips.

"Molly bought it for me in New York. Said I had to have it." He spun in a circle, showing off his figure.

Crystal grinned, "It hits your butt just right. I like it." She leaned in for another kiss and grabbed his hand, pulling him into the house. "Mel! Mason! Derek's here!"

Lulu ran down the stairs, wagging her tail and jumping on Derek's thigh. Instead of scolding her, he knelt and rubbed her head. "Lulu, I missed you." He stood up and said, "I never thought I'd say that, but that little girl grew on me."

"Lulu," Mason called, rounding the corner. He stopped in his tracks. "Hi." Lulu ran over, and Mason led her back upstairs.

Melanie moved into the living room with a dishtowel in her hand. "Hi, I'm Melanie. Nice to meet you." She dried her hand and shook Derek's.

"I'm Derek. Nice to meet you too. Wow, Crystal, the house looks great." He eyed the staged furniture that still decorated the rooms.

"Thanks. The furniture is here until the house closes, just in case the buyer falls through. It worked out perfectly since I wanted to have the party for my mom. It saved me a lot of hassle finding a place for people to sit for one day only."

He removed his jacket and threw it on the loveseat.

"Are you hungry? Food should be hot."

The three sat around the table, eating leftovers and making small talk. *Mel and Derek seem to be hitting it off*, and there were no awkward pauses between them.

"Is Mason eating?" Derek asked.

Crystal shrugged. "He woke up late and had a late breakfast. Mason's not a big fan of vegetables. He'll eat French fries, but not mashed potatoes, and rolls are his favorite part of Thanksgiving. Rolls and cookies. That's it." When Mason was younger, it bothered Crystal that he didn't have a varied appetite. As she learned his strengths and weaknesses, she recognized and celebrated the minor victories. "He'll eat apples too. He likes the crunch."

Derek looked around the kitchen. "Do you have any apples? I'm not sure what he thinks of me, but I'd love to have an excuse to go up there and talk with him. Get to know him a little better."

Crystal's body warmed at his thoughtfulness. "That would be wonderful. I think he'd like that. The apples are over in that bowl by the sink."

Derek collected their dirty plates and carried them to the dishwasher. He rinsed and loaded before taking an apple. "Peeled or not peeled?"

"Peeled and sliced. Thanks, Derek." Crystal looked at Melanie, and Melanie gave her a thumbs-up sign just above the table.

"He's a keeper," Mel whispered.

Derek cut the apple and disappeared down the hallway.

"Crystal, he seems perfect. And it's clear he's totally into you."

Crystal blushed, flattered that Melanie noticed the chemistry between them.

"It's so weird, though, because we haven't spoken much this month. Ever since that stupid movie encounter with Christina."

"Maybe he needed time to think. But it's obvious he likes you. And it's obvious he wants to get to know Mason. Maybe he's the one you've been waiting for."

Crystal drummed her fingers, thinking.

Bzzzzz. The black mobile phone on the table jittered in place. Crystal looked down, and a text message popped up.

"Is that your phone?" Mel said, picking it up.

"No, Derek's." Mel handed the phone to Crystal and Crystal glanced at the screen. A message notification stared back at her.

Christina.

Crystal's eyes widened, and she looked at Melanie. "It's from Christina." Her calm voice barely carried across the table. "What do I do?"

Melanie leaned forward. "Read it."

Crystal's wobbly voice read the message. "Hi. I got your message. Can you meet tomorrow?" Crystal dropped the phone like it was coated in lava. She spied the hallway and returned her attention to Melanie. "I got your message, Mel. That means he's texted or called her. What does that mean?" She felt tears build behind her eyes. *Crystal, stop crying.*

Melanie snatched the phone out of Crystal's hands. "No passcode," she said. She opened the text conversation and scrolled. "Let me scroll up a bit. You tell me if he's coming."

Crystal repositioned herself to see better, in case he came down the stairs.

"Okay, this whole thing started a few weeks ago. Hi, great seeing you the other day. I'd love to get together and chat. Are you free tomorrow? Derek: Yes, what time do you want me? Christina: How about two o'clock? We can meet at Phil's."

Crystal gasped. *Phil knew.* "Go on."

"Okay, this looks like a week later. Christina: Congratulations." Melanie looked at Crystal with furrowed eyebrows and a wrinkly forehead. "Congratulations? What the heck does that mean?"

Crystal shrugged; her eyes fixated on the hallway.

"Derek: Thank you. I couldn't have done it without you. You are amazing."

Crystal sucked in a moan. She swallowed loudly and choked on her saliva. *Jerk.*

"Christina: I learned a lot from you too. Do you want to get together next week and make things official? Derek: I would love that."

"Stop, stop, stop." Crystal shook her hands in Melanie's face and grabbed the phone, placing it on the table where they found it.

Quiet footsteps got louder as Derek entered the kitchen and Crystal's heart boomed like a bass drum. "Success," he said, placing the empty plate on the counter.

Crystal didn't respond. She wanted to run, but her body froze to her seat.

"You okay?" He rushed to her side. "You're pale as a ghost."

Crystal tried to smile. "I'm not feeling well, and I think you should go." She moved about the kitchen in a daze imagining him and Christina together.

Derek looked at Melanie and scrunched his forehead.

"Yeah, you should probably go. Here, let me walk you out." Melanie rose from the table, gave him his phone and coat, and escorted him to the door.

Crystal sat at the table, staring at where his phone had sat.

"Melanie, would you mind giving us a few minutes?" Derek asked.

Crystal made eye contact with Melanie, and Melanie stepped out of the room. Crystal couldn't look at Derek.

"Are you okay? What happened?" He took her chilled hands in his and rubbed them together. "You're cold as ice."

She stared at her fingers. They didn't feel like her own.

"Crystal."

She pulled everything she could muster, and smiled. "Nothing. I'm fine. While you were upstairs, you got a text. I'm feeling under the weather, and I'd like to catch up with Mel before she goes home in a few hours. I'll talk to you later, okay?" She kissed him on the cheek and walked him past Melanie to the door.

Derek looked around. "Okay. I'll call you later."

"Sure." Crystal closed the door in his face, pressed her back against the hardwood, and fell to the ground. Sobs escaped her like bubbles, and she was suffocating. Evelyn's words crashed at her, keeping her knocked down. 'He's not good enough for you, and you can't trust him.'

Melanie crouched next to her and held her tight. "Shh. I'm here. I'm here."

It was too late. Her fractured heart had broken.

CHAPTER 46: DEREK

W hat happened? Derek sat in his truck, staring at the old farmhouse. It had been ten minutes since Melanie and Crystal kicked him out. He searched his brain for something that would cause them both to flip, and nothing came to mind. *Mason and I had such a great chat, too. Damn, what happened?* He banged the leather steering wheel ring and changed the radio station to heavy rock.

The scent of gasoline filtered through his air vents as his truck noisily idled behind Crystal's car. He expected Crystal to come out and talk to him or at least check on him since he hadn't left her driveway, but the door never opened, and she never appeared.

Derek put his truck in reverse and slowly backed out of the driveway. The lonely road led to his dark, empty house, and he exhaled, knowing he could deal with his thoughts in solitude. Molly had left that morning to go Christmas shopping with some girlfriends and hadn't returned home yet.

Derek stepped into the dim kitchen and pulled out his phone. He attempted a dozen messages to Crystal before deleting the texts and putting his phone down. He paced the house and paused in front of the twenty-year-old wedding photo resting on the mantle. Vanessa's off-the-shoulder wedding gown accentuated her broad shoulders, and her pink lipstick matched the roses she carried in front of her bosom. Derek spoke out loud, and his voice wavered. "If you're here, please help me. I don't know what I'm doing with my life."

Silence answered him.

After an hour, Derek called Crystal, but she didn't answer. He couldn't get her out of his mind. The apparent hurt across her face was all he saw. It didn't make any sense.

He wanted to go over there but knew it was a bad idea with Mason in the house. Crystal was upset and angry, and he didn't want to cause a fight. Plus, he was pretty sure Mason liked him.

Instead, Derek texted Crystal repeatedly.

Can we talk?

I'm not sure what happened, but I'm sorry if I caused you pain.

Crystal, what happened?

I'd like to talk before you leave tomorrow. Can I call you?

The texts were endless. Derek wanted to drown his worry in a case of beer, but the last time he did that, he ended up at Christina's.

He distracted himself with old movies, planning upcoming jobs, and checking his email. He had an email from Chrissy, the realtor working under Tamara, about his house. They had an appointment on Tuesday to sign all the paperwork accepting the sale, but she needed to cancel and reschedule for Monday. She wrote at the bottom of the email: **Sorry to have texted you on the weekend. I hope you had a nice Thanksgiving.**

Derek scrunched his nose. He pulled out his phone and saw the message from Christina, also known as Chrissy. *Shit. When did she text me? It must have been when I was up with Mason.* Realization hit him a second before sheer panic coursed through his veins, the icy blood chilling his bones. His heart thudded in his ears, and he laughed out loud. "Is this really my life right now?" It was a horrible misunderstanding, and he needed to talk to Crystal immediately.

He flew to his car and raced to her house. It was nearly eleven o'clock. *What am I doing? I can't go in there.* He imagined her holding a frying pan, ready to assault whoever was breaking into her home. He drove past her driveway and returned home. *Tomorrow.*

He didn't sleep. Molly came home after midnight, and he heard her shuffle through the house. He prayed to Vanessa, asking for her help. Too many coincidences connected Vanessa to Crystal, and he knew Vanessa set Crystal in his path.

At six the following morning, Derek stumbled outside and cleared his car. He needed to talk to someone—Margie or Phil, it didn't matter—and he found his way to the warm, lit diner.

"Hey, Derek. Come on over. I have a fresh pot of coffee for you." Margie's welcoming smile comforted Derek.

Derek sat in the empty restaurant.

"You look like shit. Did you sleep last night?" Margie got down to his level and scanned his face.

"Got a lot on my mind." He played with his placemat and silverware.

"Wanna talk?" Margie set the coffeepot down and returned to Derek. "I got nothing else to do right now."

Everything spilled out. His house. The farmhouse. Not seeing Crystal for a month. Meeting Melanie. Bonding with Mason. Getting kicked out of the house. And finally, the text message. Margie listened without breaking eye contact. Derek concluded his story with a question. "What do I do now?"

Margie held out her hand. "Give me your phone."

He obliged, and she hit the home button. "Derek, you don't have a passcode on this thing?"

Derek shook his head. "No, I've never needed one."

Margie tsked. "Everyone needs one. Let me pull up the text." She hit some buttons, and the conversation under Christina filled the screen. She scanned the contents. "Jesus, Derek. It sounds like you're seeing this woman. You're making dates, saying how wonderful she is...if Crystal saw this, she'd think you're dating someone on the side."

"Let me see that!" Derek grabbed the phone back and banged his fist into his forehead.

"And her name is Christina? That woman, Christina, that hair stylist...she wants you bad. She's wanted you ever since that Fourth of July picnic."

Derek rubbed his temples with both hands. "Her name is Christina. That's what was written on her business card and how she signs her email, so that's what I saved her as. But in person she calls herself Chrissy. She's my realtor and selling agent."

Margie scrunched up one side of her face. "I think you've got yourself a problem. You need to get over there and explain."

Derek pulled on his jacket. "Shit. I'm such an idiot. Thanks, Margie."

He tripped out the door, squeezing past a couple coming in. He threw his truck in reverse and sped out the parking lot. His back tires squealed, and a cloud of dirt and dust circled his vehicle.

When he got to the old farmhouse, Crystal's car was gone.

CHAPTER 47: CRYSTAL

C rystal drove Mason home on Saturday night in a thick fog; searching for reasons why she always picked men who couldn't be faithful. She had growing suspicion about Christina since the Fourth of July party, but Derek always reassured her, reminding her she was the only one for him.

Bullshit. I should have known he was too good to be true.

Crystal brought Mason back a day early because she couldn't keep up the happy charade he deserved. She had texted Jeremy, but he never replied. She assumed if he weren't home, he would be home eventually. She could wait all night if she needed.

They pulled into his apartment complex, and Crystal saw Jeremy's SUV right where she had left it on Wednesday. Crystal clutched Lulu under her armpit, and Mason grabbed his bag. They made it to Jeremy's door, and Crystal knocked. Music and light danced under the door, and Crystal knocked harder.

The door flung open. "Crystal, Mason, what are you doing here?"

Basil, oregano, and garlic drifted from his apartment into the hallway.

"I tried calling, and I texted. We left the farmhouse early."

Jeremy put his arm up on the doorframe to prevent Crystal from entering. "Bad weekend?"

"Um…" Crystal felt the tears building again and built her wall higher. "Yeah, you could say that." She peered under his arm. "Is it an okay time?"

Jeremy repositioned himself. "Yeah, yeah, it's fine. Come on in. Welcome home, Mase!" Mason barreled down the hall, dropping his stuff at Crystal and Jeremy's feet.

They stood in the foyer with a coat rack on one side and a table across, wedged in like a can of sardines. Crystal smelled Jeremy's woodsy cologne and observed his cleanly shaved face. "Oh my God. Jeremy. Is someone else here?"

Redness traveled up Jeremy's neck.

"Hi, Amanda," Crystal heard Mason say in the next room.

"Mason," Crystal interrupted with a high-pitched squeal. She cleared her throat. "Come say goodbye. Mommy has to go. Now." She didn't step one more foot inside the apartment.

"It's no problem, Crystal," Jeremy said. "I should have checked my phone."

Mason ran over and hugged Crystal after he snuggled Lulu. "Bye, Mom! See you Friday."

"I'm sorry. I hope I didn't ruin your night." She hurried away from Jeremy and Amanda, down the hallway and out the building.

Even Jeremy's moved on with another woman. Her insides threatened to burst out of her body, and she screamed within the enclosed vehicle. Her rage toward Jeremy and now Derek stirred within her like a witch's cauldron, and she sobbed to catch her breath. She felt rotten inside and questioned her worth. *Will I ever find someone to love me, just the way I am?*

When she got home, she saw endless notifications from Derek on her phone. She couldn't talk to him. Not yet. He had betrayed her and lied to her when all she asked was to please be honest. She knew in her heart that she was preparing herself for this moment, preparing to say goodbye.

Crystal climbed into bed at 10 p.m. and slept until noon the next day. When she woke up, she couldn't get out of bed. *What's the point? No one needs me.*

The following week, Crystal willed herself to work. Her mushy brain resembled scrambled eggs, and she couldn't figure out what she needed to do to get ready. She pulled her shoulder-length, wild hair into a messy ponytail. Her red eyes and dark bags stressed her sadness, and she did nothing to hide them. She threw on a pair of yoga pants and a tunic before grabbing her work bag. Each day further into the week was more brutal than the one before.

On Thursday, her phone rang. Crystal let it ring four times before looking to see who was calling. Derek had been calling and texting incessantly, but Crystal couldn't pick up. She wasn't ready.

This time, it was Tamara. She sat in her bed with a bag of chips and a glass of wine for dinner. This was the third bag of chips she'd consumed since Monday. The milk went sour, she was out of coffee, and her bread grew green mold. She had no intention of going to the store.

Crystal answered the call. "Hello?"

"Hi, Crystal. How are you?" Tamara's bubbly voice busted through the phone.

Crystal summoned whatever dying enthusiasm she carried in the pit of her stomach and dragged it up to her vocal folds. "Fine. How are you?"

"I'm great. I am calling because I have some great news for you! The all-cash buyer came through, and it's a go!" Crystal pulled the phone away at Tamara's shrieking tone. "I will send over the documents for you to review and sign, and it will be official two weeks after I receive your John Hancock. Call me if you have any questions."

Crystal hung up the phone and sat, her body asleep but her mind in constant motion. *The house sold.* Crystal expected to feel joy when the news dropped, but she surprised herself with sadness. More sadness from more loss. Crystal had lost everything—her father, mother, husband, Derek, and now the house. The tornado that was the past ten years was nearly killing her.

She lay in bed, weighed down by her new reality. Her life in Farm Cove, NY, was officially over.

CHAPTER 48: DEREK

H e couldn't get in touch with Crystal. As each day passed the
urgency faded, and Derek wondered if this was Vanessa's
way of telling him Crystal wasn't the right girl after all.
Perhaps he was destined to be alone.

By the time Wednesday rolled around, Derek couldn't take the
uncertainty anymore. He found himself on the train heading south.
He called Molly, letting her know he was in town and wanted to see
her.

"Dad, everything okay?"

"I just want to be with my little girl. It's almost Christmas, and I miss
you. I thought we could grab some dinner." He watched the trees whiz
past his window.

"Are you spending the night? Because I have an exam tomorrow and
we don't have an extra bed."

Derek heard the concern behind her politeness. "Oh, no, no. I'll take
the last train home tonight. Just dinner, I promise. I feel like I haven't
seen you in forever."

"Dad, it's been two weeks."

Derek shook his head. *A lot can happen in two weeks, Sweetpea.* "That's it? It feels so much longer than that."

"Call me when you get here. I'll pick you up at the train station." Derek heard the worry in Molly's voice and imagined her rubbing her eyebrows like Vanessa did when she was thrown into an unexpected scenario.

"Will do, Mols. Love you."

Derek hung up the phone and watched the gray clouds blur into a foggy mist. It wanted to snow outside, but Mother Nature was holding it hostage. He wondered if Vanessa was holding his heart hostage.

Alternating images of Vanessa and Crystal mashed in his brain, quicker and quicker, until they blurred together. He was at his wit's end, praying for some guidance from Vanessa, or even from God himself, to point him in the right direction. His house had sold, and his entire life with Vanessa was disappearing. *Am I making a huge mistake?*

Derek continued to torture himself by conjuring memories of his past, his choices, and the infinite possibilities of his future. The weight of Vanessa's disappointment trampled his lungs, and he struggled to breathe. He stared out the window and cried silently. He hadn't cried since her funeral, but something inside him broke.

When he got off the train, Molly was already waiting. Her red parka hood covered her face, and Derek almost walked past her. "Dad!" Molly said, grabbing his arm.

"Oh, Mols. Sorry, I didn't recognize you there."

Molly looked him up and down. "Dad? Are you okay?"

Derek felt his chin quiver, and he bit the inside of his cheek to distract himself from his emotions. Pain radiated through his cheek and up to his eye. Metallic tasting blood traveled to the back of his tongue, and he swallowed. "Yeah." He looked away, searched for a tissue, and blew his nose. "Can we go talk somewhere?"

Molly drove him to town. A blanket of snow coated the two-story buildings, and slush lay across the sidewalk. "I'm broke, Dad. How much do you want to spend on lunch or dinner?"

Derek glanced at his watch. It was three-thirty, and he wasn't hungry. "Uh, is there a sandwich or deli shop somewhere?"

Molly drove him down the main drag and parked in front of a cute Italian deli. "Sandwiches it is."

They settled at the counter facing the street with an Italian sub and a Turkey-Bacon wrap. Derek chose these seats so he wouldn't have to look at Molly.

"Dad, what's going on?" She pestered him until he caved.

Oh, Molly, where do I begin? He swallowed, sighed, and wiped his mouth. "Remember when I told everyone I sold the house?"

Molly nodded. "Did it fall through?"

Derek shook his head. "No, it didn't. It's a long story, and I don't want to bore you with the details, but Crystal saw a few texts from the realtor and thinks I cheated on her."

Molly's hand sprang to her lips, and her nose and eyes scrunched together. "Huh? That doesn't make sense."

"Well, it does because her husband cheated on her, so she's struggling with trust and commitment."

Molly took a sip of water. "Okay. Got it."

"Well, she got angry. She kicked me out of her house over a week ago, and I haven't heard from her since. It took me a while to figure out what happened, but after reviewing the texts and not knowing the context, I can see it. I never told her I was selling the house because I wanted to surprise her."

Molly nodded. "And now your house sold. Did you buy the farmhouse?"

Derek looked out the window and watched a woman help an old lady avoid an icy patch on the sidewalk. He smiled and nodded to the street. "That's something your mother would do. She was always so kind."

"Dad."

Derek turned toward her. "Right. Yes. But of course, Crystal doesn't know it's me. I don't know why Molly. Why did I buy it? I've always loved that house. Crystal came around to love it, too. I imagined this beautiful romantic gesture by buying it for her, but now I feel like a fool. I wasn't thinking, and I moved too fast. Hell, I haven't even told her I love her yet." Derek felt a deepening warmth crawl up his neck and awkwardly adjusted his seat. He had never talked about this stuff with Molly before.

"You have to talk to her."

Derek slammed his sandwich on his plate. "You don't think I tried?" His voice came out louder than he wanted, and he ducked his head when the neighboring patrons stared. He whispered, "She won't return my calls."

Molly leaned closer to him. "Dad, you have to. You have so much riding on this house transaction. You must be honest with her and tell her it was a misunderstanding and that it was your realtor. You can't just hide and hope it gets better on its own." Molly's eyes darted back and forth, and Derek saw Vanessa staring back at him.

His eyes welled up with tears at the loss of his wife. He had hung on to her memory and influence over him for years. And now he was ready to move on.

"Dad." Molly placed her hand on Derek's, as the tears rolled down into his scruffy beard.

"Molly, what do I do?"

"You find her, and you tell her."

Derek's words caught in his throat, and his voice came out fuzzy. "But what about your mom?"

"Dad. Mom taught me in my early years that if you don't ask, the answer is always no. Tell her, and if she doesn't want you after the truth comes out, you can move on and figure out your next plan. But it will be a no if you don't talk to her. She deserves the truth."

Derek wiped his eyes and inhaled and exhaled, lost in thought. *She's right. Vanessa would tell me to face this head-on. To be brave and vulnerable. And if the answer is no, so be it, but if I don't tell her, I'll never know.* He kissed Molly on the forehead and said, "Thank you, Mols, for being my number one cheerleader."

That night, he went back to his home and packed his bags.

CHAPTER 49: CRYSTAL

⟨ornament⟩

Time passed. It could have been hours, or it could have been minutes. She drank too much wine, and the room slightly tilted and blurred. A banging downstairs alerted Lulu to an intruder, and the barking mixed with the banging startled Crystal. She looked outside but saw blackness. She checked the clock, and it was only 07:45.

She pulled on her bathrobe and moved down the stairs, flipping on all the lights. She peeked through the door and recognized the black and red checked flannel in her line of vision. She was too tired to be surprised. Without thinking, she opened the door. "What do you want?"

"We need to talk." Derek held a bouquet in his right hand and wore a hopeful smile. He held it out to her, and something gold hung from the ribbon.

She swatted them to the ground. "I don't want your apology." She crossed her arms and closed the door.

"Wait, wait. Please, stop." Derek's arm shot out and blocked the door from closing. "I know you're mad at me, and I know why, and I swear it's all a misunderstanding." His eyes pleaded with her, but she refused to fall for any more lies.

"I saw the texts, Derek. It wasn't a misunderstanding. That woman has wanted you since the day I met her. Everyone knew, including you, and you lied to me. You told me it was nothing, and I had nothing to worry about." Her voice cracked, and she hated herself for showing weakness. She straightened her shoulders and widened her stance. "You're a liar."

"You have nothing to worry about, Crystal. I love you."

She crossed her arms and squinted, unsure if he was being honest. She refused to allow any emotion to cross her face.

"I fell in love with you the moment I met you, but I was too afraid to recognize it. You're funny, smart, beautiful, thoughtful...everything I need. Please. Let me explain myself."

Crystal heard the words, but they bounced off the steel wall she built around her heart.

"Derek, I don't know if I can believe you. Whatever you say, I don't know if I can ever fully trust you. You broke my trust with that woman. That awful woman stormed into my house to make me jealous and then flirted with you at the movies. I saw it all, Derek. I saw everything."

"But—"

Crystal held up her hand like a stop sign and ignored him. "And then you meet up with her? I knew something had happened because you never returned my calls or texts. It was like I didn't exist anymore."

She wiped her eyes with the back of her hand. He reached out to touch her, and she jerked her body away from him.

"Don't touch me."

"Crystal, please." He dropped his arm and looked around the street. A single set of headlights drove past and then disappeared around the curve.

"Don't. Everyone told me long-distance relationships wouldn't work, and I should have listened. I'm an idiot for thinking this could work. I have to go, Derek." She tightened her bathrobe and stepped back to close the door.

"Wait!" Derek picked up the flowers. "Here." He threw them at her, and the assortment of gold, coral, and teal hit her chest. Crystal heard a metal clink when they hit the concrete steps. She leaned down to retrieve the flowers and gasped. Hanging from the thin, silver ribbon was a metal key chain with two keys attached.

"What's this?" she asked, holding the metal ring.

"My keys."

"Your keys to what?"

"The farmhouse." Derek pushed his hands into his jacket pockets and stepped back.

Another wave of anguish washed over her. *He's giving me back my keys. It's officially over.* "Thank you, Derek, but why now? The house is officially sold, and I'm closing in two weeks. The new owners will change the locks. Did you really drive all this way to give me your set of keys?"

"The locks don't need to be changed."

Crystal's head jerked up and her shoulders tensed. "What? Why?"

"I know the buyer."

"How?"

"Because I bought the house. Using my realtor, Christina, who is working under Tamara."

Crystal dropped her eyes to the keys and analyzed all the nooks and crannies that made them unique to her and her history.

"I don't understand." Her voice quivered and she looked from the keys, to Derek, and back to the keys again. She turned the keys over in her hand and squeezed them in her palm.

"The house, Crystal. I bought it for me, but I hope it can be for us. I love you, and I am in love with you. I want to wake up every morning next to you."

The tears behind her eyes finally spilled over, like a dam that broke, and she laughed from her belly. *What is happening?* Her shoulders shook in a combination of joy, sadness, and a lot of confusion, and she wrapped her arms around her stomach to keep her emotions from splashing onto him.

"For me?"

"For you. And Mason and Lulu. And Molly, when she's home if she wants."

"How can you afford to be an all-cash buyer? You can barely pay Molly's rent." Her forceful eyes questioned him.

"I sold my business to Nicky."

She leaned against the door frame and her eyes widened like saucers. "You did what?"

"I never wanted it, but Vanessa died, my dad died, and I needed it. I'm not a business owner. I can't even write up a contract correctly." His lips pulled up at the corners, but Crystal's mouth did not reciprocate.

"Like my contract?" she asked. "Is that why you were harassing me about the money?" She rocked on her heels, shoving her hands in her terrycloth pockets.

"I'm a much better worker bee, and Nicky offered to buy all my equipment and my client list. Plus, he hired me as a full-time employee. I even have benefits." Derek beamed and straightened his back, like he made the honor roll for the first time. Crystal couldn't help but smile at his apparent pride. She leaned on her tiptoes and kissed him. The chill of his lips stayed on her after she pulled away and she shivered from head to toe.

"I'll give you an A for effort." Crystal beamed back at him and held both his hands in hers. "Your hands are frozen," she commented.

"Can I come in now? It's getting cold."

She looked at the keys, still resting delicately in her palm, and looked at Derek. He bobbed on his toes waiting for her invitation. The pain and stress from the last few days escaped her eyes like a refreshing shower.

He wiped the tears off her cheek and said, "I hope I never make you cry again."

She grabbed his hand and pulled him inside.

CHAPTER 50: DEREK

erek's muscles fell into the mattress like jelly. He lay in the king-sized bed, wrapped in a sheet and a soft, chenille blanket. Memories of the past hour replayed through his mind. He rolled on his side and watched Crystal sleep, tracing his finger along her jawbone.

The stress he felt hours before had disappeared entirely. His steady heartbeat lulled him into this relaxed post-ecstasy state, and he needed it to stay with him. Everything felt right, and he never wanted to leave Crystal's bed again. The pain from his past and the fear of the future crept away. All that remained was authentic satisfaction.

They hadn't talked about the farmhouse because passion took over as soon as he closed the door behind him. Derek knew whatever path they were on was complicated, and he needed Crystal to feel comfortable. He pushed away thoughts of serious conversations and focused on Crystal's peaceful breathing. She slightly smiled in her sleep, and Derek hoped she was dreaming about him. He kissed her on her cheek and nudged himself against her body. He closed his eyes and inhaled the moment.

It seemed Vanessa was right. He needed to ask the right questions.

* * *

The buzzing alarm clock woke Derek with a start. Crystal sat beside him, fiddling with her phone. She leaned across and kissed him. "Morning, Sunshine," she said. The redness and puffiness around her eyes had disappeared, and her skin glowed. "I have to go to work, and I have to pick up Mason after school."

Derek watched her naked body climb out of bed and stroll to the bathroom. As much as he wanted to, he didn't follow her. The two of them had been on an emotional roller-coaster for the previous two weeks, and Derek didn't want to be too forward. Instead, he familiarized himself with her kitchen and çooked her breakfast.

They sat down with scrambled eggs and toast before Derek ventured back to the topic of the farmhouse.

Crystal seemed happy, but had said little about his romantic gesture. He wondered if it was borderline creepy and hoped her feelings were as strong as his.

"How are you feeling about the house?" he finally asked. The flowers sat in a mason jar in the center of the table, and Derek fingered the petals.

Crystal swallowed a bite of toast and wiped her chin. "I can't believe you did that. It's so sweet. Can I ask you something?" Her round eyes looked at him from her hunched posture.

"Sure, what's up?"

"What are your expectations? What happens next?" Crystal ripped her napkin into small pieces and piled the paper next to her plate. She didn't break eye contact, and her gaze's intensity made Derek shift in his seat.

"I bought the house for myself because I've always loved it. I understand you have a life out here, and your life is complex with Jeremy and Mason. We both have baggage, Crystal, and I understand.

But I'm a patient man. I love you. Of course, I want you by my side, and live happily ever after, but I'm not stupid. I can't just snap my fingers and have my happy ending. It's going to take time."

Crystal cupped her mug and leaned forward. "Thank you for your honesty. I love you too, Derek. I want to start a life with you, but you must be patient with me. I can't do things for me; I have to do things for Mason. I would love to move in with you. We built that farmhouse together. It's as much yours as mine, and I know we would have a beautiful life there, but I can't uproot Mason or leave my job in the middle of the year. Plus, the two of you barely know each other, and we need to strengthen your relationship with him before we can make a move like that."

Derek nodded. "I know. I'm willing to wait however long it takes."

Crystal squinted her eyes, thinking. "Ten-month plan? Let's date, get to know each other as a threesome, and I'll put my house on the market if things are still looking good in June. I'll look for a job near Farm Cove for the fall, and we'll make that transition."

She checked her watch, jumped up, and kissed Derek with the same intensity she had the night before. His stomach dropped to his toes and his heart raced. Fireworks erupted behind his eyes.

He groaned behind her lips and yanked on her bottom lip with his teeth. "I'll miss you."

Crystal looked into his eyes and traced his lips with her index finger. "I love you."

He leaned in and pressed his lips against hers, feeling her tongue trace his upper teeth. "I love you, too. I'll call you tonight."

He gathered his belongings, and Crystal walked him to his truck. "Drive safely."

Sadness and joy traveled with him home. Even though they were still attempting a multifaceted long-distance relationship, he hoped Crystal would move into the farmhouse by next fall.

CHAPTER 51: CRYSTAL

Crystal's hand shook as she knocked on Jeremy's door. Sweat beaded on her forehead, and she wiped it with her sleeve. She unbuttoned her jacket and fanned her torso. *I hope my armpit sweat hasn't stained my blouse.* She felt the sticky material cling uncomfortably to her bare skin.

Jeremy's door flung open. "Hi. You're early. Mason's bus hasn't arrived yet."

Crystal swallowed the pit of doubt. "Yeah, I need to talk to you."

Jeremy let her in, and Crystal sat on the edge of the couch. She wanted to take off her coat, but didn't want Jeremy to see her armpit stains. Instead, she brewed in the fire.

"Everything okay?"

"Yes. Yes. Everything is fine. Has Mason talked about a man in Farm Cove named Derek?"

"Yeah, the contractor, right?"

Crystal placed her hands in her lap and gripped her fingers. "Yes. That's the one. We started dating a few months ago, and he bought the house. He invited me to move in with him."

Jeremy shot up from the couch like a rocket.

"With Mason," Crystal added.

"What? You hated that house, and you barely know this guy."

Crystal bit her lip and looked at the floor. "True and true. But I fell back in love with the house. Jeremy, it looks nothing like what you remember. It's fresh and welcoming, and beautiful. I poured my blood, sweat, and tears into that house this summer. I thought I'd be happy to get rid of it, but I felt sad when I put it on the market. I needed the money, for Mason. Now I have a chance to start over, like a full circle."

Jeremy leaned against the wall and eyed her up and down. "And the guy?"

"Oh, he's wonderful." Her voice softened at the image of Derek flashing before her.

Jeremy's eyes threw daggers at her and Crystal's wall fortified.

"We're not married anymore, Jeremy. The only reason I'm talking to you about this is because of Mason. I plan on moving in during the summer. Mason may still be here most of the week, or he can come with me. We can still have the same custody schedule. I needed you to know because things may change for him again, and I'm worried about the transition."

Jeremy scoffed. "Yeah? Now you're worried about another transition? Crystal, you gave up on him. I'm the one dealing with the phone calls and emails from the school. I'm the one going to his IEP meetings, trying to figure out a behavior plan. I can barely work because all my attention is going to him." Jeremy's voice rose, and he walked the living room's length.

Crystal's breath caught in her throat. "How dare you!" She stood up and walked over to him. "You have it so hard? We did this for him. To be in a smaller school. I didn't want him to move out, but I knew Rochester schools would eat him alive. Especially at the middle school. You left me, Jeremy. You left me the first time you engaged in conversation with that woman. Don't you DARE tell me how hard your life is. You left us. And I'm sorry if being a father is inconvenient, but you can't throw him away the way you did our marriage." She tried to catch her breath, but her lungs felt underwater. She heard her heart beating in her ears, and her head throbbed. "I'm sorry if this messes up your perfect little life, but I thought you should know. Stupid me for thinking you could put our son first."

Crystal knew she had gone off the rails. What started out as a conversation about Mason's schooling had turned into a conversation about Jeremy's infidelity. Relief swept over her, saying all the thoughts that haunted her for the past three years. Just like Evelyn, she could finally let go of the hurt Jeremy had caused.

She stomped out of the apartment and down to the bus stop. The cold air numbed her body, and her mind went blank. By the time the bus arrived, her toes and fingers tingled and any movement sent fire up her limbs.

"Mason, let's get your things," she said when he climbed off the bus. "Did you have a good day?"

Mason led the way to the second-floor apartment. "Yep, great day. I got Student of the Month today."

Crystal smiled. "That's wonderful! Congratulations."

Mason and Crystal walked into Jeremy's apartment, and Crystal stood firmly at the front door. "Mason, grab your stuff. I'll be right here." Tension immediately built around her. Jeremy stood ten feet away with his arms over his chest. His long face and deep wrinkles reminded Crystal that they were getting older. *It's about time I put my needs first.*

After stepping out of the building, Crystal's body relaxed, and a feeling of freedom wrapped itself around her. The drive back to Rochester was full of chatter and jokes. Mason talked about the latest video game, and Crystal pretended she was interested. He told her about a new friend he made at school and his Student of the Month ceremony.

Crystal took advantage of Mason's good mood and asked about the bus incident from a few weeks back. Mason reiterated that a boy had made fun of his friend until his friend was crying, so Mason went to his friend's aid. "I punched him, but not hard," he said. Crystal walked through problem-solving strategies for the next time, and Mason verbalized what he could do differently.

"Mason, I'm really proud of you for recognizing what went wrong and what you can do differently. You're growing up right in front of my eyes."

Mason beamed. "When I grow up, I want to be just like you."

"Oh yeah? Like how?"

Mason looked out the window. "I want to be strong and brave. You aren't afraid of anything, and I hope I can be like that, too."

Pride billowed within Crystal. *You're right, Mase. I'm not afraid.* She pictured her and Mason in the old farmhouse with Lulu running around, Molly visiting, and Derek setting up the Christmas tree. She knew it was going to be okay.

CHAPTER 52: DEREK

⸎

"Phil, I need some help with this dresser." Derek stood on the floor of the almost-empty U-Haul.

Phil rubbed his hands together. "What made you think moving in January would be a good idea?" He stepped over a snowbank and made his way up the ramp.

"Life happens, man. What can I say?" Clouds of breath floated from his mouth to the top of the truck.

"Last one? Let's do it."

The two men struggled down the wet ramp onto the icy driveway. They skated to the front door and dropped the dresser at the base of the stairs. Phil stretched his back and removed his hat. "Never again, man. I'm too old for this."

"One more. Help me get it upstairs." They hoisted the dresser and climbed the staircase to Crystal's old bedroom.

Derek rearranged the furniture so his bed faced the door instead of under the window. This way, he could see Crystal every time she emerged from the bathroom. He missed her and couldn't wait until she lived with him.

"Are we done?" Phil asked, stretching his back. "I have to get home and help Amy with dinner."

Derek grinned. "You're such a good husband."

"Hey, man, happy wife, happy life, right?" He fist-bumped Derek and walked downstairs.

Derek handed him a travel cup of coffee. "It's not as good as this amazing diner I frequent, but it's a good second."

Phil held up the cup. "Congratulations. It's a beautiful house."

Derek followed him outside and waved as the truck crawled down the icy driveway. He stumbled back inside and scanned the stacked boxes pushed against the walls. He was too tired to open them, so he popped a beer and sat on the couch. *I can't believe this is mine.*

* * *

That weekend, Crystal and Mason pulled down the long driveway. Derek had been waiting all day, sporadically looking out the window, anticipating their arrival. Soup simmered on the stove to warm them from yesterday's snowstorm and today's arctic air.

Derek pushed a pile of boxes to the corner of the dining room and set the table. He and Phil had moved the boxes to their specific rooms, but Derek still hadn't found the energy to unpack. He rummaged through a small box, searching for a ladle.

Derek's head jerked up and he listened. *Is that a car?* A second door slammed. *They're here!* He raced outside to help Crystal and Mason navigate the snow-packed driveway and safely enter the house. Snowflakes rested on their hats and shoulders. Lulu ran through the house, sniffing at all the boxes.

Crystal and Derek kissed, and Mason hugged Derek. It seemed that weekly visits helped strengthen Mason's trust in him.

"Wow!" Mason said. "You have Xbox?" He walked over to the television and picked up the controller.

"Yeah, we'll have to play later. Hey Mason, we have to go shopping this weekend. The room you'll be staying in has no blankets or anything. Would you mind helping me pick something out?" He was careful not to say 'your room' because Crystal thought it was too early to make any drastic announcements.

"Yeah, can I get a bag of gummy bears while we're out?"

Derek chuckled. He'd buy him a sports car if he'd asked for one. Derek needed Mason to like him. "Absolutely. How about I buy you two bags?"

"Yeah. How about gummy bears and gummy worms?" Mason removed his coat and shoes and made his way upstairs.

Crystal followed Derek into the kitchen and inhaled the oniony aroma. "This smells amazing. I never knew you could cook." She wrapped her arms around Derek, and he hugged her tight. They danced in a circle in front of the stove. Crystal tilted her head back and gazed into his eyes.

"I can do more than cook. This is just a preview of what's coming."

She giggled and squeezed him tighter. "I can't wait to see what you have up your sleeve."

They sat at the dining room table and ate a bowl of homemade chicken noodle soup. The first sip burned Derek's tongue. "Oh, it's hot. Make sure you blow on it." He watched Crystal's lips round like an 'O', and his stomach fluttered. He fought the urge to lean over and kiss her.

Mason trudged downstairs, breaking up his thoughts.

"Mason," Crystal said. "Derek made soup. Are you hungry? It's delicious."

Mason sat down. "Mom, I don't like soup. Do we have any crackers?"

Derek passed him a sleeve, and Mason chomped down, leaving cracker dust on the table.

After lunch, Derek, Mason, and Crystal drove to Saratoga to buy bedding for his room. Mason picked a superhero comforter set, and hugged the packaging.

"Is that what you want?" Derek asked.

"Yep. They're my favorite." Mason bounced on his toes and examined the characters.

"You got it. Whatever you want." Derek grabbed one bag of gummy bears and one bag of gummy worms and handed them to Mason. "These are for you, too."

They spent the rest of the night watching television, playing games, and eating snacks. To Derek, they felt like an actual family.

CHAPTER 53: CRYSTAL

Winter turned to spring and the last two months of school hung in front of Crystal like a carrot swinging in front of a donkey. Crystal and Melanie spoke on the phone over coffee, while Mason played video games in the next room.

"Read me what you wrote," Mel said.

"Okay." Crystal pulled out her computer and opened the Word document. "To whom it may concern. I, Crystal Whitman, am writing to inform you that I will not be returning to Rochester Public Schools in the fall. Please contact me with any questions. Sincerely, Crystal Whitman. What do you think?"

"I think that's perfect. Short and sweet and straight to the point," Melanie replied. "I can't believe you're moving in with him."

Crystal put the phone on speaker and placed it face up on the counter. "I know. It feels right, Mel. Mason's on board, and I'm ready to start over. I'm too young to feel stuck. I have a lot of life to live, and it would be a shame if I didn't just go for it." Crystal thought about her mother, and wondered what their life and relationship would have been like if Evelyn hadn't worried so much about the future.

"Girl, my fingers are crossed that your house sells soon and you get a good price. I gotta run. Call me later."

Crystal hung up the call, printed the letter and signed it. She sealed the envelope, placed a floral stamp in the corner, and addressed it to the Superintendent's Office. She dropped it in the mail slot and breathed a sigh of relief. She had worried about this moment all year, but now it was done. In the fall, she wouldn't be coming back.

She put the house on the market, and as each day passed without an offer, Crystal doubted her decision. After nineteen sleepless nights, she finally got a phone call from her agent. Full price offer. All-cash.

Feelings of déjà vu shot through Crystal. *What are the odds? No, it can't be Derek.*

Crystal texted Derek a laughing emoji and typed: **You didn't just buy another house, did you?**

He returned the text with a surprised emoji. **Nope.**

Crystal grinned. *That would have been too weird. Maybe it was mom and dad teasing me.*

She called her agent back and agreed to the terms. She was moving and getting rid of the house that held her rocky past.

Crystal couldn't wait to restart her life. Mason decided to come with her for the summer, although they hadn't yet discussed where he would attend school next year. "We'll talk about that in August," she had told Jeremy.

Jeremy fought the move, but he had no real influence on what she did. Divorced spouses didn't have a say as long as she was upholding her end of the custody agreement. Eventually, he agreed a fresh start in a new place might benefit Mason. She wondered how much his new girlfriend influenced his willingness to let Mason move to Farm Cove, but she was grateful he hadn't made it more difficult for them all.

The days leading up to the last day of school traveled at supersonic speed. Crystal barely had time to sleep between the end-of-year events, great weather, and packing. Rejuvenating exhaustion increased her energy level.

A few days before closing, Derek drove up with a U-Haul van, and they packed the van with only the necessities. It was important that even though Crystal was moving into Derek's house, the house represented both of them. She had sold her furniture but kept the little things, like lamps, blankets, pictures, and her favorite mugs.

"I can't believe it. It's so sad." Crystal looked out the windshield at the house that shaped her adult life. The happiness from her wedding, the heartbreak from her divorce, and the struggles of parenthood all lived within those walls.

Derek placed his hand on hers. "This is to new beginnings."

Crystal leaned over and kissed him. "New beginnings." Lulu snuggled between her and Derek, and Crystal petted her soft fur.

He drove away from the small cape in the cramped neighborhood and onto the busy highway. They had three hours ahead of them and talked about the house, the summer, and their future.

"I still don't have a job." Worry creased around Crystal's forehead. "I've always had a job."

"You'll get one; any school would be lucky to have you. It'll be easy. Don't worry."

"I think I'll focus on Mason's transition for the next month, and then I'll look for something." Uncertainty settled around her, and she shook the feeling away. "It'll work out."

They pulled up to the farmhouse, and Crystal inhaled the crisp air. Something about the country used to make her anxious but now centered her. Maybe it wasn't the country but her childhood life within the farmhouse walls. *Those walls are gone. Literally and figuratively. Only happy memories now.*

Crystal and Derek unpacked the truck and roamed around the house to find the perfect places for her items. She kissed Derek and smiled up at him. "I can't wait to start our life together."

* * *

Three months later, the summer heat faded, and chilly nights overtook the humidity. The green leaves transitioned to red, orange, and yellow, and the scent of pumpkin spice was everywhere.

"Mason, time to wake up!" Crystal barged in his door and stopped at the foot of his bed.

"Mom, stop." He rolled over and snuggled under the blankets, away from her.

He was no longer a little boy, but teetered on adolescence and almost-adulthood. "Honey, it's time to get up. We're leaving in a half hour."

He sat up in bed and rubbed his eyes. He swung his feet over the edge and climbed out. "Can I have some breakfast?"

"Come on down." Crystal left his room but kept the light on to prevent him from falling asleep again.

Derek stood in the kitchen, gripping a steaming cup of coffee. His jeans hung at his hips, and his flannel shirt pulled at his belly. Crystal kissed him.

"Coffee?" He held out the cup to her.

"Thanks."

"First day jitters?" Derek asked.

Crystal raised her eyes to the ceiling. "For me? Yes. For Mason? Who knows? He's still sleeping. I have to get there so I'm fully prepared for my little angels, when they walk through the door. One of the good things about these tiny towns is that the entire school body is in one building. He'll hang out with me before I walk him to his classroom." She sipped her coffee, checked her watch, and assembled their lunches.

She pulled out a napkin and wrote: **Good luck on your first day!** And stuffed it in his lunchbox.

"Mason!" Crystal called up the stairs. "We are leaving in fifteen minutes!"

She returned to Derek and kissed him again. "I hope you have a great day, Derek. I'll try to have a nice dinner for us tonight."

Derek smiled. "That sounds great. Let's celebrate. A new year, a new school, and for me a new job. I'll be busy for the next two months, at least. Nicky won the bid for the new apartment complex in town. You may not see me until Christmas, because the project is massive."

Crystal sipped her coffee and rechecked her watch. "I'm so glad everything with Fischer Home Services worked out. You deserve to be happy, and if your dad's company caused you stress, I'm happy you let it go. I like Nicky. He seems like a quality business owner, and I think you'll go far with his company."

Derek shrugged. "All I want is to go to work, pay the bills, and spend my free time with you." He embraced her and smelled her hair. "You smell great."

Crystal breathed in his mahogany cologne. "So do you. Your cologne reminds me of camping. Want to go camping this summer?" She pulled away and he nodded.

"Anything you want," he said.

Crystal grabbed her jacket. "Mason, let's go. The train is leaving."

Mason raced downstairs and grabbed a cookie.

"Mason, that is not breakfast," Crystal scolded.

"Mom, we're gonna be late." He picked up his backpack and walked to the door. "Bye, Derek, see you later."

Derek waved above his head. "Bye, have a great first day!"

Crystal kissed Derek. "Love you."

"Love you too. Good luck. I can't wait to hear all the stories over dinner tonight."

Crystal and Mason climbed into the car to start their first day of their new life. *It's an incredible life, and I am one lucky girl.*

The End

***

To get updates, giveaways, and all the juicy info on upcoming books, sign up for the monthly newsletter at https://www.edhackettwrites.com

About the Author

E.D. Hackett loves writing, reading, and anything related to Ireland. She prefers reality television over movies, ice cream over cake, and fall over summer. She resides in New England with her loving, supportive family.

You can connect with me on:

🌐 https://www.edhackettwrites.com

📘 https://www.facebook.com/edhackettwrites

🔗 https://www.instagram.com/e.d_hackettwrites

🔗 https://www.linktr.ee/edhackett

Subscribe to my newsletter:

✉ https://www.edhackettwrites.com/contact

Also by E.D. Hackett

E.D. Hackett writes stories about love, friendship, family, self-discovery, and finding happiness.

Reinventing Amara Leventis

She wants everyone to think she's got it together. So where did it all fall apart?

Providence, RI. Amara Leventis craves validation. So when her best friend and roomie gets engaged, the twenty-five-year-old single girl fears she's losing her soulmate... and her apartment forever. Reeling from the sense of abandonment, Amara turns an interview for a work promotion into a shocking pink slip.

Humiliated and effectively homeless, the frazzled woman begrudgingly returns to rural Connecticut and her parents' Greek bakery. But when a fight gets her bounced from the wedding party and she discovers her dad's troubling secrets, Amara wonders if life will always be sour instead of sweet.

Will she ever find the right recipe for happiness?

Reinventing Amara Leventis is a richly drawn women's fiction novel. If you like relatable characters, family dramas, and laugh-out-loud moments, then you'll adore E.D. Hackett's entertaining read.

The Havoc In My Head

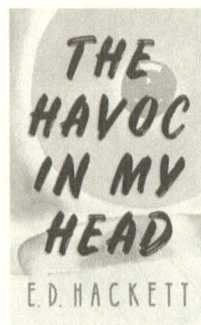

She had all she expected to achieve. But a surprise hidden in her head was about to change everything…

Ashley Martin has it all. With a high-paying job, a devoted husband, and impeccable children, the ambitious woman is living the dream life she envisioned for herself. So determined to maintain her perfect existence, she hides her odd vision problems, headaches, and confusion… until one morning she wakes up blind.

Diagnosed with a brain tumor, the terrified professional faces two difficult surgeries and a year-long recovery. And as she struggles to cope with her sudden reversal of fortune, Ashley begins to see truths she never had before.

Can this tenacious woman reclaim her health and redirect her happiness?

The Havoc in My Head is a powerful and moving women's fiction novel. If you like deeply personal journeys, overcoming impossible hurdles, and inspirational turnarounds, then you'll love E.D. Hackett's tale of extreme courage.

Hope Hanna Murphy

She sacrificed too much for them. When her real ancestry shatters her world, will she ever reclaim happiness?

Carly Davis was sure getting away from the island would help. Elated after finally freeing herself from running her late family's inn, her fresh start in Maine fizzles in the aftermath of a failed relationship. And her luck sours further still when an innocent DNA test reveals at least one of her parents had been deceiving her for decades.

Furious she gave up the best years of her life to support people she wasn't even related to, the distraught woman returns home to seek answers about her actual origins. But with her dear friend's sister marrying a guy who is suddenly Carly's cousin, the angry adoptee fears the truth could leave her more alone than ever...

Will she find the joy she so desperately craves, or will her true heritage only bring new sorrow?

Hope Hanna Murphy is the enchanting second book in The Block Island Saga women's fiction series. If you like optimistic stories, conflicted characters, and the strength of community, then you'll love E.D. Hackett's tale of courage.

An Unfinished Story

Complete strangers. A bustling B&B. Can two women help each other find their dreams?

Boston. Joanie Wilson has played it safe her whole life. But her fifteen years of loyalty to the newspaper seem like they count for nothing when her boss announces the business's impending sale. And though she doesn't really enjoy her job, the frightened reporter fights to save it by accepting a remote assignment to write articles on local flavor.

Block Island, RI. Carly Davis longs to live on her own terms. But with her father deceased and her mother's dementia dominating her world, the gregarious young woman feels trapped into running the family's bed-and-breakfast. So when a desperate journalist arrives and swaps her rent for assistance with the property, Carly seizes the chance to finally take a deep breath.

As Joanie becomes immersed in the relaxed atmosphere and meets a handsome police officer, she wonders if her need for safety is costing her happiness. And as Carly grows close to her big-city tenant, she sees a new future opening before her.

Will this accidental friendship trigger the changes both women crave?

An Unfinished Story is the charming first book in The Block Island Saga women's fiction series. If you like relatable characters, sweet romances, and beautiful settings, then you'll love E.D. Hackett's escape to paradise.

Coming September 2023

A high-achieving girl from America meets a laid-back Irish bloke. Can he show her more than just the Irish countryside?

Rory Stanley heads to Ireland for a semester of a lifetime. Things start on the wrong foot, as the Irish guy next to her on the plane gives her more than she bargains for. What's worse is that she finds him in her bedroom after her first night exploring the city. Roommates for five months, Rory struggles to live with Jaime O'Sullivan's messy ways, but no matter how hard she tries to avoid him, the universe keeps pulling them together. The problem is, she has a boyfriend, until she doesn't.

As Jaime shows her around the country, her heart warms to his silly, childish ways, and she melts into the Irish culture. When her ex-boyfriend shows up at her door, her heart dissolves under a tsunami, and everything she believes about love is destroyed.

As Rory returns to America, will she lose it all? Or will she forever be Jaime's Galway girl?

If you like fast-paced romantic comedies full of sweet moments, young adult angst, and Irish traditions, you'll love E.D. Hackett's A Match Made in Ireland.